UNKNOWN REMAINS

UNKNOWN REMAINS

A NOVEL

PETER LEONARD

COUNTERPOINT

This book is a work of fiction. Names, characters, places, and incidents either are products of the author's imagination or are used fictitiously. Any resemblance to actual events or locales or persons, living or dead, is entirely coincidental.

Library of Congress Cataloging-in-Publication data is available.
ISBN 978-1-61902-606-3

Cover design by Faceout Studio
Interior design by Domini Dragoone

COUNTERPOINT
2560 Ninth Street, Suite 318
Berkeley, CA 94710
www.counterpointpress.com

Printed in the United States of America
Distributed by Publishers Group West

10 9 8 7 6 5 4 3 2 1

FOR KEN CALVERT

UNKNOWN REMAINS

PART
ONE

ONE

Duane Cobb parked on Church Street and watched the mark get out of a taxi and cross the World Trade Center Plaza. It was 8:12 in the morning, perfect blue-sky fall day, slight breeze, when he opened the window, sun glinting off the domed glass buildings to his left. Cobb watched a couple good-looking babes cruise by, wondering what it would be like to work here, Jesus, all that tail walking around you all day.

"You going to go see him or what?" Cobb said to Ruben Diaz sitting next to him in the passenger seat. He reminded Cobb of a Puerto Rican Ray Mancini, big head, square jaw, dark hair combed forward. Diaz looked like what he was, a former boxer: bent nose, scar tissue around his eyes. Ruben Diaz wore a gray suit with white stripes and a white open-collar shirt, diamond earring, gold Rolex on his right wrist, and a silver bracelet on his left. The middle-finger knuckles on both hands looked permanently swollen.

"I give him a little time," Ruben said, heavy barrio accent. "Let him get his coffee, get settled. I want him to be relaxed."

"What difference does it make he's relaxed or not?"

"That's the way I do it. You do it a different way, that's up to you."

Cobb looked up at the 110-story building, morning sun reflecting off it like a mirror. The mark, whose name was Jack McCann, worked for a brokerage firm on the eighty-ninth floor of Tower One. Cobb glanced at Ruben Diaz. He hardly knew him. This was only their second time working together. "Miss being in the ring?"

"I miss the life. All the money and the babes coming around. It was a good life."

"I can see it. You like bling, huh?"

"I like flashy shit. Flashier the better."

"What's it like being a fighter?"

"It's about how bad you want it. Most people have no fucking idea. You think you're tough, get in the ring and prove it."

"I don't think it's a matter of being tough. It's a matter of being smart. I wouldn't get in the ring for anything, get my ass handed to me."

"I can see it. Man, you're soft."

"What does that mean?"

"Look at your hands, uh. You got hands like a girl. Make a fist."

Cobb did and Ruben wrapped his big distressed mitt around it and squeezed until it hurt. Cobb clenched his jaw trying not to show anything. "Okay, that's enough."

Ruben let go but kept his eyes on him. Jesus, this freak almost broke his fucking hand. Cobb was mad now, but thought, wait a minute, why're you letting this over-the-hill, punch-drunk idiot get to you? He sipped his coffee and got himself under control. "You say it was a good living. You looked in a mirror lately? I see your whole boxing career on your face. How many stitches you got?"

"Two hundred seventy-one."

"Were you a bleeder?"

"No, but you're going to be," Ruben said, "you don't watch it."

"I don't mean anything," Cobb said. He had to be careful with this guy. He was looking at Ruben's swollen lids and the scar tissue around his eyes, and saw how he got his nickname: Winky.

"I'm having fun with you," Ruben said with a grin, accentuating the wrinkles and creases on his face. "Don't think of it as something bad. Boxing saved me."

"Yeah, from what?"

"From me. I didn't get into it, I'd be in prison."

Cobb didn't expect this, Ruben getting philosophical. "How many fights?"

"Forty-two. I was thirty and ten. Two draws."

"Yeah? Who were they?"

"Hector Camacho. The macho man."

"I remember that little curlicue of hair came down his forehead like it was mocking you. I bet you wanted to knock it off, huh?"

"He was a good fighter. The Puerto Rican Ali. Beat Duran twice and Sugar Ray."

"Yeah, but Leonard was forty," Cobb said. "Shouldn't have been in the ring in the first place." He sipped the coffee. "What was your toughest fight?"

"They all were. But I'll tell you Micky Ward was a motherfucker. That left hook to the body would stop your fucking clock."

"You beat him?"

Ruben glanced at his watch. "What about you," he said, changing the subject. "What'd you do before this?"

"I was a debt collector in Detroit."

"But you're not from there with that accent."

"I'm originally from Little Egypt."

"Where's that at?"

"Southern Illinois."

"Why they call it that?"

"There's a town called Cairo." He didn't want to go into it, explain the whole thing.

"Oh." Ruben had probably never heard of Cairo and let it go. He paused and said, "So now you're a debt collector in New York."

"This is a little different than what I was doing."

"Lot of people skipping out on their bills in the Motor City?"

"You want to get in debt collections, Detroit is the Promised Land."

"Who you work for?"

"A collection service. Person goes crazy with a credit card, can't or won't pay the bill. After a period of time, the bank sells the debt to a buyer, who goes to a collection service, who gives it to me. We had a contest in the office every week, see how many losers we could make cry."

"You never had any hard luck, uh?"

"My job was to collect money. You don't get it if you're nice. These people spent it, decided they didn't want to pay it back."

"Or couldn't. Maybe their circumstances change," Ruben said, surprising him. "Ever been hungry? I'm not talking about you missed a meal. I mean you don't have enough to buy food. You ever in that situation, you'd be more sympathetic." Ruben paused, looking pissed off. "So what'd you do, threaten to take their car?"

"I'd call up, say I'm in the fraud department. They don't have the money in twenty-four hours, I have no choice but to hand their claim over to the district court. That got people's attention."

"That's good." Ruben Diaz grinned big, showing a gold front tooth with a diamond pattern on it. "Nobody wants to fuck with the court. Know what I mean?"

"Or I'd say, 'I know where you live, where you work'—like I'm watching them. 'You don't have the money tomorrow I'm going to tell everyone you know, your friends, your neighbors, and co-workers, what a fucking deadbeat you are.' Only I didn't really say 'fucking,' 'cause it's not professional."

"Anyone threaten you?" Ruben said, taking off the seat belt, leaning back against the door.

"Threaten me, are you kidding? They'd say things I've never heard before, yell and swear and ask my name and address. I'd say, 'My name's Duane, but giving you any more would violate my right to privacy.'" Cobb smiled, thinking about it, more relaxed now.

"Violate your privacy." Ruben shook his head. "That's good."

Cobb looked at the clock on the dash. It was 8:44. "Think he's settled enough, you can go up and see him?"

Ruben opened the door, got out, and started across the plaza.

Jack McCann walked into his office at 8:25. He'd bought a blueberry muffin and a medium coffee at a coffee shop in the mall and rode the elevator up to the eighty-ninth floor and passed through the lobby. Bonnie, the receptionist, waved to him. McCann went to his office and closed the door. He took off his sport coat, folded it over one of the chairs at his mini conference table, sat at his desk, turned on the computer, and looked north out the window at the Empire State Building. The visibility was good; he could see Manhattan, almost the whole island bordered by the rivers.

McCann checked his messages. There were fifty-seven. He went through them as he sipped the coffee and ate the muffin. Two calls from Mel Hoberman, head of account services at the corporate office in San Francisco, asking Jack to phone him ASAP.

There was a knock on the door. Mary, his assistant, came in the office. "Stewart called. Wants to see you upstairs right away. Is something going on?"

"Why do you say that?"

"It was his tone. He sounded angry. He came down yesterday, looking for you, and said he's been trying to reach you for two days."

Stu Raskin, his boss, was a VP. His office was four floors up on ninety-three. Jack knew he was going to be fired, and possibly prosecuted, although he doubted the company would go to that extreme, risking such negative publicity.

At 8:45, he got up from his desk and saw something out of the corner of his eye, an object coming toward the building. At first he thought it was a helicopter—they were common enough—but this was an airplane in restricted airspace. It was several thousand yards to the north and closing fast, Jack waiting for it to pull up, change course, but it didn't. Seconds later he felt the impact as it hit the tower. Jack was thrown to the floor, felt the 110-story building sway, thinking it was going fall over, heard the creaking sound of the steel structure flexing and felt it swing back in the opposite direction. The lights blinked on and off. The ceiling was falling on him. He was hit on the head, knocked down, and buried under a pile of debris.

Cobb looked up, saw something big coming toward the building, looked like an airplane. Jesus, it flew into the World Trade Center tower, high up, followed by a big explosion and a fireball blowing a hole right through the building, and so much smoke he couldn't see the top.

"The fuck's going on?" Ruben said, running back to the car, looking at him, stunned. Like Cobb, he couldn't believe what had just happened.

"Jesus, a plane just crashed into the building," Cobb said. Black smoke poured out of the top of Tower One, drifting over Lower Manhattan and the river, and debris and shit was raining down on the plaza, steel and glass, chunks of concrete. Sirens wailed in the distance. People stopped in the street watching, staring up in disbelief, other people were running out of the building, and way up where the flames were, people were jumping, bodies falling and the ugly sound of them hitting the plaza.

Minutes later, cops and firefighters were everywhere, and more fire engines were roaring into the scene. Firefighters carrying equipment ran across the plaza, going into Tower One. A cop banged on the side of the car, telling Cobb to move out. He started the car, then looked up and saw an airplane coming toward the second tower. Another explosion shook the ground, and a fireball bigger than the first one blew out three sides of the building, black smoke pouring out of the gaping holes.

As Cobb and Ruben drove north on Broadway, emergency vehicles, with lights flashing and the high-pitched whine of sirens, were passing them speeding toward the Trade Center.

Ruben was turned sideways in his seat, looking at him. "You fucking believe this?"

No, Cobb didn't. He pulled over to the curb and they got out, standing next to the car, looking back at the towers engulfed in smoke seven blocks away, the sidewalk crowded with people staring, people in shock, who couldn't believe what they were seeing.

"It's a bomb," a man said.

"It's not a bomb, it's a gas leak," a second man said.

"Holy shit," a third man said.

Cobb smelled smoke and burning plastic and jet fuel. He stood there next to Ruben for over an hour watching the burning towers. Then Cobb heard sounds like sticks breaking, and the south tower went down with a thunderous roar, sending up mountains of dust that drifted toward them. He heard screams and shouts, women putting their hands over their mouths, others shaking their heads.

"The whole building," someone said.

"It just collapsed," someone else said.

He could see people running, trying to escape the cloud of dust that was blowing toward them, swallowing everything in its path.

"We better get outta here," Cobb said.

They got in the car and drove north toward Tribeca, parked and got out again, joining thousands on the sidewalks. Cobb could see the top third of Tower One above the dust cloud, black smoke drifting up against the bright blue sky. Not sure what else to do, they waited almost half an hour until Tower One collapsed, sending up another mountain of dust and debris.

Ruben said, "Think he made it out?"

"I don't know, but if he did, I have a good idea where he's at." Cobb reviewed the timeline. Tower One was hit at 8:46, but didn't collapse till 10:28. That was an hour and forty-two minutes, plenty of time to get out before the building crumbled. He'd heard on the radio that there was no way to enter or leave Manhattan. The Holland Tunnel and all the bridges had been closed, and all commercial flights had been suspended.

They got back in the car. Cobb put it in gear and drove north in heavy traffic to the Village, sirens wailing around them, took a series of turns and pulled up in front of the apartment building.

Ruben squinted at him. "You really think he's in there, uh?"

"He's alive, it's a good possibility, so we check it out. McCann's there, we've got him. He's not, I don't know. You got any ideas, feel free to speak up, express yourself."

"I think is too soon. We have something to eat and come back."

"You're hungry, huh? You can eat food after what you just saw?"

"Yeah, why not?"

Cobb dropped him off at a tapas bar Ruben knew in SoHo. He sat in the car on the street in front of the restaurant, listening to Hank Jr. on the radio:

I got a shotgun, a rifle, and a four-wheel drive
And a country boy can survive.

The sidewalks were filled with people like it was the Fourth of July. Even with the windows up, he could smell the smoke and dust from the Trade Center. Either that or he'd inhaled some and it was still in his lungs.

Ruben came out thirty-seven minutes later, got in belching garlic that was almost a relief from the smell of smoke, and closed the door. It had been almost two and a half hours since the first plane crashed into Tower One. Cobb drove back to the Village and found a parking space on Sullivan Street.

Ruben sucked his upper teeth like he had something stuck in them, gave Cobb a blank look, and opened the car door. He followed Ruben into the building, and they went up the stairs to the second floor. Somewhere down the hall, a baby was crying. They stood in front of the girl's apartment, Cobb and Ruben next to each other, Ruben a couple inches shorter even with the heels, but he had a pair of shoulders.

Cobb heard a TV on inside. He knocked on the door, waited, heard footsteps, and the door opened a couple inches and caught on the security chain. He could see her face in the opening, dark hair tucked behind her ears, eyes red and swollen like she'd been crying.

The girl said, "What do you want?"

"Where your boyfriend at, uh?" Ruben said, jumping in.

"You just wake up? You don't know what's going on?"

"Invite us in, we'll talk about it," Cobb said.

"You don't leave, and I mean right now, I'm calling the police."

She tried to close the door, but Ruben blocked it with one of his Puerto Rican fence climbers, got the pointy-toed boot in the opening, then rammed his shoulder into the hardwood and the chain snapped and the door flew open. The girl backed away from them, afraid now as they entered the apartment.

Ruben said, "Where you hiding him?"

"You want to see where Jack is? I'll show you."

They followed her into the living room, the girl pointing at the TV showing a high angle looking down at the mountain of debris, what was left of the Trade Center.

"You want Jack? He's in there."

As soon as she said it, Cobb imagined people being blown up and body parts compressed in the rubble. "Gimme your cell phone."

She took the phone out of her pocket and handed it to him. Cobb checked the call log. There were seven numbers. He checked the deleted calls. Jack's cell number didn't appear in either place.

"He would've called if he could," the girl said. "I know that. And because he didn't, I know what happened." She turned and looked at the TV showing rescue workers circling the rubble, and Cobb left her there with Ruben, moving through the apartment, first going to the bedroom, looking under the bed, checking the bathroom, pulling the shower curtain open, and then checking the closet, looking behind all the clothes on hangers.

The girl came in and said, "You really think he's in here, are you kidding? Get out of here. Get the fuck out of my apartment."

Cobb wouldn't have thought a girl this good-looking could get so mad, using language like that.

He closed the apartment door and they started down the hall. "You believe the mouth on that one?"

"Man, you don't let a niña talk at you like that," Ruben said. "Listen, they gotta show respect. You gotta demand it."

"She thinks her boyfriend's dead; she's blowing off a little steam. What do you care?"

"You don't teach them, they gonna give you trouble."

Cobb wasn't listening; he was thinking about Jack McCann. He liked the situation: guy in trouble, walking away from his problems, Cobb trying to convince himself Jack was alive. It was way more interesting that way, but now they had to find him.

TWO

Cobb parked across the street from a clapboard colonial in a rural residential neighborhood. The house was nothing special but had to have cost a small fortune in this trendy town. People had been stopping by all afternoon. Ruben, quiet for the last thirty minutes, said, "Think he's in there?"

Cobb lowered the binoculars and glanced at him.

"Anything's possible. But let me ask you, if you were in Jack McCann's shoes, would you go home?" He glanced at Ruben's blank, beat-up face, gold studs looking out of place in his mangled lobes, the ex-fighter wearing a pink and white striped shirt and black blazer today, a gold bracelet on one wrist and two diamond rings, one on each of his gnarled, swollen hands. Take away the jewelry, Ruben dressed like he was going to pledge a fraternity.

Reconsidering, Ruben said, "He make it out alive, man, all he does now is disappear. Start over. His woman collects the life insurance, she all set. Know what I mean?"

"But we've got to make sure." Cobb raised the binoculars and aimed them at the big windows in front, looking through the glass at people holding plates and cocktails, socializing in the crowded living room, late afternoon on September 16. Looked like a party but no one seemed like they were having fun.

At six they drove into the town. Ruben wanted to go to Applebee's. Cobb had never been to one, hated places like this, where eating was supposed to be fun, but he didn't protest. It was happy hour, loud and crowded. They sat at a table in the bar and ordered drinks, Ruben looking at the menu, reading the words out loud: enchiladas with chicken, quesadillas with steak, fajitas with steak.

"Need some help?"

Ruben gave him a dirty look. The waitress brought their drinks, and they ordered food. Cobb studied the young girls and wished he was alone. He thought he could deal some of this young ass, but not with the over-the-hill ex-fighter next to him.

Their meals came. Ruben had ordered the sizzling skillet fajitas. Cobb grinned. "Makes you think you're back in the barrio, huh?"

Ruben ignored him, getting right to it, shoveling sizzling meat and peppers into his mouth, eating like he was being timed.

"Makes me think I'm in a second-rate restaurant." Cobb had ordered Bourbon Street chicken and shrimp that had about as much to do with New Orleans as macaroni and cheese.

They ate and drove back to the house. There were lights on, but the cars that had been lining both sides of the street were gone. "I'm gonna go, check it out," Cobb said.

"How long you gonna be?"

"I don't know. Why, you got something more important to do?"

Ruben looked at him and said, "Already tired of sitting here."

Cobb got out of the car, crossed the street, and walked up the driveway along the side of the house, looking in windows, no one in any of the rooms.

He stood next to the three-car detached garage. The rear of the house was all lit up. McCann's wife, a nice-looking blonde, was standing at the kitchen sink, washing glasses, lining them on the sideboard to drain. She turned off the faucet and brought her hands to her face. She was crying, letting go. Cobb studied her for a while with detached indifference.

Was it possible Jack McCann was alive and hiding in one of the dark upstairs bedrooms, and the crying wife and people coming by were all for show?

That was just Duane's amped-up imagination running free. He could hear a phone ringing in the house. The woman took her hands away from her face, turned her head and looked across the room. Cobb crossed the driveway and moved next to the house and saw the woman holding the phone up to her ear. He listened for a few minutes then walked down the driveway to the side door and turned the handle. It was unlocked. He opened it and went in. The woman was talking, crying, having an emotional conversation. Cobb moved along a hallway to the front of the house and went up the stairs. He stood on the landing, listening, didn't hear anything. Were there kids up there asleep? He had no idea.

The second floor was dark, the wood floor made noise, so he stopped and took off his shoes. He checked the three rooms. One looked like a guest bedroom; the second had a TV, a couch and chairs, and bookshelves full of books.

Cobb was in the master bedroom when he heard her come up the stairs. He dropped to his knees on the far side of a king-size bed and then went to the floor as she came in the room and turned on a bedside lamp. Looking under the bed, he could see her shoes with short heels. She sat on the bed and took them off, got up, crossed the room, went into the walk-in closet and came out a couple minutes later in her underthings, walked into the bathroom, and closed the door. That she was good-looking with a great body made the situation more fun. Give it a little time, Cobb thought he might be able to take advantage of the grieving widow.

He heard water running and the sound of an electric toothbrush. He walked out of the room and down the stairs, carrying his shoes. All the lights were off. He slipped out the side door, walked down the driveway, and crossed the street. Ruben was staring at him when he got in the car. "The fuck you been?"

"Seeing if he was in the house."

"Was he?"

"No."

"I could've told you that."

"An hour ago, you thought he was in there hiding. Now you say he isn't. You've got all the answers, huh? Tell me where he's at."

"Muerto. Difunto. In the rubble."

"Now you're saying he went down with the buildings, is that right?"

"I say, I think he went down. But I don't know. Just like you don't. That's why we here, uh?"

Cobb started the car, put it in gear, and pulled away. "I keep seeing him walking out of that cloud of dust lucky to be alive, and McCann saying to himself, 'All I have to do is disappear and start my new life.' How many get an opportunity like that?" He turned onto the highway in light traffic.

Ruben said, "What about his woman?"

"What about her?"

"Maybe he loves her."

"If that's true, why's he fooling around?"

"Don't mean he don't love her."

"Let me tell you she's a knockout, too," Cobb said. "Better than the other one. But there are three billion women in the world. Subtract the ones are too young and too old, there still has to be a billion and a half."

"What you think is too young?"

"Under eighteen. Where you come from, girls lose their virginity at what, eleven, twelve?"

Ruben said, "A woman is a woman, uh?"

"Try that here, they put you away."

"What's too old?"

"Over twenty-five," Cobb said with a straight face and saw Ruben grin in the dim light.

"Ever been married?"

"I look crazy? It's the ones tell you they don't want a serious relationship you have to watch. They want a piece of your soul."

"They don't want a piece; they want the whole thing."

Cobb said, "What about you?"

"Two times. I don't learn. First time, I was nineteen."

"Nineteen? Why would you do that?"

"'Cause I wanted her more than anything. Carmen was something, had the best ass I ever seen."

"Were you fighting then?"

"I was always fighting, since I was fourteen."

"What happened?"

"Carmen's perfect ass got big. Went from this to this." He showed Cobb, moving his hands from ten inches apart to two feet, and showed the gold tooth.

"Did you look at the mother?"

Ruben frowned. "What're you saying?"

"You always look at the mother to see how the daughter is going to turn out. They don't do that in Puerto Rico, huh?"

"I think is done everywhere, but Carmen's mother died before I see her."

Cobb saw the hotel in the distance and took the next exit.

"Listen, every thirty seconds in America, some guy's getting a divorce 'cause his wife got big as a cow. It's a fucking epidemic."

Ruben shook his head. "Man, you like to talk."

Cobb turned into the hotel parking lot, pulled into a space, and glanced across the interior at Ruben. "You're on tomorrow. Know what you're gonna say?"

Ruben nodded, opened the door, got out and leaned his head back in. "I know what I'm gonna say. Know what you gonna say?" Saying it mean, like Cobb had challenged him.

"You don't ever have to worry about Duane Cobb. I'm always in character."

Ruben closed the door and headed for the hotel entrance.

THREE

It had been six days, and the feeling of loss was like a weight she carried around. There'd been hope in the beginning; survivors were found alive under the rubble. One guy rode down in the collapsing building and lived. But hope that Jack was alive faded a little more with each passing day, and now it seemed impossible he had made it out.

He'd called after the first plane had hit. He'd left a message, said it was bad, fire and smoke and bodies everywhere. Jack said he was going to take the stairs—it was the only possibility. She had tried to call him but never got through. Watching the news an hour later, Diane saw the north tower go down in twelve seconds and her heart sank. She listened to his message over and over. It ended with "I love you." She'd tried calling him, and kept calling till her cell phone ran out of juice, recharged it and kept trying.

Of the 258 people in Jack's office, 243 were still missing and presumed dead. Diane had met with a group of Jack's co-workers' spouses in a banquet room at a local country club, the wives asking each other what they were going to do. How they were going to cope. How do you bury someone when there's no body? What heals your heart?

They cried and tried to cheer each other up, but for Diane the meeting was more depressing than helpful or therapeutic. She was overwhelmed and just tried to keep it together. She kept seeing the same images over and over. The gaping hole in the north tower. Plumes of black smoke. The jumpers. Burning paper raining down like confetti. The fire trucks and ambulances lined up. The noise. The feeling of panic and helplessness.

At one point Diane had taken a train to Manhattan and a cab to the Trade Center area. She walked along the missing-persons wall, looking at flyers that had photographs of people who had disappeared that morning. The flyers had notes that were typeset or handwritten. *This is my husband Paolo Minoli. If you see him, please call his wife, Inez: 646-480-6649.*

Diane found a space on the wall and took out the page she had designed on her computer. There was a photo of Jack smiling, and a headline that said *This is Jack McCann, last seen on the 89th floor of Tower One. If you see him, call 203-555-0198.* Tacking a flyer to the wall was probably crazy, but it was proactive; it was doing something other than waiting by the phone.

Diane was on the phone with her mother when she saw a black sedan park on the street in front of the house. She watched a dark-haired guy get out and start up the walk to the front door. "Mother, I've got to go. Someone's here."

"Who is it?"

"I don't know." She flicked off the cell phone and slid it into her front jean pocket, moved into the foyer, stopped and looked at her face in the mirror. Her eyes were red, and she had a streak of black on her cheek where the mascara had run. She wiped her face and dabbed her wet eyes with a Kleenex.

The doorbell rang. She took a breath and opened the door, looking at a guy in his midthirties, about Jack's height: six feet, but smaller through the chest and shoulders.

"Mrs. McCann, I'm Duane Cobb from corporate. I'm sorry for your loss."

The name didn't ring a bell, and he didn't look at all familiar. She wondered if they'd met at the office Christmas party, scanning faces of Jack's co-workers in her mind, but she didn't see Duane Cobb.

"I just want to talk," he said, "if you have a few minutes."

The last thing Diane wanted to do was rehash what had happened. "What do you want to talk about?"

"You, and how you're doing."

"I don't have much to say." She opened the door all the way and he stepped into the foyer. She closed the door and led him into the kitchen, standing across the island counter from him, self-conscious being in the house alone with a stranger.

"Would you like something, a cup of coffee?"

"That'd be nice," Cobb said.

She took the pot out of the coffeemaker and poured him a cup. "How do you take it?"

"Cream and sugar. I better do it, I'm kind a particular."

The sugar was on the counter. She opened the refrigerator, took out a pint of half-and-half, and handed it to him. She'd never seen a grown man put two spoonfuls of sugar in his coffee or use that much cream, turning it into a kiddie drink. Cobb saw her watching him, smiled, and said, "Keeps me sweet."

She was trying to place his accent. "Where are you from, Taylorville, Mattoon?"

"No, Carbondale. How in the devil'd you know that?"

"My cousin married a salesman from southern Illinois who sold combine harvesters, hay tedders, and haul-out transporters. Your accent's like Bud's."

"Sounds like you know what you're talking about."

"I don't really."

She saw him staring at the platters of baked goods lining the counter. "Would you like something to eat, a cookie or a brownie?"

"No, I'm all set." He paused. "I didn't know Jack, but I've heard what a wonderful person he was. How popular he was in the office. How much he helped young people breaking into the business."

Hearing that made her feel better, because she knew it was true. Jack had mentored a number of young brokers who'd made it, done well, and were anxious to tell Diane at company functions how Jack helped accelerate their careers, and how much everyone admired him.

The TV on the counter was tuned to a news broadcast showing the planes striking the towers in slow motion. She turned it off and fixed her attention on Cobb. "So you work in the San Francisco office?"

"I'm not actually with Sterns and Morrison."

"Who're you with?"

"I'm a grief counselor hired by corporate." He sipped his sweet coffee.

"Why didn't somebody call and ask if I wanted to talk to you?"

"I don't know."

"I don't need a grief counselor."

"I can help you work through the emotional pain you're experiencing."

"How do you know what I'm experiencing?"

"I don't really, but I can imagine. I'm trained. I went to school for this." He paused. "Tell me, Mrs. McCann, what are you feeling? Are you in shock? Are you angry? Do you feel guilty Jack died and you survived?"

"All of the above."

"Now I'm going to tell you something, and I just want you to listen." Cobb paused for effect. "Grief is a normal and expected reaction to loss. It's a process that can't be rushed. There's no quick fix. There're no shortcuts here. There are seven steps you'll go through before you're whole again."

Diane was thinking step one was to get through it on her own, and bag the other six.

"You can't go back," he said. "You can only go forward. My advice, talk to Jack, tell him what you're thinking. He can hear you."

"Really? Where is he, up there in heaven?" Diane pointed at the ceiling. "Looking down at us?"

Cobb ignored her sarcasm. "I'm sure Jack was a wonderful husband, and I can only imagine how much you miss him. He's still with you but in a different way. I can help you cope with your feelings and regain your inner strength."

"Let me stop you right there. I'm not interested in talking to you or anyone else about this. I don't want to be rude, but finish your coffee, and I'll walk you out."

Cobb pulled a business card out of his shirt pocket and tried to hand it to her. Diane wouldn't take it. He left the card on the island countertop and walked out of the kitchen. She followed him to the front door. He turned and looked at her. "Mrs. McCann, I can help you if you'll let me."

Diane locked the door, went into the living room and watched him walk to his car, wondering why someone from corporate HR hadn't called to tell her they'd hired a grief counselor. Wouldn't it have been more appropriate to ask her first? She'd have said, No way. It's personal and I'll handle it.

Her cell phone rang. It was Connie May, whose husband Jeff had worked at Sterns & Morrison and, like Jack, had gone down with the tower.

"What're you doing?"

"I just kicked out a grief counselor corporate sent over."

"What're you talking about?"

"No one's stopped by your place, or called?"

"No."

"Anyone else say anything?"

"Not to me."

"He came by out of the blue, wants to help me through this difficult time."

"What'd you tell him?"

"No thanks."

"Send him over to me, will you?" Connie started to cry. "I don't know if I'm gonna make it."

"We'll get through it," Diane said, trying to sound positive. "Come over tonight; we'll have a few glasses of wine." She heard the doorbell. "Somebody's here, I'll call you later." She slid the phone into her pocket, hoping the grief counselor wasn't back.

FOUR

Diane was about to open the front door, then stopped. She moved into the living room and looked out the big window at the front porch and saw a well-dressed, dark-skinned man she'd never seen before. He didn't look like a salesman; he looked rough. The bell rang again. After the grief counselor, she didn't want to see or talk to anyone else. The guy on the porch turned and glanced at the street, shuffled his feet, and looked at his watch. Now he came down the steps and stood on the lawn in front of the living room window. Diane went down on her knees, ducking under the level of the couch. She felt foolish hiding in her own house, but it was too late now.

She waited, hoping he'd leave, and heard pounding on the side door. Maybe there were two of them. She peeked over the back of the couch and didn't see him, got up and moved into the kitchen and heard him shake the door handle, then bang on the door. Diane was rattled now. Who was this lunatic, and what did he want?

She thought about calling the police. And say what? There's a stranger knocking on my door? He was aggressive, but he hadn't done anything. Now he was on the driveway, moving toward the kitchen windows and she retreated down the back stairs halfway to the basement and froze. Her cell phone rang. She reached in her pocket and turned it off.

Diane waited a couple minutes, went up the stairs, and saw him walk by the side door. She followed him through the house and saw him move past the den and living room windows, saw him walk down the street, and her heart stopped pounding.

It occurred to her that for the first time in a week, she hadn't thought about Jack. This guy, whoever he was, had taken her mind off 9/11 for a few minutes, made her realize this was what she was going to have to do, or she'd go out of her mind.

Diane sat at the kitchen table, shuffling through the bills she'd been putting off paying. A payment of $785 was due on the BMW Jack was leasing. Diane had tried to talk him into a Volkswagen or a Toyota, but he was all about image. "How can I look successful driving a second-rate car?" The mortgage was $4,900 a month for a house that was way more than they needed. When she'd challenged Jack—"Are you kidding? Why do we need five thousand square feet?"—Jack had locked her in his gaze and said, "We're gonna have a family, aren't we? We've gotta have room for all the kids."

Then there was the monthly bill from Darien Country Club, where they seldom went, but the average charges were $2,500 a month. What really surprised her, though, was the accumulated debt on two Visa cards and a MasterCard totaling more than $87,000. She studied the current list of charges on the Visas: two business-class flights, New York–London, three nights at Claridge's, in addition to meals at Rules and Le Gavroche. On the MasterCard were two business-class flights, London–Rome, and a suite at the Hassler.

When she and Jack fought, it was always about money. He would tell her that she spent too much and had to cut back, or get a job and contribute.

Now she went online and looked at the balance of their joint checking and savings account, thinking they had at least $50,000. Jack said it was their safety net if he ever lost his job. She studied the transactions from the previous month, checks written and Visa card activity, the portfolio summary showing a balance of $5,415.12. She was surprised to see that Jack had withdrawn $45,000 the last week of August. Why would he need that much money? He had always paid the bills, and she trusted him. What else didn't she know?

Diane felt dumb, naive. How could she not have known what was going on? The grief counselor said Jack could see and hear her. She glanced up at the ceiling. "Jack, what'd you do with the money?"

A couple nights a week, he was out with clients on a company expense account. They'd have dinner at Le Bernardin, Le Cirque, or Jean-Georges. He'd come home late, if he came home at all, smelling of cigars and booze. Some nights he'd stay at a hotel in the city, walk in the door before Diane was awake, shower, change, and go back to Manhattan. She never worried about him, never thought he was doing anything crazy. But now, thinking about all the money that had disappeared, maybe he had been gambling.

Diane couldn't remember Jack ever being interested in cards. He didn't bet on horses or sporting events that she knew of. Unless this was something else she'd missed. Then again, maybe she was judging him unfairly. Maybe he needed the money for something else. "What'd you spend it on, Jack?"

She heard the side door close. "Who're you talking to?" Connie May said, coming into the kitchen.

"Myself."

Connie hugged her, clung to her. Diane felt her friend's body heave as she let go, crying, and they held each other like that for a while until Diane said, "Let's have a drink. What do you want?"

"What're you going to have?"

"A martini."

"Really? What the hell, I'll have one too."

Diane filled a cocktail shaker with ice and vodka and added a splash of vermouth. She put the top on and shook it till her arm was tired and the shaker had a layer of ice on the outside, almost too cold to touch. She poured the cold mixture into two martini glasses, submerged an olive in each, and handed a glass to Connie. "You're not supposed to get drunk, I read, when you're grieving. You're supposed to feel the brunt of the pain. You're not supposed to dilute it with alcohol."

"Who said that?"

"I don't remember."

"The hell with it; I want to get drunk and not feel anything."

Diane held her glass up and clinked Connie's. "To us. We're gonna get through this. We're gonna be okay." She sipped her martini, tasting the cold vodka and feeling the burn in her throat as she swallowed.

Connie said, "What's Sterns and Morrison doing to compensate us?"

"Are they going to do something? I have no idea."

"That's what I heard at the last meeting. You do have savings, don't you? And Jack did have life insurance, I hope."

"I'm not worried; I'm okay. But a little extra wouldn't hurt." Jack did have a $1 million term life insurance policy. She had called Howard Zamler, their agent, to make sure.

"I got Jeff's paycheck today. That helped. But I don't know how long they'll keep sending them."

"I didn't get Jack's."

"You should call." She paused. "I'm going to go back to work. I've got to do something, keep busy."

Connie was thirty-eight, tall and blonde, a former art director who'd taken a leave of absence when she got pregnant years before, had two kids and never went back.

Diane drained the martini, and the vodka-soaked olive rolled in her mouth. She chewed it and said, "Another one?" She could feel the euphoric buzz and wanted to keep it going.

"Are you kidding? I have to drive home. I have to make dinner."

"What're you having?"

"Chicken tenders and French fries. You're welcome to join us."

"I'm gonna have another martini and get in the tub."

"I'll see you in the morning," Connie said. "Anything I can do for you before the funeral?"

FIVE

On the morning of the twenty-first, Cobb was paging through the *Times*, breathing in a mixture of fresh coffee and Ruben's cologne. It was raining, and there was a chill in the air. He turned on the radio, heard Toby Keith singing:

> *I'm not talkin bout hooking up and hanging out.*
> *I'm just talkin bout tonight.*

He turned it off when he saw a black Cadillac drive up and park in McCann's driveway. Diane McCann came out dressed in black, carrying an umbrella, and got into the Caddy. Cobb folded the newspaper and followed Mrs. McCann to St. Mary's Church in Norwalk. This was the fourth funeral they'd followed her to since 9/11.

He sat in the back of the packed church during the service, no idea who'd died until the priest said, "Our brother Jack McCann has been taken from us." After the mass, a guy walked up to the podium and said, "For those of you who don't know me, I'm Joe Sculley. And let me say: we lost a good one. I met Jack in first grade. He came up to me on the playground and said, 'A lot of us think you look like an albino.' And we've been friends ever since." He paused, took a breath. "Jack was an American classic, which is to say he was an original. I've never met anyone like him. I doubt any of you have, either. If you were Jack McCann's friend—and by the number of people here today, there are a lot of us—he would do anything for you. Jack loved his family, his mother, his sister, and especially his wife Diane, who he referred to as his soulmate. Jack loved life. He grabbed it and squeezed everything he could get out of it."

Cobb decided he'd heard enough bullshit, slid out of the pew, walked out of the church, and got in the car. Ruben gave him a blank-faced stare. "What you doing in there? Know how long I been out here?"

"I give up, how long?"

Ruben kept the hard stare on him.

"You follow the subject till you find out something that might be helpful. That's the job, waiting and watching. What's this, your first day? Maybe you're in the wrong line of work."

Ruben shrugged. "What you think I should be doing?"

Cobb pictured him in a green uniform with his name on the shirt, cutting grass. "What do you know how to do?"

"You mean like boxing?"

Jesus, there was hope for Ruben after all. "Exactly. You know the business. You become a trainer, a manager, maybe even a promoter."

"You know, that's not a bad idea."

Cobb clamped his jaws together so he wouldn't smile. He looked over, saw people coming out of the church now. Diane McCann appeared a few minutes later and got in the limo.

He followed the funeral procession going about eighteen miles an hour, forty-two cars, he counted them, to the cemetery. They sat in the car fifty yards from the burial site, watching a big group, everyone dressed in black, holding umbrellas up against a light rain.

Cobb checked out the faces of the mourners with binoculars. Anyone not crying looked like they were about to.

Ruben said, "All these people die when the building go down, right? But no bodies."

"Is there a question there somewhere?"

"What's in the coffin?"

"Personal things. Guy played hockey, they put in his stick and skates and photographs of his team and maybe shots of the man's wife and kids. Guy was a golfer, they put in his clubs. Things that have a sentimental attachment. You know, like he's playing golf, a championship course up in heaven."

"No jodas! You believe it?"

"Doesn't matter what I believe."

"I was the woman, I sell the golf clubs."

"Uh-huh."

"What would you do?"

"I was dead, it wouldn't make any difference, would it?"

It was raining harder now, drops pelting and rolling down the windshield. Cobb couldn't see anything.

"Why don't you put the wipers on?"

"I don't want to call attention to us. People are gonna see a car with the wipers on and two guys sitting in it."

"So what?"

"How can we follow the woman if she recognizes the car?"

Ruben didn't say anything. He probably couldn't think of a response, and that was okay. Cobb was tired of making small talk with this idiot.

Now a bagpiper started to play. Cobb brought the side window down a couple inches. He saw Diane McCann raise her umbrella over the bagpiper's head till he finished playing.

After the casket had been lowered, the mourners dispersed, running to their cars. Cobb followed Diane McCann in the limo to the Darien Country Club, pulling over across Mansfield Road, rain pounding the roof and windshield, watching the limo pull in.

Diane was drained, exhausted. The limo dropped her off. She went in the side door, hung the umbrella on a hook in the closet, took off the wet raincoat, and hung it in the laundry room. She moved into the kitchen, opened the liquor cabinet, brought out a bottle of port, and poured a couple inches into a short-stemmed glass. She sipped the port and checked her messages. Friends offering their condolences, and a mortuary company offering specials on gravestones, markers, and monuments. It was unbelievably bad taste.

Glancing toward the dark breakfast room, Diane thought she saw someone sitting at the table. It startled her. There was a man there. She didn't feel the glass slide out of her hand, but heard it shatter on the counter, a dark red stream running over the side of the granite onto the floor. She fumbled, opened a drawer, and brought out a cook's knife.

"I not going to hurt you." His accent sounded Spanish.

She picked up the phone. "I'm going to call the police."

"Is not necessary. I have something to show you. That's all." He was up now moving toward her, and she recognized him as the dark-skinned man who had come by yesterday. He walked into the kitchen, unfolding a piece of paper, stood on the other side of the island counter, and slid the paper to her.

"What is this?"

"Have a look."

He was well-dressed but scary looking, with ridges of scar tissue around his cheekbones and eyes, and diamond studs in his big ears. She studied the paper. It was a copy of a contract. It said Jack had borrowed $750,000 from a company called San Marino Equity. She had never heard of it. There were terms and conditions in small print she couldn't read even with her readers. "My husband is dead. I don't know what you're trying to pull. This has nothing to do with me."

"This your signature. You guarantee to pay back the debt."

"I never signed this." She looked at the signature. It wasn't hers; it wasn't even close.

"You owe seven hundred fifty grand."

"I don't owe you anything. Get out. If I see you again, I'm calling the police." Diane had been afraid, scared to death. Now she was angry, thinking this clown had broken into her house and was trying to scam her.

"Listen," he said, "this is not gonna go away. You owe this money and have to pay it back. We can start with the life insurance."

"We're not starting with anything."

"I see you again, uh?"

He left the paper on the counter, walked out of the kitchen, down the hall to the side door. Diane went after him and locked it and set the security alarm. They didn't use it when Jack was alive, but now she decided to keep it on.

Back in the kitchen, she could smell what he had left behind, an aura of bad cologne, her nose filled with it. She picked up the piece of paper on the counter. San Marino Equity, 121 Mulberry Street, New York, New York 10006. An address that was probably in Little Italy.

In spite of what she'd already discovered about Jack, this had to be a scam. There's no way he would've borrowed that much money. If anyone knew about it, she figured Sculley would. He'd been Jack's closest friend for as long as she had known him.

Another possibility: Jack was seeing someone, having an affair. Was this something else she had missed, not paying attention? There was a good-looking girl she had never seen before, early twenties, at the funeral reception. Diane didn't know her, so Jack must have.

She called Sculley and asked him if he was available for breakfast the next morning.

SIX

"How're you doing, you okay?" Sculley said, looking at her with a solemn expression and sad eyes the way everyone did. Everyone except the scammer with the bad face. He didn't seem to care about her situation one way or the other. People either overdid their concern, their condolences, or they avoided her. That was happening more often, and Diane understood perfectly. Who wanted to hear about someone's problems, talk about death? If one more person said, "Sorry for your loss," she was going to scream. Every time she heard it, she wanted to say, "I'm sorry for your loss of imagination."

Diane sipped her cappuccino, glancing at untouched scrambled eggs, bacon, and whole-wheat toast on the plate, and then looked up at Sculley's pale face, thinking about Jack calling him an albino in grade school. "Did Jack have a girlfriend?"

"Why would you ask that?"

"If he did, I have to believe he would've told you."

"Why go there? Why do you want to think anything bad about him?"

"It's hard not to. Jack cleaned out our savings and left me with a pile of bills. You don't do that unless something's going on. You have a girlfriend, or you have a gambling problem, or you're into serious drugs." Diane sipped her cappuccino. "A young, good-looking brunette showed up at the club after the funeral. I didn't know her."

"I'm not sure who you mean. She was probably somebody's wife or girlfriend," Sculley said.

"Come on. I saw you talking to her. You know who she is."

Sculley poured hot sauce on his omelet, eyes on the plate.

"What's her name?"

"Vicki Ross." He cut a piece of omelet with his fork.

She felt her heart race. "How long had Jack been seeing her?"

"Couple of months, maybe a little longer."

"Why are you telling me this?"

"Because you asked." He took a bite of the omelet, chewing slowly, looking at her.

"He'd been seeing her for a couple of months? How did I miss that?"

"It's not your fault."

"No? Whose fault is it? I obviously wasn't doing something Jack wanted or needed, or he wouldn't have been out looking."

"He wasn't looking. If you want to know: women hit on Jack all the time, and the first thing he'd say was, I'm married."

"God, I hope so."

"Jack said he met her at Ulysses, you know, that Wall Street bar. He told her he was married—"

"That did a lot of good, huh?"

"He talked to her for a while at the bar, and that was it. Jack saw her again at the restaurant where Vicki worked. He knew her for quite a while, and innocently one night, they ended up in the same bar."

"Oh, come on, Sculley, 'innocently'?" In this context, the word sounded absurd. "One of the nights he said he was working late or going out with clients, huh?" Diane paused. Jack, who she thought was perfect, was a cheater. What a thing to find out after he was gone. "What'd he do, buy her a place to live?"

"I don't know anything about that."

"He took her on trips, didn't he? Business class to London and Rome. And another trip to L.A. She went on those too, didn't she?"

"Don't think about it."

"It's hard not to. I've been living a lie. I'm the naive, trusting wife. I went along and thought everything was okay. More than okay, it was good."

"Jack loved you. He told me you were the one."

"I might've been the one when we got married, but I wasn't, as of a couple months ago. Jesus." Diane unfolded her napkin and covered the untouched breakfast. "There was a man in the house when I got home from the funeral."

"What?"

"A scary-looking guy who said Jack borrowed a lot of money from a company called San Marino Equity. What do you know about that?"

"Nothing. How much did he borrow?"

"The guy said seven hundred and fifty thousand dollars. Was he gambling?"

"Not Jack."

"Was he into drugs?"

"I can't imagine."

"I can't imagine Jack having an affair."

"There has to be a reasonable explanation."

"Yeah? Tell me what it is."

"You were married for twelve years. Jack loved you. Don't let this ruin everything."

"Where does the girlfriend work?"

"What're you gonna do?"

"Now you're worried about her, huh?" She almost said Vicki.

"A bistro on Spring Street."

"What's the name of it?"

"I don't remember. I don't even know if she still works there."

"With all our money, she doesn't have to." Diane took a breath. "I can kind of understand her coming to the funeral, but not the club. She's got a lot of nerve."

"She was offering her condolences."

"Why, for stealing my husband? Why are you sticking up for her?" She had heard enough, stood up, and put a twenty-dollar bill on the table.

"What're you doing? Diane, come on."

She walked to the door and didn't look back. Sculley made no attempt to go after her. Probably because he didn't want to be interrogated anymore. Why was she mad at him? What did he do? Sure, Sculley knew more than he was saying. But he was probably trying to spare her feelings. That's what good guys like Sculley did, right?

Diane went home and changed into jeans and a blazer. Checked her messages. There was one from Duane Cobb. "I want to see how you're doing. I'm ready to begin regular sessions when you are." Sessions? She still wasn't interested.

She sat at the island counter in the kitchen and called Sterns & Morrison's corporate office in San Francisco. Diane identified herself and asked to speak with Susan Howe in Human Relations. They had met at a company picnic at the chairman's home in the Hamptons years earlier.

Diane was on hold for almost five minutes and was about to hang up when Susan came on the line.

"Mrs. McCann, Diane, so sorry to keep you waiting. My sincere condolences for your loss. How may I help you?"

"I haven't received Jack's midmonth paycheck. Is there a problem?"

"Let me look into it, and I'll get back to you ASAP, if that's okay."

"That's fine. Thank you." She realized she had come on a little strong and backed off, taking the edge out of her voice.

She drove to the Darien train station, bought a round-trip ticket, picked up a *New York Times*, and walked out to the platform, thinking about Jack. They'd been married twelve years, had just celebrated their anniversary on August 26. Their relationship had changed, no doubt about it. The first five years, they couldn't get enough of each other. Did everything together: played tennis, went to movies, cooked, drank martinis, read in bed with matching gooseneck lamps, sat around on Sunday morning going through the newspaper, made love a few times a week and, in the past couple years, hardly at all. They were both busy and not as energetic at night as they were in the early days. Now she realized Jack hadn't been getting what he wanted at home, so he had gotten it somewhere else.

At Grand Central Station, Diane got off the train, walked outside, and hailed a cab to SoHo. She started walking at one end of Spring Street, passing storefronts, restaurants, and shops, looking for a bistro and saw Les Amis. Diane went in and sat at the crowded bar, ordered a café au lait, and studied the dining room, white tablecloths and simple French decor. A sign said, "Cassoulet served every day during winter and spring" and, under that, "Fois gras served every day for dinner."

From her vantage point at the end of the bar, she could see the entire dining room. She paid particular attention to the waitresses, didn't see Jack's girlfriend, which didn't mean anything. Maybe she worked at night. When the bartender approached, she said, "Does Vicki still work here?"

"Vicki who?"

"Vicki Ross."

The bartender frowned and said, "Never heard of her."

A well-dressed guy sitting next to her flipped his cell phone closed and got her attention. "This is your lucky day. My lunch date just canceled. I'm Bob. Why don't you join me."

"It isn't yours." Diane got up, left a ten-dollar bill on the bar, and walked out. She continued along Spring Street till she saw Balthazar, went in, approached the hostess, and said, "Is Vicki working today?"

"Vicki Ross?"

"We're old friends. I want to book a table in her section and surprise her."

The hostess paged through the reservation book. "All we have available today is five-thirty."

Diane cut over to Mulberry Street, and now she was in Little Italy. It reminded her of scenes from *The Godfather*. She found number 121, an office building over some food shops. She opened the door. She walked in and found the directory on the wall. San Marino Equity was in Suite 210.

Diane had butterflies in her stomach as she walked up the old wooden stairs to the second floor and moved along the hall that was dark and stuffy and smelled like her grandfather: mothballs and cigars.

She stood in front of a door with a beveled glass window in the top half. It reminded her of doors she'd seen in old movies. SAN MARINO EQUITY was stenciled on the glass.

She slid her hand in the shoulder bag and felt the grip of the .380 Beretta, a gift from her dad, the ex-cop. What was she doing here, trying to make things worse? Or was she trying to appeal to their sense of fairness, going for sympathy? No, it wasn't that; Diane was angry. She knocked on the door, wondering who was going to answer and what was going to happen. She'd hold up the contract and say, "This isn't my signature. I never signed this. I've hired a lawyer. I'm going to sue you." When no one came, she knocked again.

Diane heard a door close down the hall. A short, wide man walked toward her, cigar clamped in his jaw, the smell of smoke filling the hall.

"They no here," he said in heavy Italian-accented English.

"Do you know when they'll be back?"

He shook his head. "Non lo so."

She followed the man to the stairs, stood at the top, and watched him taking little steps, balancing considerable weight on his small feet, cigar smoke trailing after him.

Diane walked to West Broadway and checked in to the SoHo Grand. She had three hours till her reservation at Balthazar. She wasn't hungry, wasn't in the mood for shopping or sightseeing. So she went to the room and lay on the bed, thinking about what she was going to say to the girlfriend. "Hi, remember me? Oh, you don't? I'm Jack's wife." She'd throw that out and see how the girl reacted.

Diane wasn't sure why she was doing it or what it would accomplish. Would it make her feel better to get in the last word? Maybe it was more primitive than that. This girl, Vicki Ross, stole her husband, and Diane wanted to see her. Was she prettier? Was she sexier? Was she smarter? Was she more fun to be with?

At five thirty, Diane gave her name to the hostess and was escorted to a table. She wore sunglasses and had her hair pulled back in a ponytail. She opened the menu, using it as a prop, looking over the top at the bustling dining room, saw Jack's girlfriend taking an order a couple tables away, and studied her.

Vicki Ross was about five six and thin, but she had shape, a good butt and breasts. Her hair was dark and hung to her shoulders. Vicki was having an animated conversation with four stylish forty-something women.

A few minutes later, she walked by Diane's table and said in a sweet girlish voice, "Sorry, I'll be right with you," flashing a smile.

Diane studied the menu, thought she might order something small, an appetizer and a glass of wine, decided on Mussels Provincial, a baguette, and a glass of Puligny-Montrachet. When she looked up, Vicki Ross was standing at the table smiling. "Can I bring you something from the bar, a glass of champagne?"

"I don't have anything to celebrate."

"With champagne you don't need a reason. It is the reason."

Vicki Ross had perfect skin, plump lips, and white teeth. She was even better looking up close. Diane ordered the Puligny. Vicki moved toward the bar. As much as Diane didn't want to admit it, she could understand why Jack had fallen for this good-looking young girl. She was aware of the way women looked at Jack—like they wanted to eat him up. But she trusted him. He was married. He had given that up.

Guys hit on Diane occasionally, like earlier, the man in the French restaurant. She never took any of these advances seriously. She was committed.

Diane took off the sunglasses and put them in her bag when Vicki returned with the glass of wine, setting it on the table.

"Would you like to hear about our specials?"

"You don't recognize me, do you?"

Vicki looked at her and blinked. "Have I been your server?"

"I'm Jack's wife."

They stared at each other. Vicki looked horrified, opened her mouth, but didn't say anything.

"Why'd you come to the funeral reception? If you hadn't come, I wouldn't have found out. What were you thinking?"

"I'm sorry." Vicki was flustered. She backed away from the table and started moving toward the bar. The group of women two tables away tried to signal her.

"Miss," one of them said. "We're ready to order."

Vicki appeared a few minutes later, a jacket over her uniform and a bag over her shoulder, stopped at the hostess stand, said something to the girl, and walked out the door.

Diane got up and went after her, following her to an apartment building on Sullivan Street in the Village. Washington Square was at the end of the block. There was a sushi restaurant on the ground level. She stood on the sidewalk, looking in the windows at people having dinner, moved down the street, opened the door to the apartment building, stood in the vestibule, scanning the directory, saw V. Ross in 2B and pressed the button.

SEVEN

Jack was dead. What did his crazy wife want? Seeing the woman had freaked her out. Vicki thought she might even get fired, but she didn't have a choice. She had to get out of there. Vicki wondered who had told Diane about her, and why. Jack's wife had been so calm, sitting there saying, "You don't recognize me, do you?"

No, she didn't recognize her. Vicki had seen her once from across the room at the funeral reception, and the woman in the restaurant, with her hair pulled back, looked completely different. But when Diane said, "I'm Jack's wife," giving her that hard look, Vicki did recognize her, and Vicki's first impulse was to run, and she did, got her things, told Holly she was really sick, had to be the flu, she should have called in, and walked out. Now she was kicking herself. Why'd she go to the country club after the funeral? How dumb was that? Vicki had seen Diane on the street following her from the restaurant and was sure she'd lost her.

Jack had brought Vicki to the house in Connecticut one weekend when Diane was out of town, visiting her old college roommate in Chicago. Vicki had agreed to spend the night, but said, "Jack, I'm not sleeping in the bed you share with your wife. It doesn't feel right."

"We're having an affair. What difference does it make?"

"I don't know, but it does. And what if someone sees me?"

"Who's gonna see you?"

"A neighbor, someone coming over to borrow a cup of sugar."

"People in this neighborhood don't borrow. If they need something, they buy it."

"I still don't like it."

"I'll keep you hidden upstairs. Come up when I feel like it and have my way with you." Jack had grinned and put his arms around her. He thought they were invisible; they could do anything they wanted and not get caught.

Vicki remembered walking around the house, which was enormous, old and comfortable, beautifully furnished. She remembered looking at photos of Diane, thinking how attractive she was, wondering why Jack was having an affair. It didn't make sense.

Looking at Diane's clothes and jewelry, Vicki could see they had similar taste. Looking at Diane's life, she felt like a voyeur. Looking at Jack, seeing his marriage from a different point of view, Vicki felt guilty, that what she was doing was wrong. But she didn't have a choice.

Jack, trying to be funny, had said, "You see the movie *Misery*? It's loosely based on my marriage."

Seeing where and how they lived, and how pretty Diane was, Vicki wasn't buying it. Jack wasn't miserably married. He might've been a little bored, but didn't that happen to everyone at times?

"Diane's a drink counter," Jack had said. "We were at a party last weekend, she came up, said, 'You know how many drinks you've had?' I looked at her and said, 'Yeah, twelve.'"

Maybe Diane had been onto something. Vicki thought he drank too much, too. After a night out with clients, he'd stop by her apartment at three in the morning all slurry, and pass out. He was fun, though. No one liked to have a good time more than Jack.

He had taken her to Europe, and they had done it on the plane in the tiny bathroom when it was dark and everyone looked like they were asleep. Vicki's opinion, it wasn't worth it.

In L.A., they stayed in a bungalow at the Chateau Marmont. While Jack was at a business meeting, Vicki hung out by the pool and, in one day, saw J. Lo, Justin Timberlake, and Ashton Kutcher.

One night they went to a party at the Playboy Mansion and met Hef, who was wearing his customary robe and pajamas. They went into the famous grotto where Hef had seduced countless women. All Vicki thought was how dark and slimy it was.

"You take off your clothes in there," Jack had said, "you better get a tetanus shot."

Vicki heard the buzzer and froze. It was loud in the quiet apartment. She heard the buzzer ring a couple more times, walked over, and pressed the intercom button. "Who is it?"

"Diane McCann. I want to talk."

"I've got nothing to say."

Jack's wife didn't answer. Vicki went to the living room window, looking down at the street, no sign of her, and then there was a knock on the door.

Vicki looked through the peephole and saw her. This was insane. Jack was dead. What did she want?

"I'm gonna stand here till you come out. I don't care how long it takes."

Vicki unlocked the deadbolts, top and bottom, and opened the door. Jack's wife staring at her, as her neighbor Rachel walked by and flashed a concerned look. "Everything okay, Vic?"

"Yeah, we're fine." And then to Jack's wife, "Wanna come in?"

They sat in the living room, a coffee table separating them, the woman giving her a cold stare. It was awkward, uncomfortable, Vicki wondering if she should offer her something, but this wasn't a social call. She said, "What do you want to know?" breaking the silence.

"What was he like?"

"Excuse me. You were married to him."

"Evidently, I didn't know him as well as I thought."

No reason to pretend now, tell her the way it was. "No one had more fun than Jack. He was a blast to be around."

"How long had you been seeing him?"

"We met about three months ago. At first, I didn't know he was married. He didn't wear a ring."

"And when you found out?"

"I liked him and rationalized it somehow." There was more to it than that, but she couldn't go into it.

"Were you in love with him?"

No, she wasn't. Their relationship wasn't like that. "I don't know."

"What do you mean, you don't know?"

"We had a good time together."

"What'd Jack say about me?"

Vicki was trying to think of something that wasn't derogatory, that wouldn't offend her. "You were a great cook, a wonderful decorator."

Jack's wife made a face. "That's it? That's all he said?"

"It was more about you doing things. 'Diane and I went to a dinner party. Diane and I went to a Yankees game. Diane and I went to an event at the Museum of Modern Art.' Like that."

"How'd you meet?"

"What difference does it make? Why don't you let it go. Jack's gone. It's over."

"I want to know. It's important to me."

"We met in a bar. We talked for a few minutes; he bought me a beer and that was it. A few weeks later, he came into the restaurant. I didn't even remember telling him I worked there." Actually she was kind of drunk and had written her phone number on the palm of his hand with a red marker she had gotten from the bartender.

"And then what?"

"A couple weeks later, he showed up at the restaurant again for lunch. I was there working an early shift, covering for a friend. I usually work nights. I waited on Jack and another guy. They were nice, had lunch, and left." The coincidence was pure bullshit. Jack had called, knew when she was working. Vicki was uncomfortable sitting in the hot glare of Diane McCann's gaze, apologizing for going out with a guy that didn't seem to care about his wife. "Jack would come in regularly with clients, different groups. This went on for a while before he asked me out. I didn't see a ring, but I asked, 'Are you married?'"

"What'd he say?"

"Nothing. Shook his head." That wasn't true. Jack had admitted he was married right away. At the time, she didn't know if he was conning her or not, but she liked him. He was good-looking and funny, and the way he picked up checks, he had to have money, and that's what she needed.

"How was London? I know he took you there in early July. Jack said it was a business conference. You stayed at Claridge's, and Jack took you to Wimbledon. I saw him on TV, the quarter finals, and you were next to him. I didn't realize it until right now. After that, he took you to Rome. You stayed at the Hassler, didn't you? Sat on your balcony, looking down at the Spanish Steps. Jack takes all his girlfriends there."

How did she know that? Vicki decided not to say anything else, not confirm or deny. Diane McCann was looking across the deep room toward the kitchen now.

"Nice apartment. How long have you lived here?" Diane stood up.

"Almost a year."

Now Diane was moving through the apartment. Vicki followed her, wondering what she was doing. Diane stopped at the bedroom and went in. Vicki was embarrassed by the way it looked, bed unmade, clothes on the floor, like she was still in school. The closet door was open. Diane was staring at a couple of Jack's shirts and sport coats on hangers.

"I gave him that tie for his thirty-eighth birthday," Diane said, pointing at a blue-striped Zegna. "Why are you keeping his clothes?"

Vicki felt foolish. "I don't know."

"I'm asking myself the same thing. Why not throw everything out?"

"Seeing them makes me think he's still alive. Do you want the tie?"

"Jack withdrew forty-five thousand dollars from our account a couple weeks before he died. What did he do with the money?"

"I have no idea, but I know he was worried. There was something hanging over his head." She threw that out to deflect any further blame.

"What was it?"

"I never found out."

"Ever heard of San Marino Equity? Jack supposedly borrowed money from them."

"No, he never mentioned it."

"When was the last time you saw him?"

"September tenth."

There was a long silence after that. Vicki said she was sorry. Diane said good-bye, and Vicki followed her to the door. The meeting was over as abruptly as it had begun.

EIGHT

Diane went back to the hotel, called home, and retrieved her messages. There were four: her mom, Connie May, Duane Cobb, and Mel Hoberman, who wanted her to call him ASAP. She dialed his direct line.

"Thanks for getting back to me. Diane, we have a situation I want to talk to you about. Hang on a second, will you? I'm gonna put you on hold."

She waited a couple minutes listening to classical music.

"Diane," he said, coming back on the line. "I have Barry Zitter, our corporate counsel, here with me. I'm going to put you on speaker."

"Mrs. McCann, how are you today?"

"What's this about?"

"Apparently, there were improprieties taken with one of the accounts your husband managed," Barry Zitter said in a nasally New York accent.

"What does that mean?"

Mel Hoberman said, "Jack misappropriated a client's funds."

"Your husband embezzled seven hundred and fifty thousand dollars from an elderly woman who trusted Jack and had given him power of attorney," Barry Zitter said.

"I don't believe it. Jack wouldn't do that." Although, given what she had learned since his death, as soon as the words were out of her mouth, she wondered.

"Jack's boss, Stu Raskin, was aware of the situation and had contacted us on September tenth," Barry Zitter said. "Stewart was going to terminate his employment on the morning of nine-eleven and contact the police."

Mel Hoberman said, "I'm sorry Diane."

Barry Zitter said, "Do you know where the money is, Mrs. McCann? Your cooperation in this matter would be extremely helpful. The sooner we recover the money, the sooner we can put all of this behind us."

"You think I had something to do with it?"

"No, Diane," Mel Hoberman said. "No one's saying that."

"Take a look at my bank account, if you don't believe me. I've got fifty-four hundred dollars and a pile of bills I can't pay."

"I hope we don't have to litigate," Barry Zitter said.

Mel Hoberman said, "Barry, come on. No one's talking about litigation."

"This is unbelievable. Jack's dead, and you're trying to strong-arm me? I hope I don't have to litigate." Diane hung up the phone.

What the hell was going on? What she had discovered about Jack in the past couple weeks didn't make sense. She felt like she didn't know him; she had been living with a stranger. The idea that Jack had an affair and embezzled money from one of his clients was mind-boggling. Diane was sick to her stomach thinking about it.

She picked up the phone and tried Sculley, who worked near Wall Street not far from the hotel. He sounded surprised she was in town, surprised to hear from her. Or maybe he thought she was going to lay into him again.

"What's up?"

"I've got to talk to you."

She was at a table in the hotel bar an hour later. Sculley sat across from Diane and gave her a weak smile. He loosened his tie and unbuttoned the top button of his shirt.

"Let's say you're a stock broker," Diane said, "and you were going to embezzle a client's money. How would you do it?"

A waitress walked up to the table. Sculley ordered a Macallan's neat. Diane ordered another glass of chardonnay.

"What's this all about?"

"It's a hypothetical situation."

"I'm not a broker. How would I know how to embezzle a client's money?"

The waitress set their drinks on the table. Sculley sipped his whiskey. "Tell me what's going on, will you?"

She did, not holding anything back.

"I don't believe it. Jack was a stand-up guy; he wouldn't have done that."

"A stand-up guy with a girlfriend."

"That's a little different, don't you think?"

"What're you saying, it's okay 'cause it's not against the law? It's all right to have a girlfriend, get a little on the side?"

"I'm not saying that." Sculley was flustered. He glanced at the whiskey for inspiration, took another drink. "I'm not trying to minimize what Jack did."

"Sculley, do you have a girlfriend?" He looked nervous. "You going to answer the question?"

"No, I don't have a girlfriend."

"Why is your face all red?"

"Diane, I'm sorry about Jack, but you're way out of line."

Sculley was right, why was she taking it out on him? Probably because of his attitude about the whole thing. She didn't think he'd been entirely truthful. "I met Vicki."

"What?"

"Based on what you told me, I found her. It's interesting that you couldn't remember she worked at Balthazar, one of the most popular restaurants in the city."

Sculley shook his head. "What good did that do? What're you trying to prove?"

"Why are you protecting her?"

Sculley didn't say anything.

"I wanted to see what she was like. When a girl steals your husband, you get curious." Diane sipped the chardonnay. "You know Vicki, don't you? You knew the whole time."

"Give it a rest, will you?" He finished his whiskey. "Listen, I've gotta run. It was good seeing you."

Diane checked out of the hotel, walked to the end of the block, turned the corner, and there he was, his scarred face magnified under the brightness of the streetlight. Seeing him so unexpectedly startled her.

"You believe this?" he said. "And I was just thinking about you."

Did he follow her from home that morning? Was he on the same train?

"You have the money?"

"Yeah, right here," she patted the side of her shoulder bag.

He showed expression for the first time, a slight grin getting bigger, showing his front tooth, a diamond pattern on gold, sparkling under the light.

"Want to see it?"

He furrowed his brow, not sure what was going on. Diane reached into the bag, gripped the .380 Beretta, wanting to pull it and show this freak who he was dealing with. But now she was conscious of people moving all around her on the sidewalk. "Another time."

"What you mean, another time?"

She stepped back, moving away from him, and saw a cab coming toward her, all of it happening in seconds. She put her hand up, signaling the driver. The cab stopped and she got in. "Grand Central."

The cab passed him standing on the street corner, looking at her through the side window. He had probably been following her all day. He was good. She hadn't seen him till he wanted her to.

Diane, still tense, ordered an Absolut and tonic in the bar car and found an empty seat on the crowded train, looking out the window at commuters talking and smoking on the loading platform. She sipped the drink, thinking about all that had happened and now the Heavy, whoever he was, putting pressure on her. She was exhausted, nerves frayed, her life turned upside down. She took a couple breaths trying to relax.

The seats were configured two facing two. Her window seat faced a well-dressed guy about her age working on his computer. The woman next to her was talking on her cell phone. The seat opposite the woman was empty.

She felt better when the train started to move, distancing herself from Little Italy and the Heavy, but also knowing she'd see him again. She thought about leaving town, going someplace, getting away for a while. But where? She'd never been any good on her own, didn't like to eat dinner by herself, always felt self-conscious. She'd have to sell the house, which would attract attention, and she'd have to wait for a check for Jack's life insurance.

Out of the corner of her eye, Diane saw someone sit in the empty seat. She looked now, made eye contact with the Heavy. Instead of being afraid, she was angry, reached in her purse, gripped the Beretta and felt better. If he pursued her, she would pull the gun. If he attacked her, she would shoot him.

He glanced at her, no expression, not giving anything away. With the bling and the distressed face, he looked out of place in the first-class car, a pit bull in an art gallery. She could see the other two commuters size him up and frown, still abiding by some unwritten class structure.

The Heavy didn't say a word, closed his eyes, sat motionless for a time, and then opened them, looking past her out the window at rural New York and Connecticut. When the train arrived in Darien, he stood, got off, and disappeared on the crowded platform.

Diane looked for him as she walked to the car. The lot was full, and everyone was in a hurry, commuters moving around her, getting in their cars and driving away. Not seeing him put her more on edge than if he'd been standing in front of her. She took a circuitous route home, checking the rearview mirror to see if she was being followed. She drove past her house and parked down the street, turned off the lights, and waited. Her house was dark. Diane opened her bag, gripped the Beretta, flicked off the safety, and rested the gun in her lap. A few minutes later, a car turned down her street and stopped in front of her house, lights off. She glanced at the clock on the dash, watching the seconds tick, watching the car: ten, fifteen, twenty, and now the headlights popped on and the car was moving, coming toward her.

Diane ducked down as it passed by, then sat up, turning her head, watching it drive to the end of the street, go right, and disappear. She slid the Beretta back into her bag, pulled into the garage, and closed the door behind her. She got out of the car and stood on the side of the garage, lawn and fence to her right, looking at the back of the house, lights on in the kitchen, though she didn't remember leaving them on.

She crossed the driveway to the patio, summer furniture covered with leaves, unlocked the French doors and saw the reflection of someone, a man, in the glass panes, heard the crunch of dry leaves as he came up behind her. Diane put her hand in the shoulder bag, gripped the Beretta, but didn't take it out.

"Mrs. McCann, it's Duane Cobb. I hope I didn't scare you."

"Why would you think that, sneaking up on me in the dark?"

"I stopped by earlier, rang the doorbell."

"Well either I wasn't home, or I didn't want to talk to you."

"I saw lights on. I was worried about you. Let me be straight here, okay? Lot of people in your situation say they don't want counseling but don't mean it. They can't wait to let out all the stress and anxiety, unburden themselves."

Diane could see how this counselor dressed as a schoolboy with his folksy, laid-back delivery could wear you down. "I don't want to talk to you, Duane. Do you hear that? Do you understand?"

"Couple of minutes, what do you say?"

He wouldn't give up, and Diane was tired. She turned the handle, pushed the door open and stepped in the breakfast room, Cobb behind her. If the Heavy showed up again Duane might come in handy.

Cobb followed her into the kitchen, standing on the other side of the island counter. She put her purse on the counter behind her. Everything she'd been through today, she looked calm and relaxed. He'd underestimated her. They both had. She was tough: the way she'd gone looking for San Marino, the way she'd gone after the girlfriend, the way she'd handled Ruben.

"I'm gonna have a drink, you want something?" She had her back to him, opening a cabinet, taking out a bottle of whiskey.

"What kind is that?"

"Bulleit rye."

"I'll have a Seven and Seven."

"That's a sissy drink."

"I don't care for straight whiskey, never acquired a taste for it."

"A country boy that doesn't like the taste of whiskey, huh? You might get kicked out of the club." She grinned, pouring rye in a low-ball glass. "I don't have any Seven Up. Who the hell drinks that?" She opened the freezer, reached in, grabbed a handful of ice cubes and dropped them in the glass. "Okay, what's your second choice?"

"Vodka and Coke."

She looked at him and grinned again. "Who taught you how to drink, your fairy godmother?"

She sipped the whiskey and put it on the island counter, opened the cabinet, and took out a bottle of Stoli.

"I hope this isn't too strong for you."

Making fun of him again. A woman talking to Cobb like that would normally piss him off, but with her, he didn't mind. She opened another cabinet, brought out a can of Coke, made his drink, and put it in front of him.

"Tell me what's so important you come calling nine o'clock at night. Don't grief counselors have a life? Don't you take time off?" She took a drink and held the whiskey in her mouth before swallowing it.

"I'm worried about you. Last time I was here, you were definitely in denial," Cobb said, reciting one of the seven stages of grief.

"Well I'm not anymore. I'm now in acceptance."

Was she putting him on or what? "I'm pleased to hear it. That's what we call progress."

She drained the whiskey and poured a little more over the ice cubes, which had shrunk to half their size.

"But that isn't," Cobb said, pointing at her cocktail. "Alcohol is a crutch, an impediment that's gonna prevent you from healing." Jesus, that sounded good. He glanced at the vodka and Coke, wanted to pick up the glass and drink it more than anything, drain it in two swigs, but held off.

"If you had the kind of day I had, you'd be drinking it straight and fast. It's got nothing to do with grief."

"What happened?"

"I don't want to go into it right now."

"Better to let it out. Holding it in is gonna create more stress, more anxiety, more problems." Jesus, he was on a roll.

She drank her drink. "As it turns out, my husband wasn't the man I thought he was."

"Would you care to elaborate?"

"It doesn't matter now."

"This is what I'm talking about." Cobb held her in his gaze. "You have to purge that negative point of view and reconcile your feelings."

"Drink up, I've got to go to bed."

"You can tell me how you feel about what happened, whatever it is. I don't judge, and the conversation doesn't go any further than me."

"You don't have to write a report and send it to HR?"

"Whatever you say to me is strictly confidential." Maybe it was the booze, maybe it was the low light, but Diane McCann looked sad now. He wanted to seize the moment, take advantage of the situation.

"Not tonight. I'm tired."

"You'll feel better, I promise you." Cobb wanted to keep pushing but cautioned himself against overdoing it. Wait till the next session, he told himself—thinking like a grief counselor. He left the untouched drink where it was, moved around the island counter, reached out like a preacher, and took her hands in his. "We're gonna get through this," he said like it was his problem, too. Diane McCann had tears in her eyes, all the toughness gone out of her, acting like a little girl now. He hugged her and she hung on. He could feel her breasts against his chest. Cobb wondering, in her vulnerable state, should he make a move, try to get some, but she pushed out of his embrace and looked away, probably embarrassed 'cause she'd let her guard down. "Would you mind if I called you tomorrow?"

"Okay."

He'd hit a nerve. Jesus, he'd hit something. "Hang in there," Cobb said, moving toward the French doors. "I'll let myself out."

She followed him anyway, and when he was outside on the patio, he heard her lock the door.

He went to Friday's across from the hotel and saw Ruben sitting at the bar, trying to deal a bleached blonde with big knockers, Ruben talking, gesturing with his hands. The woman looked bored. Ruben took off one of his diamond rings, big ugly thing set in yellow gold, and handed it to the woman. She looked at the ring and handed it back, got up, said something to Ruben, and walked toward the restrooms.

Cobb came up behind him. "What'd you do, scare her?"

"She wants me to take her home. Husband's out of town."

That wasn't the way it looked to Cobb. "Yeah? Where is she?"

"In the can." He picked up his glass and took a drink. "All it takes is confidence. Doesn't matter what you look like. Know what I mean?"

Ruben said that a lot: "Know what I mean?" Like what he was saying was some big fucking mystery.

"Tell her you were a fighter?"

"I might've mentioned it."

Might've mentioned it? It was the first thing out of his mouth, before he said his name. Cobb signaled the bartender and ordered a 7 and 7.

"How'd you do with McCann's wife?"

"I softened her up. She's almost ready to talk, wants to tell someone about her problems. You've got to be patient, look for the right opening, the right opportunity. Like boxing, huh?"

Ruben glanced at him without expression, big hand wrapped around the lowball glass. "What do you know about it?"

"I see them as parallels, similar or corresponding situations."

"Hey, Duane, why don't you go fuck yourself."

Cobb didn't take offense. He thought of Ruben as a gorilla or an orangutan, the man doing everything on instinct. Out of the corner of his eye, he saw the woman Ruben'd been talking to coming back to the bar. Cobb couldn't believe it. He'd have bet the farm she didn't want anything to do with the charming ex-fighter. "I'll see you in the morning."

NINE

Cobb sipped his coffee and put the cup back on the saucer. "Tell me about your general state of mind."

"It's unsettled. I'm anxious, agitated, pissed off, rattled—not necessarily in that order."

"That's perfectly understandable after what you've been through." He cut a piece of quiche with his fork and stabbed it, but didn't bring it to his mouth. "Do you blame yourself for surviving?"

In a moment of weakness, she had agreed to meet Duane Cobb for breakfast. He seemed harmless enough, and she kind of felt sorry for him in the sweater vest, the plaid shirt, and striped tie, like he'd been beamed from a Catholic prep school. Diane thought sweater vests had gone out with dickies and earth shoes, but nobody had told Cobb. "I'm not in denial, and I don't blame myself. Am I angry? You bet."

"Are you angry because Jack's gone, and you didn't get to say goodbye, tell him you loved him?"

"I found out he had a girlfriend."

Cobb shoveled the forkful of quiche in his mouth, chewed, and swallowed before he said, "How'd that make you feel?"

"In a way it was good. It took my mind off missing him, but that's not how I want to remember Jack. It makes me feel like a fool."

"There's nothin' about it that's fair." Cobb pinched a strawberry between his thumb and index finger. "Tell him what you think. I believe Jack can hear you. Tell him you're disappointed in him."

"I'm a little more than disappointed." She sipped the cappuccino.

"Don't hold back." He popped the strawberry in his mouth.

They were in a bistro in downtown Greenwich. Diane didn't want him in her house. Cobb ate the last bite of quiche. Still chewing, he said, "I hope Jack had life insurance, and you're set financially. Have you received a check from the insurance company yet?"

"You're getting a little off track, aren't you?"

"It's all part of the process. It's part of your overall well-being. Mental, spiritual, financial. Do you own your house, or do you have a mortgage?"

"I have a mortgage."

"Are you able to meet the payments?"

"If I can't, I'll sell it."

"I know a financial consultant, a good one. I can have him set up a meeting if you want."

"Thanks for your concern, but I'll handle it myself." What was this sudden interest in money? It didn't sound right, didn't feel right. She'd had enough of Cobb and decided it was time to go. She stood up.

"What're you doing?"

"I'm going."

"May I leave you with a thought?" He took a beat. "'What we have once enjoyed we can never lose. All whom we have loved deeply become part of us.'"

"Is that from your book of uplifting recitations to live by?"

"No, it's from Helen Keller."

"Now you're quoting deaf, dumb, and blind teenagers, huh?"

The next afternoon, Diane saw the mailman on her side of the street a couple houses away. She parked in the driveway, went inside, and watched Lloyd, in his blue uniform, come up the front walk. She opened the glass storm door and greeted him.

Lloyd was a good guy but he was a talker. One time she asked him how many miles he walked in a day, and he gave her a fifteen-minute answer. The moral of the story: never ask a mailman a question.

"How're you doing, Diane? I'm sorry to hear about Jack. I hope you got my card."

"I did, thanks." He'd been calling them by their first names since they moved into the house a year ago. Diane thought it was odd. Lloyd delivered their mail and probably thought he knew them.

"Here you go." He handed her a pile of magazines and envelopes.

"Lloyd, let me ask you something. Have you noticed anything unusual in the past couple weeks?"

He glanced at her and shrugged. "Not sure what you mean."

She wasn't, either.

"There have been a lot of funerals."

"Anything else?"

"I saw these two guys sitting in a car out front a couple times."

"What were they doing?"

"First time, I thought they were looking for an address, stopping by to pay their respects. But then I saw them again a couple days later."

"What do they look like?"

"One was clean-cut and fair, wore a shirt and tie. The other one was dark, not a black man, but ethnic and mean-looking."

The descriptions fit Cobb and the Heavy. Why would they be together? It didn't make sense, couldn't be right. "What kind of car?"

"A dark sedan, a Toyota maybe, or a Honda."

"If you see them again, let me know, will you?"

She stood at the kitchen counter and called the corporate headquarters of Sterns & Morrison in San Francisco and asked for Susan Howe.

"Mrs. McCann, I hope you're doing well. How can I help you?"

"I'm surprised that someone from your office didn't call or e-mail to say a grief counselor would be contacting me."

"I'm sorry, I'm not sure what you're talking about. You think Sterns and Morrison hired a grief counselor for you? We didn't."

"He said he was hired by the company."

Susan said, "What's his name?"

"Duane Cobb."

"I've never heard of him, and I can assure you we did not hire Mr. Cobb." Susan paused. "If this man contacts you again, I'd suggest you call the police. Is there anything else I can help you with?"

Another surprise. If Cobb wasn't a grief counselor, what did he want? Diane would have to wait for him to show up. She'd decide what to do. One thing was clear: she was on her own. There was no one she could go to for help.

TEN

Cobb studied Jack McCann's cell phone bill again from the comfort of his room at the Holiday Inn. There were two calls made on the morning of 9/11. One had been recorded at 9:14 AM, from New Jersey. He didn't recognize the number; it wasn't the girlfriend's. He dialed and listened to it ring several times before a man's voice said, "Hello."

"Is Jack there?"

"You've got the wrong number." Flat midwestern accent.

"Who's this?"

Guy disconnected, cut Cobb off. He'd have to find out whose number it was and where he lived. Jack had called the number about half an hour after the first plane hit. Jack was in the middle of an emergency, a life-and-death situation, and made a phone call to someone.

The second call was to his wife's cell phone at 9:23 AM. Cobb's guess, either McCann didn't think he was going make it out of the tower and called her, or when the plane hit, he saw a solution to his problems, came up with an exit strategy, called, and told her the situation looked hopeless. The call lasted one minute and thirty-seven seconds, awfully short for a final good-bye.

Cobb had also been opening cards: condolences from friends and relatives saying nice things about Jack McCann, cute stories and remembrances, and a few that just said, I'm sorry for your loss. He had taken the funeral registry, the list of everyone who had come to the funeral home, from the McCann's house. He'd noticed it on the kitchen counter the first time he'd stopped by, waited one morning for the wife to leave, and went in and took it.

The registry was leather bound and had a color photo of a golf course on the cover. Every name and address listed was in the area, either New York, New Jersey, or Connecticut. The three out-of-towners who sent cards were J. D. Hagan from Denver; Chris Beard, not sure if it was a guy or a girl, from Scottsdale, Arizona; and Keith Mullen from Tampa.

Cobb tried the first number Jack had called the morning of 9/11 again, and when the man said hello, Cobb said, "Am I talkin' to J. D.?"

"Who is this?"

"A friend of Jack's."

Guy hung up on him again.

He called Kathy Zack, an old high school girlfriend he'd stayed in touch with who worked for the Illinois State Police.

"Corporal Zack," she said in her girlish voice.

"Can you help out an old altar boy?"

"Duane?"

"How'd you know?"

"Who else but Duane Cobb would say something like that? How're you doing, you well?"

"Not bad."

"Duane, you settled down yet?"

"I had, you'd know about it."

"You calling 'cause you miss me? I must say I still do think about you."

"That was one hell of a night," Cobb said, like it had just happened. "I left the next day to make my fortune."

"You got there yet?"

"I believe I'm close."

"You're gonna call me when you do, aren't you? We got to celebrate."

"You can count on it," Cobb said. "I got a phone number. I need to find out who it belongs to and where the person lives. Think you can help me out?"

"You know that's against the law," Kathy said in a serious tone of voice, followed by a few seconds of silence and then laughter. "Well, what're you waitin' for, Duane? Give it to me."

"I forgot what a kidder you are." Cobb read her the number, and she said, "It's gonna take a half hour or so. Where can I reach you?"

ELEVEN

"Find him yet?" Frank DiCicco said. His Mafia name was Frankie Cheech. That's how he was referred to on the street, though Cobb would never say it to his face. Frank was sitting at a table with Dominic Benigno, Dapper Dom, in the almost empty restaurant dining room. The two big men had their elbows on the table and looked like they were crowding each other. Frank had a white cloth napkin tucked in the neck of his shirt and wiped his mouth after every bite.

"Sit down, how can I eat, you clowns standing there?"

Cobb and Ruben sat. Now Dominic Benigno whispered something to Frank in Italian, got up, and glanced at Ruben. "I seen Micky Ward kick your ass. Now you're tiptoeing for chili, uh?"

Ruben stared at him without expression, Cobb wondering what he was thinking. Dominic Benigno grinned, patted Ruben on the cheek, and walked out of the dining room.

Frank's bodyguards sat at another table about twenty feet away, keeping an eye on them. They looked bored. Val, the one with the ponytail, yawned. Cobb didn't like watching someone eat, but Frank was the neatest eater he'd ever seen. Wouldn't let his fillet touch the mashed potatoes and gravy or peas. Cobb thought it was a mortal sin. He'd have taken a big glob of potatoes, dipped it in the gravy, then pressed the potatoes into a mess of peas and shoveled it in his mouth.

"We're not gonna find McCann," Cobb said. "'Cause he's dead."

"You seen his body, know that for a fact?"

"We went to his funeral."

"What does that prove?" Frank could be a real asshole.

"There's a death certificate."

"You know how easy it is to get one of those?"

"We've been hanging around the house; he's not there."

"I could've told you that."

"We had a nice talk with the girlfriend," Cobb said.

"Let me guess, she don't know where he's at, either."

"She hasn't heard from him, is convinced he went down with the tower."

"Uh-huh. Why's this my problem?" Frank ate the fillet first, taking tiny bird bites and wiping his mouth. Then the peas, one thing at a time, still nothing touching, and then the potatoes and gravy. Cobb had grown up on scrapple: pork scraps and trimmings his mother would pour white gravy over, and he'd dip bread into. That was eating.

"Just telling you," Ruben said, "what we know."

"Just telling me," Frank said, mimicking Ruben. "You ain't opened your mouth, but you just tellin' me, uh?"

"I checked his phone bill," Cobb said. "Last call Jack McCann made was at nine twenty-three the morning of nine-eleven."

"So he got a new phone," Frank said. "That ever cross your mind?"

Frank dabbed his mouth with the napkin, picked up his wineglass, took a sip, and wiped the rim with his index finger where there was a little smudge of food.

"Owes me seven-fifty. The man's dead I'm gonna have to collect it from someone else." Frank pointed his fork at Cobb like he might stab him with it. "How 'bout you, Duane? You gonna give it to me?" Now he aimed the fork at Ruben. "Or how 'bout you?" Frank drank some wine. "Or get it from the wife. That occur to either of you?"

Cobb said, "How do you suggest we do that?"

"Send Ruben in, scare the shit out of her."

Ruben looked at him with a blank face.

"One of you knows more than he's saying is what I think."

Cobb said, "What's that supposed to mean?"

Frank took a sip of wine and looked at him. "I know how this works. You tell me he's dead, keep the seven hundred and fifty grand. I'd probably think that way too I was in your situation."

"There's only one problem," Cobb said. "McCann is dead. I think you're gonna have to write this one off."

Cobb wondered why Frank was squeezing lemon on his hands and drying them with the napkin. Now Frank bent his fingers and turned his big hairy hands, so he could look at his manicured nails, which had a semi-gloss finish.

"You got a week. You don't get the money, I'll be going to your funeral. Both of yous."

Cobb nodded at Ruben, and they got up and walked out of the restaurant, Cobb asking himself why he thought Frank would just take his word for it, accept the fact that Jack McCann was dead. Cobb didn't believe it himself, and Frank didn't have to.

"What do you think?" Ruben said when they were driving back to Connecticut. "Why's this our problem?"

"'Cause Frank made it our problem."

"You believe what he says?"

"What exactly are you talking about?"

"He's gonna come after us we don't get the money."

"Oh, I believe that. Frank thinks what he wants to think, and reality's nowhere in sight."

"Somebody come after me, I'm gonna put the motherfucker down."

"You think they're gonna challenge you to a fight, 'Hey Ruben, let's get in the ring'? They're gonna hit you when you least expect it. They're gonna shoot you or run you over and dump your body in a landfill or a construction site. They'll put you in the foundation of a building." Cobb paused. "We've got to put more pressure on McCann's wife, get her to give us the insurance money, get Frank off our back."

Ruben said, "Who's the asshole sitting at the table we came in?"

"Dominic Benigno, Frank's enforcer."

Ruben shook his head. "That's him, uh? He don't look like much."

"Tell that to the people he's killed. He shoots his victims in the head, then stabs them through the heart. Hangs the body over a bathtub and dismembers the person. Wraps the body parts in plastic and buries them. No body, no crime." Cobb glanced in the rearview mirror. "He kidnapped the twelve-year-old son of an informer, Placido Gaspare, tortured the kid, sent pictures to the old man, a federal witness, so he wouldn't testify against Frank. Ended up dissolving the boy's body in a barrel of acid. The family couldn't bury the kid, couldn't mourn properly. Dominic Benigno's a psychopath. You don't want him after you. Believe me. That's why we need to get the money, get this over with."

"You think I'm afraid of him?"

"You're not, you should be."

Cobb parked in the Holiday Inn lot and told Ruben he was going to his room. Ruben said he was going to drive to Darien and drop in on Diane McCann. Cobb's phone beeped. He took it out of his shirt pocket and saw that Kathy Zack had called and left a message.

According to Kathy, the phone number Jack had called the morning of 9/11 was registered to a guy named Joseph Sculley, who lived in a Jersey suburb called Ridgewood, forty-five minutes from Manhattan by car. Cobb remembered him. McCann's friend with the fish-belly-white skin who gave the eulogy.

He debated whether to bring Ruben with him and thought it might be easier to take care of this one alone.

TWELVE

Pushing her cart along the cereal aisle, Diane stopped to pick up a box of Cheerios and saw someone coming toward her. Jesus, it was him. She left the cart where it was and ran the other way, gunning it past shoppers who looked at her like she was crazy—not used to seeing a well-dressed thirty-seven-year-old woman sprinting through a Big Y. She ran down the dairy aisle toward the checkout counters, running out the door and across the parking lot to her car, glancing over her shoulder as she ran. She made it to the car and got in, locked the door and fumbled putting the key in.

He appeared at the side window and banged on the glass with an open hand. She started the car. Diane, staying in the moment, didn't stop or panic, but put the car in reverse and backed out of the space, the Heavy moving next to her.

He held on to the window's edge, running next to the car, till she floored it and left him in the rearview, out of breath, bent over, holding his knees.

Diane didn't know if she should go to the police or go home. She reached in her purse and gripped the Beretta, brought it out, resting the gun in her lap. If she went to the police, what would she say? This scary-looking guy stopped by her house a couple times, and she just saw him at the grocery store. It sounded lame. What would the police do? He hadn't done anything other than scare the hell out of her.

The clock on the dash said five thirty. She drove home and sat in the living room, gripping the Beretta, looking out the window, expecting a car to pull up, expecting to see the Heavy get out and pound on her door.

At six thirty, Diane went in the kitchen and turned on the outside floods, lighting up the driveway and backyard. She made a drink and a ham and cheese omelet and sat at the kitchen counter, watching the evening news.

She rinsed the dishes and put them in the dishwasher, turned off the TV. She set the security alarm and went upstairs, looking out the bedroom window at the front yard and empty street. Diane soaked in a hot bath for twenty minutes and felt relaxed for the first time since she had seen the Heavy in the grocery aisle. She put on flannel pajamas and got in bed, placing the Beretta within reach on the night table. She read two Raymond Carver short stories, eyes heavy, the book slipping out of her hands, decided not to fight it and turned out the light.

The noise woke her, a sound like glass shattering. A few minutes later, she heard the stairs creak, grabbed the Beretta, ran into the bathroom, and locked the door. She knew who it was. Diane sat on the side of the tub. The night-light was on, and she could see the sink and toilet and the beveled squares and rectangles on the paneled door. The handle shook back and forth, and then he was putting his weight into the wood, trying to break the door open.

"The police are on their way and I've got a gun." She pulled the hammer back. "You hear that?" Diane held the Beretta with two hands, trying to steady herself. If he tried anything else, she'd put a couple rounds through the door.

Ruben watched the patrol car pull in the driveway, surprised they got there so quick. Two cops, guns drawn, moved toward the house. Jesus, that was close. He was about to break the door down when the McCann woman had said the police were on their way and she had a gun, and the way she said it, he believed her.

She must've heard it when he broke the window, and must've had a security alarm. Three in the morning, he thought she'd be asleep and he'd go upstairs and have a talk with her, explain the seriousness of the situation. This one had not gone well from the beginning, Ruben reviewing the moves he'd made, but didn't think he'd fucked up. It was just bad timing, bad luck or something.

When the cops disappeared, walking up the driveway with guns and flashlights, he started the car and drove to the end of the street with the lights off, turning them on before he got to the highway. He went back to the motel, thinking about Duane Cobb, who'd given him some bullshit excuse about not feeling well. Ruben went to Cobb's room, and he wasn't there. Ruben had never trusted Cobb. What the hell was Cobb up to?

In the opposite corner, he had Frank DiCicco, Frankie Cheech, to deal with. Frank was playing him and Cobb against each other. Nothing felt right. Everything that looked good a few weeks ago had turned to shit in a hurry, and Ruben wasn't sure how it was gonna end. He needed to find McCann's money. He'd walk away if he could, but that didn't look like an option, unless he took off, went to Puerto Rico or Miami, work again as a bodyguard. Protect some rich asshole, wait around till the guy wanted to go somewhere, or drive his wife or girl-friend to the beauty parlor, sit in the waiting room till they got their hair done. Or take the guy to a restaurant for dinner, sit in the car a few hours till he finished. Ruben had gotten paid to take a lot of shit and it was tough.

Diane was still in the bathroom when the patrolmen came upstairs and called her name. "Mrs. McCann, officers Garner and Turowski, Darien Police Department. Please open the door."

She looked out the window and saw a patrol car in the driveway, slipped the Beretta in her robe pocket, and unlocked the door. The cops were big and young, helpful and reassuring. Officer Garner questioned her in the kitchen. She sat at the island counter and he stood across from her, writing in a pocket-size spiral notebook. Officer Turowski said he was going to check the house and walked toward the living room.

OFFICER GARNER: Mrs. McCann, tell me what happened.

DIANE: I was sleeping and heard a noise and woke up.

OFFICER GARNER: The perp broke a window to gain entry.

DIANE: I heard him come up the stairs and ran into the bathroom.

OFFICER GARNER: Did you see his face?

DIANE: No.

OFFICER GARNER: Do you know him?

DIANE: No.

OFFICER GARNER: Anything distinctive about his voice?

DIANE: Nothing.

OFFICER GARNER: Anything else you remember?

(Diane shook her head.)

OFFICER GARNER: I'll hand this over to the Detective Bureau. I'm sure you can expect a call sometime tomorrow.

THIRTEEN

Diane was in the bathroom putting on makeup the next morning when she heard a car and looked out the window. A Chevrolet sedan pulled into the driveway, and a man got out. Must be a detective from the Darien police following up. She heard him knock on the door, ran downstairs, and opened it.

"Mrs. McCann, I'm Detective Marquis Brown." He showed her his shield. "Do you mind if I ask you a few questions?"

"I've been expecting you."

"Have you now? Why's that?"

"'Cause of what happened last night. Come in."

Diane led him into the living room. He slipped out of the overcoat and folded it in half next to him on the couch, took off the hat and placed it on top of the coat. His clothes smelled of cigarettes. She could see the outline of a pack in his shirt pocket. Diane sat in a chair across from him. He looked older without the hat, head shaved clean, chocolate-colored skin that had an oily sheen in the morning light. His sport coat opened when he sat, and she could see a semiautomatic in a holster on his hip.

Detective Brown said, "What happened last night?"

"They didn't tell you?"

"Who's they?"

"The two officers who were here. Someone broke in, and I called the Darien police. Isn't that what you're here for?"

"I'm with NYPD Homicide investigating a murder that occurred in Greenwich Village."

"Whose murder?"

"Victoria Ross."

"My God." Diane wasn't expecting that. She didn't especially like Vicki but didn't want anything bad to happen to her.

"When was the last time you saw Ms. Ross?"

"The day before yesterday." She crossed her legs.

He opened a small notebook and wrote something. "Where'd this meeting take place?"

"Her apartment." Just tell him the truth. She had nothing to hide.

"How long have you known Ms. Ross?"

"I don't really know her."

He gave Diane a questioning look. "You don't know her, but you went to her apartment? That sound as odd to you as it does me?"

Yeah, it did. Diane was nervous, uncomfortable now.

"Where did you and Ms. Ross meet?"

"The restaurant where she works. Balthazar."

"What was your relationship with the deceased?"

"We didn't have one."

"Vicki Ross had been your waitress earlier that evening. You confronted her. What did you say? What happened that made her leave the restaurant in the beginning of her shift? Hostess said Vicki didn't feel well, but that didn't happen till she saw you."

His dark eyes held on her and she looked away. "Why do you think I had something to do with it?"

"Mrs. McCann, what'd you say to Ms. Ross?"

"I asked her if she recognized me," Diane said, looking at him.

"But you'd never officially met, is that right?"

Diane shook her head.

"You'd seen her before, though, hadn't you?"

"Uh-huh."

"Where was that at?"

"My husband's funeral. He was killed on nine-eleven. His office was in the World Trade Center, the eighty-ninth floor, Tower One."

"Your husband and Ms. Ross were friends."

"Apparently more than that. Isn't that why you're here?"

"Tell me about it."

"She showed up at the funeral lunch, a good-looking young girl I'd never seen before, and I asked one of Jack's friends who she was."

"You were suspicious, thought your husband was having an affair?"

"Not at all. I trusted Jack. I had no reason not to."

"How'd you feel when you found out?"

"I was shocked, couldn't believe it. Hearing it was like getting the wind knocked out of me." Diane paused. "We got along, liked each other. I thought our marriage was solid, our relationship was good."

"Why'd you want to meet her?"

"I was curious. My husband had had an affair with this girl, and I wanted to see her. You don't understand that?"

"So what'd Ms. Ross say when you asked, did she recognize you?"

"She gave me a blank look and said no. I said, 'I'm Jack's wife.' She took off, hurried away from the table, and left the restaurant. I followed her to her apartment, and we talked."

"About what?"

"Jack, what do you think? She still had some of his clothes in her closet. There was a tie I had given him for his birthday last year. Seeing it in Vicki's closet was strange, unexpected."

"Did it make you angry?"

"No, it made me sad."

"How'd you and Ms. Ross get along?"

"Okay, considering. It was an uncomfortable situation. She made an effort."

"Did it bother you, Ms. Ross and your husband had an affair?"

"Of course it bothered me."

"Enough to go back later that night and kill her? You did it, didn't you?"

"Why? Jack's dead. The relationship's over. What would be the point?"

"You're getting even. Girl stole your man, people've been killed for a lot less than that."

"You really think I had something to do with it?"

"You had motive, and you have a permit for a Beretta .380."

"My father gave it to me. He was a PO."

"So you know how to shoot, huh?"

"I can hold my own."

"I bet you can. Where's the gun at?"

"Upstairs."

"Let's go have a look."

She stood and he followed her upstairs to the bedroom. "It's over there," Diane said, pointing to the night table on her side of the bed. "In the drawer."

Detective Brown put on a pair of rubber gloves, opened the drawer, picked up the Beretta, and ejected the magazine. Now he took out a Ziploc plastic bag, opened it, picked the gun up by the trigger guard, dropped it into the bag along with the magazine, and sealed it closed.

"You can just come and take my gun? You don't need a warrant or a court order?" After what had happened last night, Diane needed it for protection.

Detective Brown took a folded, wrinkled piece of paper out of an inside sport coat pocket and handed it to her. "It's signed by a judge. Gives me permission to search the premises and confiscate evidence." He paused. "Victoria Ross was killed with a thirty-eight cartridge. Ballistics will do a comparison with evidence recovered at the crime scene and determine if your gun is caliber-compatible, determine whether or not it's the murder weapon."

"It isn't. I'm telling you, I didn't do it. I couldn't do it. I'm not a violent person."

"But you have a semiautomatic, and it fires the type of round that killed Vicki Ross. You admit you were at her apartment the day before yesterday in the evening. Ms. Ross was murdered several hours later. Think this is all just coincidence?"

"You find any shell casings?"

"Why do you think it was more than one?"

"I don't. I don't know anything. It wasn't me."

"Who was it?"

It was going from bad to worse, and now Diane wondered if she should refuse to say another word and call a lawyer. But that might make her sound like she was guilty. "Jack supposedly borrowed money from a company called San Marino Equity. The office is on Mulberry Street in Little Italy. A scary-looking guy has been showing up here trying to collect the debt."

Detective Brown wrote in his notebook and glanced at her. "Why'd he borrow money?"

"Maybe he was supporting Vicki, buying her things, taking her on trips."

"You know this for a fact?"

Diane shook her head.

"You said your husband died. Why they coming after you?"

"The guy showed me a contract for seven hundred fifty thousand dollars—a contract that I supposedly signed, making me responsible for the debt. Someone forged my name. The signature wasn't even close."

"You have it here? I'd like to see it."

"It's in the kitchen."

He swung his arm toward the door, gesturing for her to lead the way. "After you."

Diane had left the San Marino contract on the counter, right there next to the salt and pepper shakers, but it wasn't there now.

"There a problem?"

"I've been a little scatterbrained lately. I must've put it somewhere else." She could see by the look on his face he didn't believe her.

"What'd your husband do for a living?"

"He was a broker at Sterns and Morrison."

"Successful?"

"He made about three hundred thousand last year."

Detective Brown whistled. "Man makes that kind of money, why he need to borrow more?"

"I have no idea."

"So you were surprised when you found this out?"

"I was wondering what else I didn't know; then I discovered Jack was having an affair."

"Who's this guy you say keeps showing up, what's his name?"

"I don't know. He never introduced himself."

"What's he look like?"

"Dark skin, beat-up face, about five seven and thick through the shoulders. He has a Spanish accent. If I had to guess, I would say he's Puerto Rican. I ran into him on the street after I left Vicki's apartment. He must've been following me all day." She told Detective Brown about the guy showing up on the train.

"This the one come by last night?"

"I think so. I never saw him."

"But you heard his voice."

"Yeah, I'm pretty sure it was him."

"Why didn't you call the police the first time he harassed you?"

"I don't know; I should have. I've had a few other things on my mind."

"Like what?"

"Like my husband getting murdered. That can throw you off."

"Was your husband's body recovered?"

"No but a death certificate was issued. As I said, Jack worked on the eighty-ninth floor of Tower One. After the first plane hit, that was it. Jack never made it out."

"You think the PR knew your husband and Ms. Ross were having an affair, went to see her?"

"I don't know. I guess it's possible."

"You say the PR on the train rode back to Darien, is that right? Sat in your row, looked at you, but never said a word."

"That's right."

"Then he turned up again yesterday? Tell me what happened."

"I saw him in the cereal aisle at the Big Y."

What'd you do?"

"Ran."

"Man's determined, I'd say."

"You think?" Diane paused. "Another guy's also been coming around, says he's a grief counselor hired by Jack's company, but the company doesn't know anything about him. My mailman says he saw two guys sitting in a car in front of the house and described them in detail."

"Your mailman?"

"Mailmen see things."

"I guess they do. Never thought about it. You think these two are working together? One scaring you, the other one trying to gain your confidence: good cop, bad cop."

"Which are you, detective?"

He smiled now, showing big white teeth. "Isn't it obvious?" Brown paused. "Why don't you come visit me at the station house. We'll take a look, see these two are in the system."

"When do I get my gun back?"

FOURTEEN

Duane Cobb stopped at a diner before he got on the road and had meatloaf, fried potatoes, gravy, and a side of creamed corn, mixing everything together. He thought about Vicki, couldn't believe she was dead. Vincent had called and told him. There was a small one-column story in the *New York Times* with a picture of Vicki on page eighteen of the main news section. The headline said: "Waitress Murdered in Greenwich Village Apartment." The article went on to say: "Police discovered the body of Victoria Ross after a neighbor in the building noticed blood under the door. The victim had been shot, in what appeared to be an execution-style killing. NYPD Homicide are investigating."

Cobb remembered the night he met her, stood outside her apartment, and followed Vicki to a SoHo bar. He ordered a 7 and 7, watching guys hit on this sultry brunette with a knockout body, looked like she could suck the chrome off a bumper with those lips, and she drank Guinness.

Cobb walked up to her. "If I said you had a great body, would you hold it against me?

She smiled. "Not bad."

"Stick around, I've got more."

"I'll bet you do."

"I'm Duane, by the way."

"Duane By-the-way, huh? That's an unusual name."

He grinned. "What do you do when you're not being a smart-ass, tempting guys in bars?"

"I'm an aspiring actress working as a waitress, waiting to be discovered."

"Is that right? Well this might be your lucky night."

"Why's that, 'cause I just met you?"

She hoisted the pint of Guinness and got a foam mustache on her upper lip. Cobb would've paid serious money to lick off, but she wiped it with a bar napkin.

She said, "What's your claim to fame?"

"I'm still working on it."

He liked the girl giving him a hard time, getting in his face. "You say you're an actress, huh? What have I seen you in?"

"A McDonald's commercial. I'm sitting at a table with another girl, we're smiling at a hot-looking guy eating a Big Mac."

"That was you?"

She grinned. "Come on, you don't remember that, do you?"

"Course I do. Can I have your autograph?" He took a pen out of his shirt pocket and handed it to her. "Sign this, will you?" He slid a drink napkin across the bar top to her. She looked at him, smiled, and signed her name in flowing blue script. He picked up the napkin, studying the signature. "Okay, I give up."

"Vicki Ross." Smiling as she said it.

Cobb sipped his 7 and 7. "Well, Vicki Ross, I might have a job for you."

"Doing what?"

"Acting." He paused for effect. "Think of it as the biggest, most important role of your life."

She placed her pint of Guinness on the bar and gave him a skeptical look. "Are you serious?"

Cobb looked her in the eye and said, "Like a heart attack."

"What do I have to do?" Vicki said, giving him her full attention.

"Get close to a rich guy, make him fall in love with you."

"Why?"

"So he'll assume your debt."

"Why would he do that?" She picked up her Guinness and took a sip.

"'Cause he won't be able to help himself, won't be able to resist you."

"So you work for the Italians, huh?"

"You're a little genius, aren't you? Figured it out without any help whatsoever. I'm impressed."

"I'm going to pay back what I owe."

"We're all aware of that and very appreciative. But it looks like you need some help, and that's why I'm here. How good an actress are you?"

"Good, I think." She paused. "Who's the rich guy? Is he married?"

"What difference does it make?" Cobb didn't have a specific rich guy in mind. All he had was a vague idea how it might work.

"I don't date married men."

"You won't be dating. You'll be acting, playing a part, remember?" Cobb sipped his 7 and 7. "What was your last starring role?"

"*Oklahoma*. It's a play."

"*Oklahoma*, no kidding. That was the Broadway version, I'll bet."

Vicki grinned. "Yeah, right."

Cobb had heard of it, but had no idea what the story was about. "What character were you?"

"Laurey Williams," she said with a big grin. "I was the lead."

"Well, of course you were."

"She was an independent woman of the times."

"That's what you are living in New York City in the New Millennium."

"Laurey, if you recall, marries Curly McLain, a cowboy."

"This fella you're gonna meet is a cowboy too, a Wall Street cowboy."

He stopped talking and looked at her. "This sound like something you can handle?"

Her eyes fluttered, and she picked up the Guinness and drank. She made a face. "What if I don't want to do it?"

"I urge you to, or you're gonna be paying the debt back in another way."

She frowned. "What does that mean?"

"We'll keep you in a room and have you entertain gentlemen for the next five years. What's that, thirty, forty guys a week, one hundred and twenty-five or so a month?"

Vicki looked nervous, afraid, for the first time, and Cobb believed he'd finally gotten through to her.

Two days later, Cobb took Vicki to Ulysses, a Wall Street hangout. She'd worn a skirt and had her hair up, moving through the packed room full of Wall Street hard-ons in their outfits, confident rich assholes wearing fancy suspenders under their jackets, and shirts that had different-color collars and cuffs, every eye in the place on Vicki Ross.

Cobb stood off to the side, watching guys hit on Vic, come up and deliver their best lines. She'd look, smile, and keep going. He saw groups of Wall Streeters staring at her, following her as she moved through the room, and then, like he'd planned it, she was talking to a good-looking guy at a cocktail table. The guy signaled a waiter, bought her a drink, and looked like he was hooked.

An hour and a couple drinks later, they walked out of the bar together and got in a cab. Cobb followed them in another cab to a bar called McSorley's, one of the oldest pubs in the city.

Cobb entered the loud, crowded room but kept his distance, had a peach schnapps at the far side of the bar, watching the guy and Vicki having a good time. A little after ten, Vicki and the guy walked outside, he kissed her on the cheek. She put her arms around him and kissed him hard like the world was gonna end. He looked happy as he got in a taxi and it drove away. Vicki started walking along Seventh Street. Cobb caught up to her and said, "Looked like you had him where you wanted him, but you struck out."

"You following me now?"

"How'd it go?"

"I gave him my number." She handed Cobb the guy's business card, Jack McCann. "Said he worked for Sterns and Morrison, Wealth Management Division, as a registered representative."

"He say he was gonna call?"

"Yeah, but we'll see."

"What's your success rate with guys?"

Vicki made a face.

"Listen, why don't you come over, we'll get better acquainted, plan your next move."

"You go ahead, start without me."

God she was sexy, standing there in a miniskirt and a blue jean jacket, a scarf wrapped around her neck, goosebumps on those long, skinny legs sticking out of a pair of knee-high black boots.

Cobb was a hundred percent positive the guy was going to call her the next day, but he didn't. Didn't call the day after that, either—waited a full week and showed up at the restaurant where she worked, sat in her section, left Vicki a hundred-dollar tip on a fifteen-dollar glass of champagne. Poor guy couldn't help himself was how Cobb viewed the situation, and as it turned out, he was right on the money.

All that had happened about three months before 9/11.

It was dark driving west on the freeway in light traffic, rush hour long over, to Ridgewood, an upscale Jersey suburb. Joe Sculley, whose number Jack McCann had called the morning of 9/11 after the plane hit, lived on Prospect Street, which curved through the tree-lined neighborhood, stately houses set back. He drove past Sculley's, a big modern place with sweeping roof lines, made a U-turn, and drove by again. It was only nine fifteen, too early to get a closer look at the house, which was partly concealed by trees.

He drove back to the freeway, passed a couple cheap motels, picked one that looked the best, a motor lodge, parked, and checked in to a room that smelled of cigarettes and disinfectant. There were two double beds. He put his suitcase on one, opened it and took out a sap, a set of picks, a screwdriver, a penlight, and a hunting knife with a six-inch blade. If Jack was in the house, he'd know in a few hours. If Jack wasn't in the house, Cobb would find out where in the hell he was at.

He turned off the light, pulled the spread and blanket down, and stretched out on the bed. The neon motor-lodge sign blinked through a crack in the curtains, casting a shadow on the wall. He closed his eyes and fell asleep.

It was after midnight when Duane Cobb awoke. He splashed cold water on his face and brushed his teeth. He put on black jeans, a black T-shirt, and a black fleece jacket. He fit the tools and knife in a money pouch and strapped it around his waist and headed out to the car.

The neighborhood off Prospect Street looked different now. He cut the lights and turned onto Carlisle Terrace, a dead end. He pulled over, turned off the engine, and looked around. The sky was overcast, no moon, no one on the street.

Cobb opened the glove box and took out the Ruger Lc9, eased off the safety, and racked a round into the chamber. He slid the gun in his belt behind his back and covered it with the fleece. He could hear himself breathe. He could hear the muffled sound of the door opening, the swish of leather as he slid out of the car, and the click of the door closing as he leaned his hip into it. Sculley's was three houses north.

He walked through the woods and came out in Sculley's front yard.

The house was dark. Cobb walked along the east side, peeking in windows, seeing the shapes of furniture. He worked his way around to the back and stood on an empty slate patio, looking at the yard that sloped down to a pool with a covering over it. If things went sideways, he'd circle back through the woods to his car.

Cobb turned facing the house now, looking through French doors at the dining room, crouched, took out the penlight, and studied the lock. Took out the pick set, selected one, maneuvered it in the lock, and opened the door. He stepped in and listened, not a sound. He liked the adrenalin boost he got when he broke into a house, liked the energy, the excitement. "Let's see how good you are, boy." It's what his dad used to say when they were hunting white tail. Cobb always said it to himself, trying to psych up.

There was a paneled room with a desk. He sat, opening drawers, used the penlight to identify the contents, looked through stacks of envelopes, bank statements, an insurance contract, phone bills—everything in the name Joseph R. Sculley. Cobb found an address book in the second drawer, took it out and opened to M, went down the names till he came to McCann. Jack's cell, office, and home phones were listed, and his address in Darien.

Sculley, it appeared, also had an apartment in the city. Cobb copied the address on a Post-it. He took off the money belt that held the tools, removed the sap and put it in his pocket, and left the belt on the desk.

The living room was thirty feet long with a big fieldstone fireplace at one end. Cobb walked across the room to the stairs and went up, gripping the gun, wood steps creaking under his weight. He should've been nervous, but he wasn't. It was called believing in yourself. For some crazy reason, he liked situations like this, bust in a house, get the lay of the land, and scare the shit out of the occupants. Wake a guy up with a gun pointing at him, see what he'd do. Ninety-nine out of a hundred people went subservient in a nanosecond, did exactly what they were told.

There were four bedrooms. Three of the rooms had beds that were made. In the master, he could see two shapes under the covers of the king-size bed. The man, who had to be Sculley, was snoring. Cobb held the Ruger, moving toward the bed when the phone rang, and God almighty it was loud. He ducked into the bathroom and listened. It rang four times before he heard a man say hello.

And a woman say, "Joe, who's that calling in the middle of the night?"

"The police. They're here."

"What . . . ?"

Cobb looked out the window and saw a cop car in the driveway, two cops getting out with guns and flashlights. He glanced at the counter where the sinks were and saw a cell phone in a charger. He grabbed it and slipped it in his pocket. Now Sculley came in the bathroom, reaching for the light switch, and Cobb hit him on the side of his face with the sap. Sculley fell back against the wall and went down on the tile floor.

Cobb stepped over him into the bedroom. Sitting up in bed, Sculley's woman screamed like a veteran of horror films. He ran out of the room and down the stairs, looked out the window. One cop was knocking on the front door. He ran through the kitchen to the dining room and saw the second cop coming around the side of the house with a flashlight.

Cobb opened the French doors and ran for the woods, crouching just inside the tree line. Flashlight beams swept over the back of the house, and then the cops started coming in his direction. Cobb moved deeper into the trees and got down as low as he could. The leaves were dry, and if he ran, they'd hear him for sure. He froze as the flashlight beams swept over him.

In a few minutes the cops gave up and went back to the house.

FIFTEEN

Marquis Brown called and asked Mrs. McCann to meet him at the San Marino Equity office in Little Italy, and be sure to bring the contract with her signature on it. "I want to show you something."

Mrs. McCann arrived by taxi an hour later and called Brown's cell number. He told her to come upstairs. He was standing outside the office as she approached and said, "Did you ask them about Jack?"

Marquis, wearing a Borsalino and a black suit, opened the door, motioned her inside, and watched the look of surprise on her face as she walked in the room and looked at him. "Where'd they go?"

"You say your husband borrowed money. When was this?"

"I didn't say he borrowed money; the Puerto Rican did."

"The PR say who he worked for?"

"No, he didn't give his name or anyone else's."

"You bring the contract?"

"I couldn't find it."

Marquis looked at her like, *that's what I thought you were gonna say.*

She was frustrated. "You think I made this up?"

Yes he did. It was the only reasonable conclusion based on what he knew. "Manager said San Marino moved out more than six months ago."

"Then they must have an office somewhere else."

"They don't, nothing listed anyway. I checked."

"What about my Beretta? If you did the lab analysis, you know it isn't the murder weapon."

She was changing the subject. Marquis had to hand it to her, she was good. "Gonna take a few more days. We get a lot of homicides in Manhattan."

"What about the two guys who've been bothering me? Think I made them up too?"

Marquis did, but didn't say it. Her wild eyes held on him. Most bullshitters, in Brown's experience, were nervous and couldn't look at you. This one never looked away, almost made him uncomfortable.

"Are we going to the station to see the mug shots?" Now she was challenging him.

"Is that what you'd like?"

"I thought that's what you wanted me to do. You suggested it."

Someone with something to hide didn't volunteer to come to the station house. It's the last place a murderer would want to go. So now he was curious. "How'd you get here?"

"Taxi."

"You can ride with me." This was good, get her in a situation, throw her off balance, and start asking questions.

They went down to the street and got in his department-issue Chevrolet and drove to Homicide in silence. He escorted Mrs. McCann through the bullpen, the detectives checking her out as she walked by their desks, a sexy woman never failing to attract attention. He took her into one of the rooms they used to question suspects, invited her to sit, asked if she wanted something to drink: water, coffee, a soft drink?

"Got any bourbon?" Mrs. McCann said, straight-faced.

"I think we all out. I'll check the machine."

Now she grinned. Okay, what was up with this girl? Like she's thinking, *I got nothing to hide and I'm smarter than you, Marquis. Got the chops to bust me?* Challenging him again.

Marquis brought in a laptop and set it up on the desk in front of her.

"You know how to scroll?"

"No, what's that?" she said, looking at him, fucking with him. "Yeah, I know how to scroll."

"Well, then go to it. See a familiar face, come and get me."

Marquis walked out and went to his desk, thinking, man, this fine white suburban woman liked bourbon, liked to give him a hard time, get his attention. He could see himself with this girl, wouldn't life be fun?

He picked up the Victoria Ross file and started to read his own investigator's report:

Victoria Emilia Ross

Height: 5' 6" Weight: 117 Hair: Brn Eye Color: Brn

DOB: 6-12-80 SS: 367-54-0229 Age: 21 Sex: F

Police were called to 142 Sullivan Street on a fatal shooting. At the scene and in charge from Homicide Section are Sergeant M. Brown, badge #11978, and Ofc. Jimenez badge #170313.

Murder scene:

The scene takes place inside the deceased's apartment. The apartment building sits on the east side of Sullivan Street in Greenwich Village. The body is resting on an Oriental rug in a pool of coagulated blood. Head north, feet south, mouth open, eyes closed. Single gunshot wound through-and-through. Bullet entered the back of the head and exited through the forehead. Spatter is consistent with single shot to the head. The shooting was fatal. Manner of death was ruled to be homicide. The deceased was pronounced dead at 11:19 pm, September 22, 2001, and conveyed to the Medical Examiner's office. Sergeant M. Brown will testify to his observations.

Victoria Ross had been a beautiful girl, but she wasn't anymore. Marquis studied the gritty reality of the photos, putting himself back at the crime scene. He remembered the wineglass on the coffee table a few feet away. Vicki Ross was dressed like she was going out for the night. No sign of a struggle, which might suggest Vicki Ross knew her assailant. And there were two bullet holes in the bedroom window, like the shooter was firing at someone on the catwalk, part of the fire escape. He'd talked to everyone, all the tenants on the floor, and the kitchen crew from the restaurant behind the apartment building. Not one person remembered hearing gunshots.

Now his attention went back to Diane McCann. How could this sexy, well-dressed suburban woman murder someone in this manner? His conclusion: she couldn't. His guess, Diane McCann's Beretta was clean, because if she was involved, she hired out to get it done. Maybe the two guys she'd been talking about. They sounded real because they were. They weren't hustling her; they were in on it. But how did she find them? Darien, Connecticut, wasn't the kind of town you'd run into a contract shooter for hire. How could he connect those dots? One thing kept coming back to him, one thing for sure: Mrs. McCann most definitely had motive.

Now he looked at the medical examiner's photographs, close-up detail of the small cylindrical entrance wound that was visible after a rectangle of Vicki Ross's hair on the back of her head had been shaved. The next shot showed the destruction on the opposite side, what the round did, blowing out part of her forehead. The victim's nose and cheek also showed signs of trauma, which could have resulted when she fell forward on the floor. Could also have happened when Vicki Ross opened the door and someone stepped in and hit her with a fist.

One of the evidence techs had dug a bullet frag out of the plaster wall. The frag had been tagged and taken to the lab for analysis. Other than the positive ID of Diane McCann by Victoria Ross's neighbor, none of the other tenants in the building saw or heard anything. The neighbor did respond when Marquis had shown her a photo of Jack McCann. "I used to see him leave Vic's apartment occasionally, in the morning."

From what Marquis had learned, Victoria Ross was born in Brooklyn, an only child, and her parents had passed, drowned when their cruise ship capsized off the coast of Malta in 1998. Brown had also talked to Ross's work associates and learned that she had had little or no contact with anyone outside the restaurant. Didn't date any of the waiters, bartenders, managers, busboys, or hostesses.

Once again, Marquis added up what he knew. No one had motive except the wife. No one was even close.

Diane had been in the room a little over an hour when Marquis returned and sat across the table from her. "See anyone looks familiar?"

"I think this is one of them." She turned the laptop toward him and pointed to a mugshot. "His name's Ruben Diaz. I looked at hundreds of photos of murderers, armed robbers, and rapists—black guys, white guys, Asians, and Latinos—before I recognized him."

Marquis was watching her pale skin get red as she got into it, seeing her as a good-looking woman: the blonde hair tied in a ponytail, the slim white neck, the small nose and those lips had some plumpness to 'em. "He's kind of handsome in this photograph."

"It was taken in 1979, when he was arrested for assault. You know who he is? Ruben Diaz, a former middleweight, a journeyman. Tough guy. Why would Ruben be coming after you?"

"He works for San Marino."

"Uh-huh."

"You don't believe a thing I say, do you?"

He didn't confirm or deny, and his blank gaze held on her for a time.

"You tell me you went to Vicki Ross's apartment, and a few hours later, she was found shot to death. You tell me there was a contract with your signature from San Marino Equity, but you can't find it and the company doesn't seem to exist. You tell me two men have been harassing you, and now you point out one of them, a former prizefighter. You understand why I'm having trouble with all of this?"

"A former prizefighter with a record."

"That was more than twenty years ago."

"My husband was killed in a terrorist attack. I found out he was having an affair. I found out he spent most of our savings and borrowed a lot of money, and you're blaming me?" She glared at him. "This is unbelievable. Listen, I didn't shoot Vicki Ross. Everything else was out of my control. I'm the victim. Do you hear me? Am I getting through to you?"

He didn't say anything, and now she got up and walked out of the room.

Marquis wanted to arrest Mrs. McCann, he was so sure she did it, and if ballistics confirmed her gun was the murder weapon, he'd be able to. But as it was, he didn't have anything that'd hold up. Marquis was thinking about this as he drove to the poker club where Vicki Ross had worked. He talked to Vincent Gallo, trying to ascertain some information. The interview went like this:

MARQUIS: Know who killed Vicki Ross?

(Gallo shook his head.)

MARQUIS: That don't cut it. Got to say something verbally.

GALLO: You tell me.

MARQUIS: Vicki worked for you and so forth.

GALLO: Uh-huh.

MARQUIS: In what capacity?

GALLO: I don't understand the question.

MARQUIS: What did she do for you?

GALLO: She was a dealer.

MARQUIS: A dealer, huh? That unusual, a young girl dealing?

GALLO: Vicki knew cards.

MARQUIS: Anyone have a problem with her?

GALLO: What do you mean?

MARQUIS: Somebody she worked with?

GALLO: Everybody liked her.

MARQUIS: Customer ever get pissed off, she didn't deal the right cards?

GALLO: Not that I saw.

MARQUIS: Well somebody did. (He paused.) How long have Duane Cobb and Ruben Diaz worked for you?

GALLO: Never heard a them.

MARQUIS: They don't work for you?

GALLO: No.

MARQUIS: Tell me about Jack McCann.

GALLO: Who's Jack McCann?

That was the end of it.

PART
TWO

SIXTEEN

Jack opened his eyes and coughed smoke from burning jet fuel. He could feel the heavy weight of wallboard and a section of ceiling on his chest. Jack turned on his side, got on his hands and knees, and climbed out from under the rubble. The sprinklers were on. Everything was wet.

He looked up to where the ceiling had been and saw flames and smoke engulfing several floors, and pieces of the airplane, a row of seats with dead passengers still strapped in place. The executive offices of Sterns & Morrison, including Stu Raskin's, were in the impact zone. It didn't look good for anyone up that high.

Jack went through the trading room, a bullpen of cubicles on the other side of the building that had been badly damaged by the blast. "Anyone in here?" he yelled. No answer. There were charred bodies on the floor. Then he saw a leg in black pants sticking out of a pile of debris, pieces of the aircraft: a five-foot rectangle of sheet metal and a fiberglass inner cabin wall with the oval window still intact. He uncovered the body. It was Chuck Bellmore, a good friend, whose skull had been crushed. Jack crouched over the body, felt for a pulse and got nothing. He took Chuck's wallet and keys. Jack would call Chuck's folks in Denver, tell them what happened and help any way he could.

Jack stood up and looked south, saw the top half of Tower Two engulfed in smoke. It was a terrorist attack, had to be. He could see people standing at the gaping opening in the building, and then they were jumping, choosing the way they were going to die.

He ran to the lobby, no sign of Bonnie. The floor and walls were cracked, a twisted metal frame hanging where the ceiling had been. He ran to the hall; the bank of elevators had been blown out. The smoke was thick, it was difficult to breathe, difficult to see. His eyes were burning. Jack ripped off his shirt and tore it into strips, tied a sleeve over his nose and mouth, climbed over a pile of debris, and moved to the stairwell on the northwest side of the building.

He raced down twelve flights before he caught up with people on the seventy-seventh floor. He'd seen some of them before: in the mezzanine and in the mall, riding the elevators up or down, but didn't know anyone by name. The stairwell was packed now, people moving slowly but calmly, friends joking, no one seemed to have an idea what had happened. One guy said it was an earthquake. Another guy thought a gas main had exploded. No one, including Jack, thought the building was in any danger of collapsing. Jack moved shoulder-to-shoulder with a guy in a suit carrying a briefcase. They went quickly down a few floors and then had to stop for a few minutes before they could move again.

On the fiftieth floor, a big man in a wheelchair was blocking part of the landing and people had to squeeze by him. Jack offered to help. The man said an emergency rescue team was coming to get him. On the forty-third floor, a scared woman was sitting on the stairs crying as people pressed past her. Jack stopped. "Let me help you."

"I can't move, I'm too afraid."

"Just relax. You're going to be okay. What's your name?"

"Kimberly."

"That's a nice name." The woman stood up. She was a load. "Lean on me," Jack said, hoping she didn't take them both down. Kimberly took tiny frightened steps, stopping and waiting for the line to move, people entering the stairwell on almost every floor, firefighters in full gear, passing them, going up.

It took forty-eight minutes to reach the lobby, which looked like it had been hit by a bomb. The elevator doors had been blown out, the frames around them scorched black. A transit cop and two med techs met him and put the woman in a wheelchair, and that was the last time he saw her.

It was raining. The fire sprinklers were on, and he was soaked. He was walking in several inches of water, shoes crunching on broken glass, the air thick with smoke and dust. Above him, it sounded like the building was cracking, falling apart. He tried to walk out to the plaza, but a cop told him all the exits were closed because of falling debris and people jumping. Through the windows, he could see crumpled, flattened bodies and pieces of the aircraft: a row of empty seats, a section of the fuselage, luggage and shoes strewn around, and a snowstorm of burning paper floating down from the towers.

Jack was escorted by police down a broken escalator to the mall. He was moving through the concourse past storefronts when he heard what sounded like sticks breaking and then a deafening rumble, a train approaching at high speed. The ground shook, and he felt an enormous concussion. He was thrown off his feet, and everything went black.

He awoke in darkness. People were moaning, some were screaming, but he couldn't see anything. Jack moved with his arms out in front of him, feeling his way, no idea what direction he was going. Even with the shirt sleeve over his nose and mouth, it was hard to breathe, everything engulfed in the smoke.

In the gloom ahead, he saw a flashing light, a medical emergency vehicle that had been destroyed by falling debris, its light bar still intact. A voice said, "Come this way. You have to evacuate the building." And then he saw lights coming at him, firefighters and cops with flashlights, and he was escorted along a maze of corridors and through a door. He was outside now, disoriented and short of breath, walking into a tidal wave of dust, the sun blotted out, eyes stinging, watering. It smelled like burning plastic, burning jet fuel, and odd things he couldn't identify.

Jack was on a street, walking past abandoned cars, the sound of sirens coming from every direction. He looked back at the towers, but only one was still standing. He headed north, moved past a police barrier, two cars with their lights flashing and barricades set up blocking the street.

A cop said, "Sir, are you hurt? Do you need medical attention?"

Jack shook his head and kept going. A few blocks further, he walked out of the cloud, squinting in the bright sun. He was covered in white dust and ash. He pulled the shirtsleeve off his mouth and sucked in fresh air, felt the heat of the sun on his back, and heard the sounds of the city around him. A woman handed him a bottle of water and said, "Are you okay?"

Jack nodded. He didn't want to be recognized. He broke the seal on the cap, unscrewed it, rinsed the dust out of his eyes and mouth, and guzzled the rest of the water. The streets were lined with people, and everyone was looking south at the Trade Center. Jack turned as Tower One started to collapse, the people around him screaming, yelling, feeling the tragic effects. It took about eleven seconds for the 1,368-foot building to crumble in an explosion of dust and debris.

Jack glanced at the street signs: W. Broadway and Murray. He kept going north and cut over through Tribeca. Chuck Bellmore, the friend and co-worker he had found dead in the office an hour and a half earlier, lived alone in a loft on Hudson Street. Jack had been there a couple times for parties. He used Chuck's key to open the front door, crossed the lobby, no one around, to the elevators and rode to the fifth floor.

There was a big floor-to-ceiling mirror in the main room. Jack stood in front of it, but didn't recognize himself. Except for the flesh-colored circles around his eyes, he looked like a ghost.

In the bathroom, he turned on the shower and stood under the hot water in his clothes, rinsing off the white coating that swirled around the tile floor and went down the drain. Jack took off his clothes, threw them in a pile on the shower floor, and saw cuts on his arms, shoulders, and head, and felt shards of glass and fibers that were still embedded in him. He coughed dust and spit it out, washed his mouth out with warm water. He washed his hair twice and turned off the shower, opened the glass door, and stepped out, looking through the window where the twin towers used to be and felt sick to his stomach.

On his knees in front of the toilet, Jack coughed, heaved, and puked up water and bile, took a couple breaths, wiped his mouth with a wet towel, and flushed the toilet. He found tweezers and a tube of Neosporin in the medicine cabinet and a metal bowl in the kitchen. He took everything into the living room and sat naked on a towel in front of the giant mirror. The incredible thing, he had shards of glass all over his body and hadn't felt anything until now. Using the tweezers, he pulled eight jagged pieces out of his forearms and shoulders and dropped them into the metal bowl. Jack leaned close to the glass and studied his face. It looked like he had little patches of light brown hair high on his cheeks. He touched the bristles. They felt like plastic fibers.

With the tweezers, he pinched one and pulled out a two-inch strand. What the hell was it? There were twenty-two in all. He pulled them out and rubbed Neosporin on the pin-dot holes. The wet clothes in the shower, he stuffed into a plastic trash bag along with the shards and fibers he pulled out of his body.

Now he had to find something to wear. He went into Chuck's bedroom, opened the top drawer, and grabbed a pair of boxers. He got them on but felt like they were cutting off his circulation, so he snipped the elastic waistband with scissors. This wasn't a surprise; Chuck weighed about 160, and Jack was 195. He found a pair of warm-up pants with a drawstring waist that fit okay and a polo shirt that was skintight but fine for now.

At the kitchen table, he dumped out the contents of his own wallet and cut up his driver's license and credit cards and slid the pieces off the table into a sandwich bag.

Now he turned on the TV, watching the continuous 9/11 coverage, seeing the plane he saw, American Airlines Flight 11, smash into the north tower at 8:46 AM and explode between floors ninety-three and ninety-nine. No way his co-workers, Stu Raskin included, could've survived.

He watched United Airlines Flight 175, coming from the opposite direction seventeen minutes later, crash into the south tower, floors seventy-five through eighty-five. The accompanying explosion blew out three sides of the building.

At 9:37 AM, hijackers flew American Airlines Flight 77 into the western facade of the Pentagon. And at 10:07, United Flight 93 crashed in a field in Somerset County, Pennsylvania.

Jack watched the Trade Center towers collapse in great clouds of dust, people on the street staring in disbelief, and turned off the TV. He'd seen enough. The events were difficult to comprehend. It seemed impossible. How could it have happened? He was wound up, angry, didn't know what to do with himself. He went into the bedroom and lay on Chuck's bed, staring at the ceiling.

After what had happened today, his problems seemed insignificant, but it didn't change what he was going to do. He wanted to call Diane, tell her the whole story, tell her he was sorry, tell her to move on, but he knew that wasn't possible.

Jack fell asleep and woke up at 5:00 AM. The loft was dark. He got dressed in clothes that were too small and a Yankees cap he adjusted to fit his head, took the elevator down to the lobby, which was again deserted, and went outside. He walked down the empty street, discarding pieces of his driver's license and credit cards in the sewer drain. Jack McCann no longer existed.

He walked for a while, a faint smell of burning chemicals in the air. He stopped in an all-night diner, sat at the counter, ordered scrambled eggs and sausage links, and read the *New York Times*. The headline on the front page read U.S. ATTACKED. HIJACKED JETS DESTROY TWIN TOWERS AND HIT PENTAGON IN DAY OF TERROR.

Jack read the article. Everyone thought Al-Qaeda was behind the attacks. Osama bin Laden denied involvement. He finished eating and went back to the loft.

SEVENTEEN

For the next ten days, Jack kept a low profile, stayed inside until after midnight, trying to recover. His lungs were filled with smoke and dust, and he was weak and lethargic and slept a lot.

He felt safe in the apartment—at least for the time being—knowing that Chuck's only relative was an elderly aunt who lived in Denver. She had left a message on day one: "Charley, honey, it's Aunt Mary. I am worried sick about you. Please call and tell me you're okay."

Occasionally the girl across the hall would come over and stand at the door, knocking lightly. Jack would stare at her through the peephole. She always looked sad, and he wondered if Chuck had had something going with her.

And one morning, a balding, energetic, dark-haired man who identified himself as Dick Marcey, the super, showed up and pounded on the door. But other than that, it had been quiet.

On the morning of the twenty-second, he went to a pay phone down the street and called Sculley, his best friend since grade school.

"Sculley, it's Jack."

Sculley was silent for several beats. "Tell me what the hell's going on, will you? Tell me you're in the hospital, you've been dazed or unconscious, but now you're okay."

"I wish I could go back, change things, do it over, but I can't."

"I don't know what you're talking about." Sculley paused. "I had breakfast with your wife this morning."

"How is she?" He pictured Diane making coffee before he left for the train station, hair pulled back, wearing her horn rims.

"She wanted to know if you were seeing someone before you were killed."

"Where did that come from?"

"Vicki showed up at your funeral and the reception at the club. Vicki walks into a room, she gets noticed, you may recall. Diane didn't know her, so she thought you must have. Diane saw me talking to her."

"What did you say?"

"I told her Vicki was probably somebody's wife or girlfriend."

"She believe you?"

"Are you kidding? Diane asked me her name, and how long you'd been seeing her."

"I said, 'Why do you want to think anything bad about Jack?' I told Diane you loved her." Sculley paused again. "But somehow she knew about Vicki. Maybe Diane smelled her on you when you came home one night. Maybe she followed you."

"She wouldn't do that."

"Diane wanted to know how you met. I told her Vicki was a waitress, and of course, Diane wanted to know where she worked." Sculley took a breath. "She's pissed off. Diane had a lofty opinion of you that's been seriously compromised. You cheated on her and cleaned out your savings. She wants to know why. Can you blame her?"

"She's got the house, and she'll get the life insurance," Jack said, trying to make himself feel better. "Diane's tough; she'll get through it."

"That's all you have to say?" Sculley paused. "Diane said someone was in the house when she got back from your funeral, a scary-looking guy waiting for her. The guy said you had borrowed a lot of money from some company called San Marino Equity. The guy showed her a contract with your signature and hers."

Jack pictured Ruben Diaz, surprised, didn't think they'd go after Diane. He had never heard of San Marino and had never signed a contract. Neither, of course, had she. It was all bullshit, and they were going for what they could get.

"You still there?" Sculley said.

"I'm thinking."

"I hope so."

"Did he threaten her?"

"I don't know. What if he did? What are you going to do about it?"

Jack felt helpless and stupid. It wasn't supposed to go this way. He'd disappear, start his new life, and Frankie Cheech would have to eat the debt.

"You see what's going on here?" Sculley said. "You left Diane in a tough position. You didn't pay whatever you owe, so they're going to get it from her."

"Once they realize she doesn't have any money, they'll leave her alone."

"So you do owe money?"

"Tell her to call the police."

"That gets you off the hook, huh? Now you can put it out of your mind, wipe your hands clean, is that it?"

"I'm in trouble."

"Tell me you got hit on the head. You're not thinking clearly."

Jack didn't say anything.

"Tell me what happened."

"I don't want to go into it right now. I'll tell you this: you're the only one I can trust."

"Jack, this doesn't sound like you." Sculley paused. "You want help, tell me what the hell's going on. Who's after you?"

"I'll tell you when I see you."

"What about Diane? She's in bad shape—can you imagine?"

"She'll be better off, believe me." Jack took a breath. "There's no other way out of this."

A woman walked up to the phone booth, stood close, and tapped on the plastic door panel. "I have an emergency. I have to use the phone."

This was the last thing Jack wanted to do, call attention to himself. He put his hand over the phone. "Just a minute."

Sculley, breathing through his nose, said, "What do you need?"

"Nothing."

The woman banged on the phone booth door and gave him the finger. "I have an emergency. Get off the fucking phone."

"What was that?"

"Some angry woman. I've got to go. I'll get back to you."

He hung up and stepped out of the phone booth as the woman brushed past him and said, "Asshole."

At a J. Crew on West Broadway, he bought a new wardrobe: shirts, khakis, a jacket, and paid for everything with Chuck Bellmore's Visa. On the street with two shopping bags, he hailed a cab and had the driver go by Vicki's apartment. Cobb and Ruben were sitting in a dark sedan parked on her street.

Jack directed the cab driver to Tribeca and took his new purchases back to Chuck's loft, keeping the brim of the cap low over his eyes, carrying the shopping bags as he passed people in the lobby, getting in the elevator.

He rode up to the top floor with a girl in a fedora. She had a silver ring pierced through one of her nostrils and wore a skirt with black tights and high-top tennis shoes. Jack could see her looking at him.

"You didn't work at the Trade Center, did you?"

He glanced at the floor and said no.

"You believe that? Wasn't it the worst thing that's ever happened?"

Jack nodded, holding the shopping bags.

"At first I thought you were Charlie. He wears a cap like that." She paused. "You're new here, aren't you? I haven't seen you around."

"Just visiting." He was hoping she wouldn't ask who, and she didn't.

"My neighbor worked in Tower One. I don't know what happened to him."

The bell rang, the elevator stopped and the doors opened. Jack waited for the girl to step out and watched her walk down the hall, hanging back, taking his time. She slowed down and fumbled with her hand in her purse, found the key and opened the door to the loft across the hall from Chuck's.

Jack went in the apartment, put his bags on the kitchen table, opened a beer, and guzzled a third of it. He sat and cut the tags off his new clothes. There was a knock on the door. He crossed the main room and looked through the peephole. It was the girl from the elevator, her face without the hat, distorted in the wide-angle opening, purple hair tied in a ponytail. She knocked again and then turned and went back across the hall.

At ten the next morning, there was a knock on the door. Jack assumed it was the girl. He looked through the peephole at the super and an elderly woman who looked vaguely familiar.

"Mr. Bellmore, it's Dick Marcey. Your aunt's here from Denver."

It now occurred to Jack, the woman looked familiar 'cause there were photos of her on a bookcase in Chuck's living room.

"Charlie, it's Aunt Mary. Are you in there? Open the door."

The super knocked again. "Mr. Bellmore, can you hear me? Your family's worried about you." He heard a key slide in the lock and saw the handle turn. But there were deadbolts top and bottom, and the door held fast. Now he could hear them walking down the hall to the elevators.

He opened the door and looked toward the elevators. The hall was empty. He grabbed his gear and stepped out.

"Where's Charlie?" The girl was standing in her doorway.

"He died when the first plane hit. The ceiling came down on him."

"Who're you?"

"A friend. I worked with him."

"Charlie and I were lovers. I miss him." The girl glanced toward the elevators. "You're in trouble, aren't you?"

Jack looked at her but didn't say anything.

"They're coming back with a locksmith. Thought you'd want to know."

Jack took the stairs down to the lobby, pulled the Yankees cap lower over his eyes, and stepped outside. A cab took him to the hotel. Jack checked in with Chuck Bellmore's American Express card and went to his room. He figured he could use Chuck's credit cards a while longer. What he really needed was a new identity. He sat on the bed and phoned Sculley at his office. "I need an ID. Know anyone does that kind of thing, passport, driver's license?"

"I'm a tax attorney. Why would I know someone that does that?"

"Call your friend the prosecutor, find out, will you?"

"What's the charge for helping someone fake their own death?"

"You can ask him that too."

"Where are you going to go?"

He hadn't figured that out yet.

EIGHTEEN

When it was dark, Jack walked out of the hotel, hailed a cab, and took it to the Village. There was an alley behind the building where Vicki lived. He moved past the sushi restaurant and heard voices and the loud clamor in the kitchen. The rear door to the apartment building was locked. He looked up five stories, lights from apartments illuminating the alley.

He climbed onto a dumpster, grabbed the bottom rung of the fire escape, and pulled it down. He went up to the second floor and moved along the building on the metal walkway to Vicki's apartment, looked in the window at the tiny kitchen, and saw Vick, her back to him, pouring a glass of wine. He stared at her dark hair hanging over her shoulders and at the hard roundness of her ass in tight jeans, taking his time, enjoying the moment. He didn't think he'd ever see her again. She turned, gripping the neck of the bottle, opened the refrigerator, and put it in. He watched her, feeling his heart race.

And when he couldn't wait any longer, Jack tapped on the glass. Vicki came over, made a visor with her hand to block the light. She put her hand over her chest and stared at him. It felt like a long time before she turned the lock and lifted the window. He got down on his butt and shimmied through the opening feet first, and when he was standing in the room, she came to him and he held her, neither of them saying a word. He could feel the soft curve of her breasts and her heart beating.

After a time, Vicki put her hands on his shoulders and pressed her lips to his, but the kiss had no feeling, no emotion. Her eyes held on him. "They've been here. They're looking for you. I told them you went down with the tower 'cause that's what I believed." Vicki paused. "You said you had the money. Why don't you give it to them? Let's end it and get them out of our lives." Vicki walked over, picked up her wineglass, and took a drink.

She was different than he'd ever seen her, distant, preoccupied, and now he couldn't help but wonder if she'd been in it for the money from the beginning.

"Were you really in debt? Or was the whole thing a performance?" She wouldn't look at him. "You were good, I'll tell you that. You had *me* convinced." Jack felt like a fool. "Is that the way it was?"

Vicki looked at him and said, "No. I was in trouble and I still am. You disappeared, but the debt didn't. Jack, come on, where's the money?" She was frantic now.

There was a knock on the door. Vicki said, "Go in the bedroom and don't make a sound."

"Who is it, you got someone new already?"

Jack stood in the dark, the bedroom door cracked open an inch or so. He didn't trust her and was glad he didn't mention the money.

Vicki was at the front door, looking through the peephole. She unlocked the deadbolt and opened the door. A dark-haired guy in a suit came in and closed the door. What struck Jack as odd, he was wearing gloves. The guy asked Vicki something, and she shook her head. He punched her in the face, and she went down on the Oriental rug. The sudden unexpectedness of it stunned him. She struggled, getting up on all fours, and now she sat up unsteady, her back to the guy, legs bent under her. He pulled a silenced semiautomatic from his belt, aimed it at the back of Vicki's head, and shot her from a couple feet away, spraying the wall with blood and brain.

Jack shifted his weight and leaned against the door. It made contact with the jamb but didn't close all the way. The shooter glanced at the bedroom and started toward him. Jack pushed the door all the way and locked it. He was on the catwalk when he heard wood splinter and saw the shooter come in the room waving the gun. The shooter fired two shots that punched holes in the glass.

Jack ran along the catwalk to the ladder, looked over his shoulder and saw the shooter climbing out the bedroom window, aiming the gun. Jack jumped to the fire escape ladder and started down, sliding with his shoes on the outside of the rails. He looked up from the alley floor as a shot pinged off the concrete next to him. The alley was dark. He ran in the shadow of the building wall, rounds hitting next to him, behind him, and over his head. He came to Bleecker Street, turned right, and saw a cab, signaled the driver and got in, picturing the gunshot that ended Vicki's life and feeling guilty he didn't do something. But what the hell could he have done?

The shooter didn't see his face, but could describe him. The Italians, he figured, had wanted to believe he walked away from the Trade Center, and now they would know for sure.

Jack went back to the hotel and sat in the bar, too revved up to sleep, couldn't get the image of Vicki out of his mind. He thought about going to the police, turning himself in, but what good would that do? He'd go to jail, and Vicki would still be dead.

"Maker's and soda," Jack said when the bartender approached. Jack watched him make the drink and set it on the bar in front of him on a red cocktail napkin.

The bartender said, "Want to see a menu?"

Jack shook his head, took a sip, and tasted the heavy strength of bourbon. He pictured Vicki walking through Ulysses that evening about four months ago, every eye in the bar on her, as she stopped at his table.

"Looking for someone?" he had said.

"Not really."

"What're you drinking?"

"Nothing."

"What would you like?"

"A cosmo up."

Jack signaled the waiter, ordered the cocktail for her and another whiskey for himself. He could see guys staring at her. "This how it usually is?"

"What do you mean?"

"All the attention you're getting."

She didn't answer, put her shoulder bag on the table.

"I'm Jack." He offered his hand and she shook it, surprising him by the strength of her grip with those long, beautiful fingers and red-painted nails.

"Vicki."

"You a Teamster?"

"A pipe fitter, local 636."

"I had a feeling. You have that look." Jack finished his whiskey.

Vicki smiled. "My dad was."

The waiter brought their drinks. Vicki picked hers up and clinked his glass.

"I'm an actress waiting to be discovered."

"What have I seen you in?"

"The new Brooklyn Chevy Dealers spot. I'm in the showroom with my dog. I look at three different models, and then I'm standing next to the Malibu and the dog barks, and I go, 'You like it boy?' And to the salesman I go, 'That's the car for me.'" Vicki sipped her drink.

"You pick a car 'cause your dog likes it?"

"It's a TV commercial. It's supposed to be funny." Vicki paused. "What about you, Mr. Serious? What do you do?"

Jack smiled. "I'm a registered financial representative, a stock broker."

"No wonder you don't have a sense of humor."

That's how it started.

From there they took a cab to McSorley's, Jack's favorite pub, and drank pints of Guinness. Jack wasn't used to a girl keeping up with him, matching him pint for pint. Vicki was easy to talk to and a lot of fun, and she was a stunner. He wasn't looking for a girlfriend, wasn't planning to see her again. He was happily married.

Jack said he had to go home. He walked her outside. "Need a ride?"

"I only live a few blocks from here."

"Nice meeting you." He leaned in and kissed her on the cheek.

"You can do better than that, can't you?" Vicki put her arms around him and kissed him hard, slipping him her tongue, an electrical charge going through his body. "When I'm not appearing in commercials, I work nights at Balthazar, if you know where that is."

Jack thought about Vicki the whole way back to Darien, and she was the first thing on his mind when he opened his eyes the next morning, staring at her phone number in marker on his palm, and then at his wife sleeping next to him. He told himself he wasn't going to see Vicki again, knowing what would happen, holding out for five days before he booked a dinner reservation in Vicki's section, nervous as he rode in the taxi from Wall Street to SoHo, feeling like a high school kid on his first date.

He arrived early, sat at the bar and ordered a flute of champagne, watching her moving through the dining room. Seeing things he had missed the first time: her hair tied in a ponytail accentuating high cheekbones and a slim, delicate neck, her high can and long legs in tight-fitting black slacks.

Jack waited till Vicki went in the kitchen before he made his move, walked to the hostess's stand, identified himself, and was escorted to a booth. His face was hidden behind the menu as Vicki approached. He brought the menu down and saw the look of surprise on her face.

"My name's Vicki," she said. "I'll be your server." Not showing even a hint of recognition.

"I should've called. I think your number's still on my hand."

"What can I get you?"

"Bring two glasses of champagne and join me?"

She gave him a half smile now. "That'd go over well."

"Meet me later. What time do you get off?"

"What do you want?"

"You." They stared at each other for a few seconds. "Where do you live?"

She walked to the bar and came back with a glass of champagne, put it on the table, took a business card out of her apron, wrote an address on the back, and handed it to him. "I should be home by one."

Jack was standing in front of her building on Sullivan Street, holding a chilled bottle of Dom Pérignon in a paper bag, a Wall Street wino. The neighborhood was alive at twelve fifty, cars driving by and late-night revelers passing him on the sidewalk, the blur of lights, the smell of cigarettes, the sounds of the city around him, Vicki in his head, on his mind as she had been nonstop since he'd met her. Jack wondered why she'd had such an impact on him. He couldn't explain it. He'd had a few brief affairs over the years, but never felt anything close to this.

He stepped into the small vestibule and scanned the directory, saw Vicki's name, pushed the button, and heard her voice: "Who is it?" Her tone serious.

"It's Jack."

She buzzed him in, and he walked up to the second floor, Vicki standing in the open doorway as he approached.

"I'm kind of grubby; I'm gonna take a shower, you mind waiting?"

He followed her into the apartment and closed the door. He put the champagne on a table, moved toward Vicki and took her in his arms and kissed her long and hard, Vicki giving it back to him with the same energy and eagerness, and when they finally paused he said, "I've been wanting to do that for five days."

"Why'd you wait so long?"

"I'm married."

"Then why're you here?"

"Why do you think?"

"You can't live without me, huh?"

"I can't stop thinking about you, I'll tell you that."

"You seem like you know what you're doing. You've done this before, haven't you?"

Jack didn't say anything.

"How long have you been married?"

"Twelve years."

"Are you happy?"

He wasn't happy, but he wasn't unhappy. They'd settled into a steady routine. It wasn't boring, but it wasn't exciting either.

"What're you doing here? Go home to your wife."

"Is that what you want?"

"No, I want you to stay, but I'm being selfish. I've been thinking about you too. I was hoping you'd call or show up, and here you are." Vicki paused. "Do me a favor. Think about what you're doing. I'm gonna go take a shower. If you're not here when I get out, I'll understand."

Jack was in her bed when the bathroom door opened, releasing a cloud of steam, and Vicki appeared, entering the room, untying the sash, pulling the robe apart and letting it slide off her shoulders. Jack watched her naked body moving toward him, breasts bigger than he would've guessed, bouncing, a small trimmed landing strip of dark hair between her legs, the only contrast to her olive skin.

He slid over and she got in next to him, their bodies coming together, Jack feeling her warmth, trying to slow things down, take his time, but it didn't happen that way.

Jack woke early and took a taxi back to Darien, in a daze from lack of sleep, reliving the night, feeling guilty as he walked in the house and up to the bedroom and saw Diane asleep on her side of the bed. He showered, dressed, and went downstairs and made coffee. Sat at the counter, staring out the window at the backyard, picturing Vicki slipping out of the robe, coming to the bed and getting in next to him.

"What time did you get home?" Diane came up behind him and wrapped her arms around his neck and kissed his cheek.

"About thirty minutes ago."

"I don't like sleeping alone." She paused. "What's this? You cut yourself."

He was so out of it he hadn't noticed. She pulled a Kleenex out of the box on the counter, turned on the faucet, got it wet and dabbed his cheek. "What'd you do last night?"

"Took clients out to dinner, Cipriani, and went back to Chuck's and fell asleep on the couch."

"You must be exhausted."

"And I might have to do it again tonight."

"You poor guy. How about some breakfast?"

"I'll get something on the train." Jack sipped his coffee. "I've got a meeting in L.A. next week"—which was true—"Wednesday through Friday."

"All you do is work. Am I ever going to see you?" Diane grinned now. "Hey, I've got an idea, why don't I go with you? We could stay at the Beverly Hills Hotel, or somewhere in Santa Monica."

"I'm not going to have any time. We're in strategy sessions all day, and long boring dinners at night. You know how it is," he said, scheming, thinking about Vicki coming with him.

Jack took the train to Grand Central Station and a taxi back to the Village. It was eight twenty. Standing outside Vicki's apartment building, he called his office and talked to Mary.

"What's up?"

"I'm going to be late. See if you can move my ten thirty to this afternoon. Anytime after one."

Jack was waiting in the tiny vestibule as a young woman in business attire came through the door. He held it for her and smiled. "Morning." In the blue Zegna suit and striped Zegna tie, he didn't get a second look.

Upstairs, Vicki's door opened a crack and then all the way. Vicki's hair was disheveled and she was wearing a T-shirt that came just past her hips. She was holding a coffee mug, steam rising from it.

"Where'd you go?"

"I had to change."

"You look nice."

He stepped in the apartment, closed the door, and kissed her, tasting coffee and a hint of toothpaste. She put her arm around Jack's waist and walked him into the bedroom, placed her mug on the night table, turned, reached for his tie with both hands and undid the knot, and unbuttoned his shirt. "How much time do you have?"

"How much do you want?"

"I've got to be at work at five."

He pulled up the T-shirt, she was naked underneath, teased one of her nipples with his thumb and index finger, and brought the shirt over her head. She unbuckled his belt and pulled down his pants and he stepped out of them, pulled off his boxers and sat on the bed. She knelt in front of him, kissed his thighs and took him in her mouth, brown eyes looking up at him, saying, *you're mine*, and he was.

He awoke at noon, Vicki's warm, naked body still pressed against him. He slid out of bed and dressed, tied the tie in the bathroom mirror, getting the knot just right.

He looked through the doorway at Vicki in bed, hair across her forehead, angling down, covering her right eye. He walked into the bedroom. "What time do you get off?"

"Eleven, but I'm working tonight. I'm a dealer at an after-hours poker club. I've been doing it for about a month, couple nights a week."

"Why?"

"Money, why do you think? I can make three, four hundred in tips—more than I make waitressing." She sat up naked, pillows propped behind her, sheet to her waist.

"I thought you were an actress?"

"If I had to rely on that, I'd starve. I've got student loans to pay off, and I have to live."

Jack walked over and sat on the side of the bed. "How do you become a poker dealer?"

"It helps if you've been around cards all your life like I have. My dad ran a game in our house. There were always guys stopping by to play five-card and blackjack. He didn't charge admission, but made money off the rake."

"The rake, huh?"

"It's a percent of the pot. My mother made sandwiches and served drinks."

"How do you get a job as a dealer in an after-hours poker club?"

"You know someone. A friend of my dad's is a dealer. He called, said they were looking."

"Isn't it against the law? The place gets raided, you get busted, right?"

"The club's owned by Frank DiCicco, ever heard of him?"

"The Mafia guy?"

"I'm sure he's paying the police to leave us alone."

"Do you have any other hidden talents you want to tell me about?"

Vicki smiled. "Come back later, I'll show you. I can give you a key, you can spend the night. I'll wake you up with a blow job when I get home."

In the morning, Jack called Sculley. "Listen, I've got to get out of town. What did you find out?"

"The prosecutor said he heard there were a couple places in Brooklyn, convenience stores on Flatbush Avenue. Of course, he wanted to know why. I told him I have a friend who was doing research for a novel."

"He believed that?"

"What do you care."

"Flatbush and what?"

Jack got out of the taxi at the corner of Flatbush and Tilden. He walked north several blocks, crossed the street, and walked south back to Tilden and kept going. He came to a small market that had a sign in the window: IDs. Went in, looked around. He felt especially out of place in his J. Crew outfit.

He waited by the checkout counter for the cashier to ring up a woman's groceries and pack everything into paper bags. When the woman wheeled her grocery cart away from the counter, the cashier, a black man with short dyed blonde hair and a ring through his lower lip, said, "Look like you lost. What you need?"

"An ID, driver's license. I lost mine. And a passport."

"Cost you two fifty for the license. Don't do passports."

"Do I pay you?"

"See anyone else standing here?"

"First, I want to see the finished product."

"Got concerns, take your biz elsewhere."

This wasn't a time to negotiate. Jack took a wad of bills out of the pocket of his new khakis, counted the money, and handed it to the man. The cashier folded the money and put it in his pocket. He came around the counter, said, "Yo, over here," and escorted Jack to the back of the store, opened a door, and motioned him inside. Jack followed the guy through the stockroom into an office with bare walls that needed paint. There was a teenager sitting at an old metal desk.

The cashier said, "Yo, Reg, y'all take care of my man here? Needs a license."

The kid looked up from his computer, stood and moved behind a makeshift plywood counter that had a camera with a tripod on it. "Yo, want to come over here, gotta take your pitcher."

The cashier left the room. Jack stood in front of the camera, and the kid said, "Go back couple inches. Stop. Okay, now look here, don't move."

Jack heard the camera click several times.

The kid paused, looking in the viewfinder. "I think we got it. Have a seat over there."

There was furniture on the other side of the room, a beat-up couch facing a couple beat-up chairs. He sat and paged through yesterday's *New York Post*.

"Need your name and address, what you want it to say." The kid offered Jack a piece of lined paper and a pen. "Write it down for me, okay?"

Twenty minutes later, Jack walked out of the market with an authentic New York driver's license that said he was Richard Alan Keefer, born October 6, 1960, his real birthday. Had brown eyes, was six feet tall, and lived on West 59th Street in Midtown.

Now he could get out of the city, disappear.

NINETEEN

Cobb showed Jack McCann's picture to the Latina hotel clerk. "He worked at the Trade Center. He's gone missing. We've checked all the hospitals, and now we're checking Manhattan hotels. I wonder, you seen this fella around the property?"

"You with the police?"

"Private investigator hired by the man's wife, who is extremely distraught about her missing life partner she fears is deceased. Man has some issues upstairs," he said, pointing at his temple. "Isn't right in the head." Cobb had read that many 9/11 survivors had ended up in New York hospitals without identification, and others were dazed, wandering the streets of the city. Many people living close to ground zero had to evacuate their homes. Cobb didn't think he had to say anything else. There was a lot of emotion surrounding the events of 9/11.

The hotel clerk said, "I have friends who lost their husbands that day." She took a breath, eyes getting moist. "We're not supposed to give out any information on our guests. I will tell you this, I have seen him in the hotel, but he is not registered as Mr. McCann."

"Do you happen to have a Charles Bellmore checked in by any chance?"

The hotel clerk typed on the computer keyboard in front of her and glanced at the monitor. She wrote something on a piece of paper and handed it to him.

"You didn't get it from me."

"Get what?" Cobb said and winked.

He took the elevator up to the fourth floor and walked down the hall to room 410, put his ear up close to the door, but didn't hear anything. He knocked and waited, but no one came.

Duane Cobb sat at a table in the tiny bar with a clear view of the reception desk and elevators. The call log on Sculley's cell phone had led him to the Michelangelo Hotel. Of the twenty-seven calls listed, only three weren't identified by a name. According to Cobb's old girlfriend with the state police, one number was a phone booth on Leonard Street; the second was listed to a Charles Bellmore, lived on Hudson Street, and the third was the hotel he was sitting in.

Earlier, he'd picked up a map of Manhattan and found the two streets. Leonard and Hudson were in Tribeca, ran into each other. Now he pictured Jack McCann escaping from Tower One, walking to Chuck's apartment, and ending up staying there. If that was true, why'd Jack use a phone booth to call Sculley?

Cobb found the phone booth on Leonard Street, and right around the corner was the apartment building. He went in, saw C. Bellmore on the directory, and took the elevator up to the fifth floor.

Cobb knocked on the door. No one came. He tried the door across the hall. It opened, and a girl with a ring in her nose said, "If you're looking for Charlie, I haven't seen him since nine-eleven. I don't think he made it."

"I'm looking for a friend of his, guy named Jack." Cobb showed her the photograph.

"He was here, but now he's gone. I saw him leave with a suitcase."

"When was that?"

"Couple days ago."

"How long was he here?"

"I don't know for sure, a week, maybe more."

Cobb had nursed two Cokes and eaten a hamburger and fries at the Michelangelo bar. Normally easygoing, he'd gone into full impatient mode while he waited, the waitress looking at him like, *hey, slick, you've been holding this table for a couple hours now, ever going to leave?* And then a guy in a Yankees cap walked past him in the lobby. Cobb caught him in profile for several seconds. It was the man's size and the way he moved that told him it was Jack McCann. Cobb took two twenties out of his wallet, left them on the table, and hurried to the elevators.

Jack was looking at his perfect New York driver's license, amazed it had been made in the back room of a neighborhood market. He heard a knock on the door. Hotel employees usually announced themselves. He got up and looked through the peephole, didn't see anyone, and swung the safety bar in place. There was another knock, but whoever was on the other side of the door didn't want to be seen. He slipped out of his loafers, picked them up, and quietly walked back into the room in his socks.

He stood at the window, looking down at cars zipping by on the street in front of the hotel. Whoever was in the hall—and he assumed it was Cobb or his partner—knocked again. He sat on the foot of the bed, looking at the door. He got up and went to the phone, pressed the front desk button, and heard a woman's voice say, "Mr. Bellmore, how can I be of assistance?"

"There's a drunk guy in the hall, banging on my door."

"Oh dear. I'll contact security right away."

Jack repacked the suitcase and set it on the floor. A few minutes later, there was a loud knock. "Mr. Bellmore, it's hotel security."

Jack opened the door, looking at a heavyset man in a blue blazer.

"Sir, there's no one out here. Tell me what happened."

"I rode up in the elevator with a guy who was hammered, started giving me a hard time. I don't remember what it was about. Followed me down the hall to my room. I went in, and he banged on the door a few times, and I called the front desk."

"What did he look like?"

"Five eleven, dark hair, I don't know, maybe a hundred and seventy."

"What was he wearing?"

"I don't remember."

Jack went down to the front desk with the security guy, scanned the long, narrow lobby, and saw Duane Cobb on a couch, reading the newspaper, hotel guests moving past him, coming in and going out.

"There he is," Jack said, nodding at Cobb.

The security guy said, "Over there, in the leather jacket?"

"That's him."

"Mr. Bellmore, do me a favor, wait here."

Jack waited till the security guy was halfway to Cobb, turned and walked down a hallway, through the kitchen and out a door that led to an alley. Two Asian men in burgundy aprons and smoking cigarettes glanced at him but didn't say anything. He walked to Seventh Avenue, looking around, making sure he wasn't followed, and hailed a cab.

Cobb saw Jack McCann talking to a big guy in a blazer, had security written all over him, and now Mr. Security was coming across the lobby, moving toward him. Cobb was surprised, didn't think Jack would play it this way.

Up close, he looked even bigger, the size of an NFL linebacker. "Sir, I'm with hotel security. I'd like to have a word with you. Would you come with me, please?"

Cobb relaxed, in control, folded the newspaper and placed it on the couch next to him. "What's this all about?"

"Sir, are you a guest in the hotel?"

"No. I'm here visiting one. Just waiting for him to come down."

"What's the guest's name?"

"Charlie Bellmore."

"Mr. Bellmore said you were harassing him."

Cobb gave him a big good ole boy grin. "He's putting you on. See, Charlie's a practical joker."

"Sir, have you been drinking?"

"No, I have not. Like I said, Charlie's a kidder. He goes to great lengths to embarrass his friends."

The security man looked like he was being conned. "Then you won't mind having a word with Mr. Bellmore, so we can clear this up."

Cobb had taken his eye off Jack for a few seconds, and when he looked again, Jack was gone. "No problem. Let's go."

When they got to the reception counter, the security man looked around and said, "I asked Mr. Bellmore to wait right here."

"Maybe he's in the bar," Cobb said. Although he knew Jack was long gone.

The security man said something to the female clerk behind the counter.

She shook her head.

"Try his room, will you?"

She punched in a number. Cobb could hear it ringing. The woman shook her head again and put the phone down.

The security man moved to the bar area, which opened to the lobby. There were only three tables occupied. He came back and said, "Sir, I owe you an apology. It seems Mr. Bellmore was having a little fun at my expense."

"He is convincing, isn't he? That's why the gag works so well."

"I'm going to have a word with him, I can tell you that."

"I'd give him hell," Cobb said.

"Oh, you can count on it."

Cobb walked out of the hotel, looked across the street, and saw Ruben in his car, sitting at the curb in a no-parking zone. He crossed over and got in the front passenger seat. Ruben glanced at him, said, "Where's he at?"

Jack checked in to the Omni on East 52nd Street with Chuck Bellmore's American Express card and no luggage. "The airline lost it," he told the Omni receptionist, who didn't react or say, That's too bad, or say, When the bag arrives, I'll have it sent up. She handed him a keycard and pointed to the elevators.

He'd left his suitcase at the Michelangelo, so he didn't have clothes or toiletries. He couldn't have taken the elevator carrying a suitcase with the security guy. It wouldn't have looked right, and after seeing Duane Cobb in the lobby, he wouldn't have had time to go up and get it.

Staring out the window at Madison Avenue, he called Sculley's office.

"Jesus, where are you?"

"Fifty-Second and Madison. Know what I'm talking about?"

"I'll meet you in the bar in half an hour."

Jack was at a table in the far corner of the room when Sculley came in and signaled him. Sculley was sitting before Jack noticed his swollen jaw. "Jesus, what the hell happened?"

"I had a visitor last night. Somebody broke in, came through the French doors in back, triggered the alarm. The police called. I got up, went in the bathroom, there was a guy standing there. He hit me with something, knocked me out. Ilene said she screamed and he ran downstairs. The police came in the house responding to the alarm, and surprised him, chased him, but he got away. They checked the garage and the yard but didn't find him. They took me to the hospital, three thirty in the morning. I had my jaw X-rayed. It's bruised but it's not broken. Ilene's a basket case, won't go in the house, went to stay with her parents in Syracuse for a few days."

"If I were you, I wouldn't go back there either. Stay in your apartment in the city, and watch yourself. I don't think they're going to bother you again, but why take the risk?"

A waitress walked up to the table, and they ordered drinks. A Stella for Jack and a Macallan's ten-year-old with a couple ice cubes for Sculley.

"The only thing missing is my cell phone. Why take someone's cell phone?"

"See who you've been calling and who's been calling you. Sure there weren't two of them?"

"I don't know how many there were. I was unconscious."

"What did the guy in the bathroom look like?"

"I only saw him for a second. Ilene said she thought he had dark hair and was about my height."

"Sounds like Duane Cobb. His partner's an ex-fighter named Ruben Diaz. I'll bet they came looking for me. Cobb probably knows I called you the morning of nine-eleven, so it must've been important."

"He thinks you're alive?"

"He doesn't think it; he knows it. Cobb came to the hotel, saw me in the lobby, followed me upstairs, and knocked on my door."

Sculley picked up a water glass and held it against his swollen jaw, eyes watering in pain.

"You okay?"

"I'll have to get back to you on that."

The waitress brought their drinks and put them on the table. Sculley picked up the whiskey, took a sip, closed his eyes and made a face.

Jack said, "Vicki's dead."

Sculley stared at him.

"The killer came to her apartment and shot her, executed her. I watched it and didn't do anything."

Sculley frowned. "What the hell were you going to do?"

"The shooter came after me. I went down the fire escape and got away."

"Was it the two who are after you?"

"No, but they all work for Frank DiCicco, a Mafia underboss. Ever heard of Frankie Cheech?"

"What's his interest in you?"

"I owe him money."

"He's the loan shark?"

Jack nodded.

"How did Vicki get in debt to a loan shark?"

"She played high-stakes poker, a private game, got in over her head."

"How much over her head?"

"Originally it was a couple hundred grand." Jack drank his beer. "But the debt kept multiplying."

"Why didn't you talk to her?"

"I didn't know about it. She had ten days to pay the original debt. She couldn't come up with the money, and the meter kept spinning."

"This girl you had just met and barely knew asked you to bail her out? Come on."

"She didn't ask. She told me what happened, and I offered."

"Why?"

"I liked her, and I didn't want anything to happen to her. By the time I got involved, the debt had spun out of control. They were taking advantage of Vicki."

"I think they were taking advantage of you."

"It crossed my mind but not till later." Jack paused. "I set up a meeting with Vincent Gallo, who ran the poker room, told him I was assuming Vicki's debt and to leave her alone."

"You had that kind of money after buying the house?"

"Not even close. I cashed in most of our savings, which wasn't much. Then I decided to borrow the full amount from an elderly client who had given me power of attorney."

"Are you out of your mind? If the loan shark doesn't get you, the SEC will."

"That's what I've been trying to tell you. I see myself going to prison, and when I get out, Frankie Cheech will be waiting."

"Jesus." Sculley shook his head, sipped his drink, and made a face. "How long will it take Sterns and Morrison to find out?"

"They already know. My boss had been trying to reach me for a couple days before nine-eleven, and called again just before the first plane hit, wanted me to come up to his office on the ninety-fourth floor. I'm sure he was going to fire me on the spot." Jack took a drink of beer. "I was going to give Cobb and Ruben Diaz a cashier's check that morning."

"What did you tell Diane?"

"I didn't tell her anything. Nine-eleven happened, and I thought, This is my way out."

Sculley sipped his whiskey. "You still have the money?"

Jack nodded.

"Why don't you give it to them."

"You think they're going to forget what's happened, take it, and wish me good luck?"

"Then you're going to be looking over your shoulder for the rest of your life."

"I already am."

"They're not going to stop till they find you. If you're not worried, you should be." Sculley sipped his whiskey. "Am I getting through to you?"

"Why do you think I'm leaving?"

"What about Diane? Don't you feel anything for her? You've put her in a tough situation."

"I feel bad, but there's nothing I can do about it."

"Call her, tell her you're alive, tell her what happened."

"And then what?"

TWENTY

That evening, Jack took a taxi to the airport and bought a one-way ticket to Fort Lauderdale in the name Richard Keefer, showed his new driver's license to the ticket agent, and paid in cash. He waited at the gate thinking about Diane, feeling guilty after talking to Sculley, picturing her in the big house alone and afraid. There was nothing he could do. They'd threaten her, but he knew they wouldn't hurt her. She would just have to get through it.

The plane landed at nine thirty. As they taxied to the gate, the pilot announced that the temperature was seventy-eight degrees. He walked out of the terminal and felt the warm, humid air. Jack had the new driver's license, but no credit cards to go with it. He had Chuck Bellmore's American Express and license, but he and Chuck looked nothing alike.

He took a cab to Pompano Beach and got out at Atlantic Boulevard and A1A. He walked toward the flashing neon motel signs and stopped at the Sands, a beige two-story building on the beach, with a swimming pool behind it. Beyond the pool he could see the Atlantic Ocean. The white Sands sign flashed on and off, and under it a smaller sign said Vacancy. He checked in and went to bed.

Jack was getting dressed, fitting cufflinks through holes in the cuffs, buttoning the shirt and tying the bow tie, finally doing a passable job on the fourth attempt. He sipped a Stoli and tonic, trying to settle his nerves. He had been jittery all day, which somehow seemed fitting, since he was getting married in an hour. He wasn't worried that he'd made the wrong choice in a wife. He had not been attracted to another girl since he'd met Diane two years earlier. What might've thrown him off a little, he was going into uncharted territory. Jack had never lived with a woman. Sure, they had spent part of every week together, but he could go back to his place and she to hers. After today, there was nowhere to go.

He had met Diane Jackson at Joe Sculley's wedding. Ilene, the girl Joe was marrying, and Diane were friends. Even before the wedding, Sculley had bugged Jack about asking her out. "I'm telling you she's something. Trust me, will you? You're going to thank me."

And then he saw Diane in the church before Joe and Ilene's ceremony, and he felt something in his gut. Jack and Diane were paired during the wedding, walked down the aisle together, sat next to each other at dinner. Jack couldn't believe he had put her off for so long, although it was more about not trusting Sculley's taste in women.

On their first date, Jack picked Diane up at her apartment and took her to a bar. They had drinks and dinner, talked about books and movies. Jack suggested seeing *Wall Street*, a midnight show at a multiplex not far from where they were. On the way to the theater, he stopped and bought a bottle of cabernet, a couple plastic cups, and a corkscrew. They sat in the last row so no one could see them drinking. They finished the bottle, and Diane started nodding off. That was the last thing Jack remembered. He woke up first. The screen was black, the lights were on, the theater was empty. He looked at his watch and woke Diane. She looked around and said, "Where is everybody?"

"Gone. It's four in the morning."

"What? Why didn't someone wake us up?"

"Good question." They got up and went in the lobby. The lights were on but no one was there. "Let's get out of here." The doors they had entered four hours earlier were now chained from the inside. He looked out at the dark empty parking lot and saw his car. Now what?

Diane said, "Should we call the police?"

"I left my phone in the car."

"We'll use the pay phone. Do you have any change?"

Jack dug his hands in his pockets and shook his head. He turned, scanning the lobby, walked over to a furniture grouping, and picked up a leather chair with a metal frame that weighed as much as a bag of cement. He dragged it to the doors.

"What're you going to do?"

He picked up the chair and swung it into a floor-to-ceiling window flanking one of the double doors. The chair exploded through the glass and landed outside the building. Jack kicked out shards until the opening was big enough to fit through, and they ran to the car, jumped in, looked at each other, and started laughing.

They were inseparable after that, Jack telling Diane it was the best first date he had ever been on, and two years later, they got married.

Jack remembered how good Diane had looked in church, coming down the aisle, escorted by her father, the ex-cop who'd struck it rich running a successful home security company. He remembered scenes from the reception, his drunk groomsmen running down the first fairway at ultraconservative Darien Country Club, hoping Diane's father didn't get put on probation for sponsoring boorish behavior.

He remembered the same group, later, jumping off the diving board into the pool in their rented tuxes. Diane's father told Jack it was okay to shake things up, give the country club rule-followers something to talk about.

They honeymooned in Tahiti, an island off the coast named Moorea. The hotel rooms were grass-roof huts built over the turquoise water. He and Diane were in love; all he wanted to do was touch her and kiss her.

Jack now felt the hot sun on his face and opened his eyes, blinking in the bright glare, forgetting for an instant he was in a motel room in Florida, morning sun streaming through the open slats in the blinds.

He turned on the shower and stood under the water. He dried off and put on the same clothes he had worn for the past two days. He had an ocean view and stood at the window, looking out at the waves crashing on shore, wondering what he was going to do. After all that had happened, coming to southern Florida seemed like a good idea. He knew the area and had everything he needed to start over, start his new life. There were a couple of problems he would have to take care of first: getting a credit card in his new name, then renting a car and finding a place to live. He also needed a cell phone and clothes.

First he went to the post office and got a post office box. You had to have an address to get a credit card. Then he went to the SunTrust Bank he had passed earlier, opened an account with three grand he'd withdrawn a few days before 9/11, and filled out an application for a Visa. Darlene, the assistant manager, said it usually took a few days, but she could expedite the proceedings because he opened the savings account with cash money.

"Are you new in town, Mr. Keefer?"

"I arrived yesterday."

"You're gonna love it here," Darlene said, smiling. "I'll tell you that. The Arbor Day Foundation named Pompano a Tree City USA community for its commitment to forestry for the fifteenth year in a row, but don't quote me."

"No kidding," Jack said, already bored. "That's wonderful."

"And don't miss Music Under the Stars the second Friday of every month." Darlene paused. "Do you like shells, Mr. Keefer?"

Jack gave a fake smile, not sure where she was going with this.

"You have to see the Broward Shell Show. It's at the Emma Lou Olsen Civic Center—all these super-talented shell crafters showing off their works of art. And there's way more than that too."

Jack got out of there as fast as he could, worn out from small talk.

There was a shopping center across the street. He walked through the parking lot and moved along the concourse passing storefronts, stopped at a men's clothing store that had outfits for old-timers in the window, mannequins decked out in casual resort wear. He went in and bought a couple pairs of shorts, four golf shirts in assorted colors, a bathing suit, sandals, socks, and underwear.

At Pompano Drugs, he bought a toothbrush, toothpaste, shampoo, razors and shaving cream, a beach towel, tanning lotion, and sunglasses. He took everything back to the motel, shaved, brushed his teeth, and changed into the bathing suit. Now he stood in front of the medicine cabinet mirror, looking at his pale chest and stomach, imagining Diane in the room, hearing her say, "Jack, how could you do this to me? You were my rock."

TWENTY-ONE

"You were McCann, where would you go?"

"Somewhere warm," Ruben said.

"That narrows it down." They were in Cobb's Toyota parked on Ericson Place across from the apartment building. It was cold out. You could see your breath, and there was frost on the windshield.

"I guess it depends how much money I had. Puerto Rico for sure."

"Yeah, they'd never think to look for you there."

Ruben, all churched up in a black sport jacket and striped shirt, gave him a dirty look.

"Hey," Cobb said, looking out the side window. "There he is, blue overcoat, tan sport cap, briefcase." He watched Joe Sculley come out of the apartment building and head south along the outer edge of the sidewalk close to the street. Sculley walked to the end of the block, turned right.

Ruben said, "Sure it's him?"

"Trust me."

"Let's go get him then, uh?"

"You want to take him now, in broad daylight?" They were creeping in heavy morning traffic on Varick Street.

"Why not?"

Cobb could think of a few reasons—all of them breaking the laws of New York City. "What're you gonna do?"

Ruben told him, and it didn't sound too bad, New Yorkers being uncaring, who-gives-a-fuck kind of people. Would anyone care if something happened to a lawyer with a briefcase? Then Cobb thought, hold it, kidnap a lawyer, people might cheer them on, give them a medal. Up ahead Sculley walked, occasionally looking over his shoulder.

"What's he doing?"

"I don't know. Maybe he's paranoid, thinks he's being followed. You might be too, someone broke into your house, hit you with a sap."

"You think I'd let that happen?"

"Well, if someone snuck up behind you, you didn't see it coming. *Bam*." Cobb slapped the dashboard with an open hand.

"I'd hear the motherfucker."

"What if you didn't? You get hit, you're out cold."

"I can take a punch. I don't think it would put me out."

Was anything easy with this guy? "Well, everyone else in the fucking universe, it would, okay?"

"You don't know that."

"Just go do the job, how's that sound?"

Ruben made a fist, gaudy diamond ring on the middle finger, making a face, faking like he was going to throw a punch, and broke into a big smile. "Thought I was going to do it, didn't you?"

Jesus, Ruben, would've been a psychiatrist's dream. Thirty-nine going on twelve. Cobb slowed down and let him out. The car behind him honked. Cobb opened the window and motioned the driver to come around him. Guy in a Benz drove up next to Cobb and flipped him off. Cobb grinned and nodded, wanted to follow the guy, shoot his tires out. "Count your lucky stars, asshole."

Ruben was almost to Sculley, closing the gap fast, when Sculley got into a taxi and shut the door. Cobb went fifty yards, picked up Ruben, and followed the cab to a high rise on Wall Street, pulled over in a no-parking zone. "Why don't you wait here," Cobb said. "I'll see where he's going."

For once Ruben didn't say anything. Cobb got out and Ruben got behind the wheel. He followed Sculley into the building, into a crowded elevator up to the fifty-fifth floor, and down the hall to a law firm, Cobb hanging back, letting Sculley put some distance between them.

This was the difficult part, trying to figure out what someone was going to do. Should they wait for Sculley to go to lunch? Or wait for him in front of his apartment? Cobb saw himself sitting in the car all day, breathing Ruben's cologne. Maybe there was another way.

Cobb went through the big floor-to-ceiling glass door that had four names on it, into the lobby, and up to the slick granite reception counter. The receptionist wore a black tapered headset, talking to someone as Cobb approached. She finished the call, looked at him, and said, "May I help you, sir?"

"Duane Cobb here to see Mr. Sculley."

"Do you have an appointment, Mr. Cobb?"

"I do not. But I'll bet Joe will make some time for me. Tell him I was recommended by Jack McCann."

Cobb wandered over to one of the couches, sat and picked up a *National Geographic*, opened it to an article on the headhunting tribes of Borneo, Cobb wondering where Borneo was. There were pictures of shrunken heads and Dayak warriors who carried spears and machetes and looked like native chinks. Apparently headhunting was a sport in Borneo. Jesus, it took all kinds.

Maybe they should do that to Jack when they caught him, cut off his head, shrink it in boiling water, and give it to Frank as a souvenir, let him hang it from the rearview mirror of his limo.

"What can I do for you?"

Cobb looked up at Sculley standing in front of him, closed the magazine, and put it back on the table. "Somewhere we can go and talk?"

"About what?"

"The mysterious whereabouts of Jack McCann."

"I'm sorry to have to be the bearer of bad news. Jack passed away tragically on nine-eleven. We believe he died when Tower One collapsed."

"Except that I saw him in a Midtown hotel day before yesterday."

"I'm sure you're mistaken."

"No, I saw him all right, and I know you've been talking to him."
Cobb paused. "He called you that morning, didn't he? First plane had
already hit, Jack dials your number, called you before his own wife.
What'd he say?"

"The building was severely damaged, a lot of people were dead.
Jack didn't know if he was going to make it out."

"How's your jaw, by the way?"

Sculley gave him a knowing look. "What'd you hit me with?"

"A lead-shot sap."

"Don't be surprised if the Ridgewood Police show up at your door.
They got your license number."

"You're making that up. They never saw me. Tell you what, I'll give
you one more chance."

"Are you threatening me?"

"I'm telling you the way it is. Where's Jack?"

Sculley raised his voice. "Get the hell out of here." He turned and
glanced at the receptionist. "Ann, call security."

"That's how you're gonna play it, huh? Okay, I'll see you around, Joe."

TWENTY-TWO

Mel Hoberman had called and said he and corporate counsel Barry Zitter wanted to talk to Diane face-to-face, explain the severity of the situation, and try to resolve the matter in question. They took the red-eye from San Francisco and met in a conference room at the Four . Seasons on West 57th, Diane insisting on a neutral site. She could have had an attorney present but decided not to.

There were scones and Danish pastries on a plate on the conference table, and pitchers of regular and decaf coffee.

Mel was six three and lean, wore a suit coat without a tie, sat across the table from Diane, and drank decaf. Barry Zitter had a reddish-brown perm. He was short and chunky and sat at the end of the long table to her right and fixed his immediate attention on a blueberry scone, breaking it into pieces he stuffed in his mouth with pale, plump fingers, with nails that looked like they had been chewed down by a wild animal.

"Diane, again, let me offer my condolences, I'm sorry for your loss." Mel sounded like he was reading a passage from a book on coping with death. "This is an extremely delicate and difficult situation. I wanted to give you the courtesy of a full and candid explanation. I knew Jack, not well, but I liked him. He was at heart a good man, but sometimes even good men make mistakes." Mel paused and drank his coffee. "We're here in good faith. We want to avoid litigation."

"Mrs. McCann," Barry Zitter said, wiping scone crumbs off the front of his blue suit. "This is what we know: your husband misappropriated seven hundred and fifty thousand dollars from Barbara Sperrick, a Sterns and Morrison client."

"How do you know?" These corporate assholes annoyed her, especially Barry Zitter.

"Your husband had power of attorney," Barry Zitter said. "The woman, Mrs. Sperrick, is elderly and incapable of making intelligent decisions regarding the management of her wealth. Your husband managed her portfolio. Your husband sold equities totaling seven hundred and fifty thousand."

"Isn't that what brokers do, buy and sell stocks?"

"Yes," Barry Zitter said, "but they don't embezzle their client's money."

"And you're positive Jack did that? What proof do you have?"

"We have a record of the transactions," Barry Zitter said. He reached a finger in his mouth and dislodged a food particle, took it out, examined a little piece of masticated blueberry and wiped it on a napkin.

Mel Hoberman said, "We would appreciate you granting us permission to review your bank statements."

"As I told you the last time we talked, that money was never deposited in our joint cash management account."

"We want to look at your bank accounts," Mel Hoberman said.

"I told you, I've got a little over five grand and a pile of bills I can't pay."

Barry Zitter said, "If you force our hand, we'll have no choice but to subpoena your statements."

"It's an interesting story. A grieving widow whose husband was killed on nine-eleven is being harassed by his former company. I wonder if the *New York Times* might want to pick up a story like this? Or how about CNN?"

Mel Hoberman said, "We don't want this to get ugly."

"I'll bet you don't."

"We assume Jack had life insurance. We can settle this quietly without tarnishing his good name," Mel Hoberman said.

"That's correct, Mrs. McCann," Barry Zitter said. "We just want to do what's right, what's fair."

Now she was convinced Jack had taken the money. But why? What else didn't she know? "Jack's dead, and I don't have Mrs. Sperrick's money. And if you think I'm going to give you his life insurance, you're out of your mind." Diane stood up and walked out of the room.

Duane Cobb was parked in front when she got home. He was walking up the driveway as she stepped out of the car. He looked different in jeans and a black leather jacket, his hair slicked back. As he came closer she said, "Can I see some ID?"

Cobb didn't react. Maybe he didn't get it.

"You vaguely resemble someone I know, but he wore ties and sweater vests. What did you do, come out of the closet?"

"Can we talk?"

"Isn't that what we're doing?"

"I mean inside."

"You going to tell me the seven stages of grief again?" She started down the driveway to the side door, opened it, and went in. "Can I take your coat?"

"That's okay."

She hung hers on a hanger in the back hall closet and walked into the kitchen. "How about a cup of coffee?"

"No thanks."

"At least take your coat off; you're making me nervous."

He did and fit it on the back of a chair at the island counter. Cobb was wearing a Western shirt with pearl buttons tucked into the jeans and a belt with a big oval buckle that had a bull embossed on it. "Looks like you're on your way to a rodeo?"

He didn't react.

Still all business, Cobb said, "Did you get the insurance money yet?"

"What does that have to do with grief? Oh yeah, I remember, something about balance, right? Mental health and financial health, isn't that it?"

"I made that up. Sounds pretty good, doesn't it?"

"What else did you make up?"

"A lot of it. I'm not a grief counselor. But I could be, don't you think?"

"What are you?" Although she had a pretty good idea. "Why the confession, does your conscience bother you?"

"You owe us seven hundred and fifty thousand. It has nothing to do with conscience. I collect money."

"You're with the Puerto Rican, aren't you? I wouldn't want to wake up in the morning looking at him."

"Just be glad you're not looking at him all day." Cobb grinned now. "The surprising thing—and I know you're gonna find this hard to believe—Ruben attracts women. I've seen him in action."

"Yeah, I can understand how some girls might go for a guy like that 'cause he's a brute. There's an element of danger. You're more my type, Duane. I like guys that are handsome. Jack was a good-looking man."

"You coming onto me?"

"No, I'm giving you my opinion. And I have to say, I like you better in the Western outfit a lot more than the schoolboy clothes. But the sweater vest and tie helped convince me you were the real thing. Perception is reality. But not really, huh?"

"Let's get back to the debt," Cobb said.

"Whatever Jack did is on him. You say he borrowed money, it's his problem. I didn't know about it. I didn't have anything to do with it. And I never signed that bullshit contract."

"Where's he at?"

"I'd like to say up in heaven, but after what I found out, I'm not so sure."

"You're not in contact with him?"

"How exactly would that work? You think I'm having séances at night, sitting here with a Ouija board, communicating with Jack's spirit?"

"I'm saying if he wasn't dead, if he didn't go down when the tower crashed, if he faked his own death."

"Don't tell the insurance company. I need the money."

"How much are you getting?"

"Come on, Duane, are you kidding?"

"I can get you out of this jam you're in, offer my employer a lesser amount, see if he'll accept it under the circumstances."

"Under the circumstances, I don't owe you anything. Why do you think this is my problem?"

"My employer Mr. DiCicco says as Jack's wife, you're responsible for the debt. There's nothing I can do to change his mind."

"You've been conning me since day one, and you're still at it. I don't think there is a Mr. DiCicco. I think you and the Puerto Rican are running this scam on your own. San Marino Equity is out of business, so you used the name and probably had some fake contracts printed or used their old ones. Does that sound familiar?"

"I'm gonna ask you to think about this before it gets out of hand."

"It already is out of hand. You're out of hand. Jesus. Do you ever quit?"

"I'm looking out for your best interests."

"As long as my interests agree with yours, huh? I wish there was some way I could turn you off, flip a switch and you'd stop talking. I can't listen to any more of your bullshit."

"Sleep on it, you'll feel different tomorrow; I guarantee that. I'll stop by, we can continue the dialogue."

"I see you again, Duane, I'm going to call the police."

Cobb was staring at the mail piled on the countertop. He picked up a stack of envelopes and started shuffling through them.

"What do you think you're doing?"

Cobb ignored her and she moved around the counter and swatted the envelopes out of his hand and they dropped on the granite surface.

Cobb, giving her his full attention now, said, "Looking for the check from the insurance company."

"I spent it."

"Uh-huh." Cobb put his coat on. "It's been friendly up till now. How we proceed from here will depend on how cooperative you are."

Diane watched him walk out and close the door. She'd had it, decided she wasn't going to put up with any more, grabbed her purse, went out the French doors to the garage, and got in Jack's BMW. She adjusted the seat, revved the engine, backed out, turned around, and gunned it. Cobb's Toyota was halfway down the block when she got to the street. She followed him, all the way to the Holiday Inn in Stamford, parked in the lot, and waited.

Half an hour later, Ruben and Cobb appeared, carrying suitcases they put in the trunk of the Toyota. It was strange seeing them together; they were so different. After taking another shot at her, it looked like they were giving up, leaving town. Diane had finally reached her breaking point. Now she could try to turn things around, find out where they lived and who they worked for.

She followed the Toyota to the freeway and all the way to an apartment building on 2nd Avenue in the East Village. Cobb pulled over, Ruben Diaz retrieved his suitcase and went in the building. Diane wrote the address on a piece of paper in her purse. When she looked up, Cobb's car was moving again. She followed him to Houston, went right and right again onto 6th Avenue and took that to West 21st Street.

Cobb parked on the street, grabbed his suitcase, and entered an apartment building. Diane found a parking space across the one-way street and sat for a minute trying to calm down. She had butterflies in her stomach, and wondered if she should phone Detective Brown now or trail Cobb a little longer and see what he was going to do.

She got out and walked to the building, went in and saw his name on the directory: D. Cobb apartment 312.

TWENTY-THREE

Jack picked up his new Visa card and rented a Honda Civic. He wanted to blend in, not call attention to himself, and it was the perfect car for that. He put on a pair of shorts and drove up the coast, stopped in Del Ray, and had grilled red snapper and a Heineken at a restaurant on the beach, thinking about Vicki. He remembered how excited and appreciative she had been when he took her to London. She had never flown business class and had never been to Europe. They stayed at Claridge's and saw the sights: Buckingham Palace, the Tower of London, and Big Ben. They went to a fourth-round match at Wimbledon and saw Roger Federer beat Pete Sampras. Diane had seen Jack on TV and asked him about the girl sitting next to him, the one he kept talking to. Of course he lied to her.

They went out to dinner, made love, slept late, and ordered room service for breakfast. One day they rented a car and went to the Cotswolds, Jack driving on the right side of the car and the right side of the road, shifting with his left hand. It was an adventure.

They had lunch in Cheltenham and drove back to London at rush hour, and neither of them was stressed out or lost their cool despite the difficult driving conditions. Jack was thinking, you want a test to see if you're compatible with someone? Rent a car and drive around London.

From there they flew to Rome for a couple days and stayed at the Hassler Hotel. They had coffee on their private balcony, looking down at the Spanish Steps and out at the dome of St. Peter's Basilica in the hazy distance.

A month after they returned from Europe, Jack went to Vicki's apartment after work one evening. He hadn't seen her in more than a week, and he could tell right away something was wrong. She was lying on the couch under a blanket. "What's the matter, you sick?" He sat next to her on the arm of the couch and touched her face, felt her forehead. "You don't feel like you have a temperature."

"Nothing's the matter."

"Come on, I know you."

"It's not your problem." Vicki looked up at the ceiling, avoiding his gaze, and then looked at him. "I owe a lot of money to a loan shark."

It sounded like a line, like she was putting him on, but he could tell by her expression she was serious.

"I told you I was a dealer at the poker room. I usually made between three fifty and four hundred a night in tips—cash, tax-free. I worked three nights a week. In a year, I'd saved forty-five thousand dollars. I told Vincent, who ran the place, I didn't want to be a dealer anymore, I wanted to play."

"And that was okay?"

"I had money, and that's what gets you in. I told the restaurant I had to take a leave of absence to care for my sick aunt who had cancer, and played high-stakes blackjack every night from ten till two, three in the morning. I won fifteen grand the first night, got overconfident, upped my bets, and it worked. The next night, I won twenty grand. Two nights, I'm up thirty-five thousand dollars, which is about half of what I earn at Balthazar in a year. I had seventy-five thousand dollars, more money than I've ever had in my life."

"Why didn't you quit and put it in the bank?"

"'Cause I wanted to keep playing; I wanted to stay in the game. That's all you care about. You get in the zone. It's a rush, and you want to stay there as long as you can." Vicki squinted and rubbed her temples. "I was up and down the next couple nights. Then I lost seventeen, and then twenty-two, and by the end of the week, I was broke."

He could see the stress on her face.

"I asked Vincent to loan me fifteen grand, which I lost, and borrowed twenty more. Did that a few times. I got into debt faster than the Fourth of July."

"Why would he keep loaning you money?"

"That's what he does."

"How were you going to pay it back?"

"I was going to win. But I didn't. You know what happens when you borrow from a loan shark?"

Jack glanced at her. He had an idea how it worked, but didn't say anything, let her keep talking.

"The first fifteen came due, and of course I didn't have it, so they tacked on their percentage."

"You worked for the guy, Vincent, right? He wasn't sympathetic, young girl gets in over her head? I would be."

"If he was, he wouldn't have given me the money."

"This was all going on while I was seeing you? Why didn't you say something?

"I thought I could work it out."

"What do you owe? How much will it take to get you out of this?"

"I don't know exactly. Every time I miss a payment, it goes up."

"Give me a ballpark number."

"Five hundred grand."

"Five hundred grand? Come on, you're not serious?"

"I've got a week to pay it off, or they're going to put me to work turning tricks."

"Why don't you go to the police?"

"What are they gonna do? Nothing's happened. Vincent works for Frank DiCicco. Know anything about him?"

"I see his name in the paper every once in a while."

"He's a bad guy."

"You know him?"

"Not really. He'd show up every once in a while."

"Tell whoever you have to tell I'm taking over your debt. Find out how much it is, and set up a meeting."

"It's not your problem."

"I'm making it my problem."

They met Vincent Gallo at the poker room in Little Italy. Vincent was short and heavy and had a three-day beard. Two of his men searched Jack, Vincent saying, "You better not be wearing a fucking wire." Then saying, "I don't think this's ever happened, someone taking over someone's debt. She must be good in the sack, uh?" Vincent glanced at Vicki. She didn't react, didn't give him anything.

Jack said, "How much is it?" He and Vicki stood facing Vincent and the collectors, a room full of green felt-covered tables behind them.

"You paying today? It's seven hundred fifty thousand," Vincent said.

Jack looked at Vicki. "You said five hundred." Now Jack looked at Vincent. "You can't do that, charge whatever you feel like. It's usury. It's against the law."

"What law you talking about? She borrowed the money." Vincent grabbed Vicki's ponytail and turned her head toward him. "You asked for it, right, babe?"

Vicki's face tightened. Jack took a step toward Vincent. He let go of her. "I said at the time, 'You know how this works?' Did I say that?" He glanced at her. She nodded and looked at the floor. "I own her. She's mine. You want to buy her, show me the money. You don't, I'll sell her to someone else."

"It's going to take a little time."

"That's your problem. Take as long as you want, but just so you know, it's rolling over. That means it's multiplying, getting bigger. Don't come back, play dumb like you don't know what's going on."

"The deal is, I take over the debt, you leave Vicki alone, understand? I'll be back in a week with the money."

"Long as you know what you're doing."

"First I want assurances from Frank DiCicco. I want his guarantee that when I pay, it's over."

"Who the hell you think you are?" Vincent said, keeping his hard stare on him. "Get the fuck outta here."

Jack glanced at Vicki and said, "Let's go."

When they were outside Jack said, "What the hell's going on? You said it was five hundred grand."

"I don't know." Vicki shook her head. "It's crazy. Vincent's crazy. He can do whatever he wants. Listen, if you don't have the money, I understand."

"I'll get it." He put his arm around Vicki and walked her back to the apartment. "Who are the two guys that work for Vincent?"

"The dark-skinned one is Ruben Diaz, a former boxer, which is probably obvious looking at his face. The other one is Duane Cobb. They're collectors. They keep the pressure on. One of them might be standing outside my building when I go to work, or standing outside the restaurant when I get off. Thing about it is, it's on my mind every second I'm awake and probably when I'm sleeping, so they're wasting their time." Vicki paused. "I don't know how to thank you for what you're doing. I've never felt so stupid in my life. It's a lot of money. Can you really cover it? If you can't, it's okay. It's my fault. I got myself into this."

Now they were walking on Sullivan Street, stopping in front of Vicki's apartment. "I'm not going to come up. I have to go to the office. I have to get moving on this."

Jack withdrew forty-five thousand dollars from his and Diane's joint account and had an idea where he would get the rest. He pulled up Barbara Sperrick's account on his computer. She had almost six million in equities, bonds, and cash.

Jack decided to sell a fund of blue chips that had gained 21 percent in the past twelve months. He thought it was his most defensible move if the Sterns & Morrison compliance group ever looked over his shoulder.

He also decided to take the full amount from Mrs. Sperrick. Why use his money if he didn't have to? He had more debts than cash as it was. And his client would never know the difference.

Jack had converted the Sperricks' stocks to cash and deposited $750,000 in a new account he'd opened at a local bank. Everything had hinged on Jack's freedom to buy and sell without permission. Mrs. Sperrick and her son Buzz had given him free rein to manage the account any way he wanted.

What he didn't expect was the son, David "Buzz" Sperrick, a forty-year-old unemployed former meth addict, spending thirty days in rehab and coming out a new man, alert and interested in his mother's estate for the first time ever. Buzz had reviewed the August statement, saw the equities that had been sold, and called Jack on September 7.

Jack said, "How's your mother doing?"

"I don't think she's going to be around much longer."

"What happened?"

"Old age. She's losing it. Doctor says it's dementia or Alzheimer's." Jack heard him light a cigarette or a joint and inhale. "I see you sold one of the blue chip funds. Not sure I agree with that, but it made an acceptable profit."

That was by far the most intelligent thing Buzz Sperrick had ever said.

"According to our analysts, those stocks are going to get banged up in the next few months—that's why I sold them. You made twenty-one percent in a year. It seemed like a good time to cash out."

"That's not why I'm calling. I'm looking at the statement. The stocks were sold for seven hundred and fifty thousand dollars, right? But I don't see the cash."

"Let me pull it up." Jack looked north from his window at the Empire State Building in the distance, counted to ten, and said, "Okay, I've opened your mother's account. Hang on, let me find it. Just a second. Yeah, there it is. I'm looking at a cash balance of one point four million.

I don't know what happened. The full deposit didn't get recorded in time to make it on the August statement. You'll see it next month."

"Oh, okay. Will you print that out and fax it to my mother's house? I'll stop by later today and get it."

"Sure," Jack said. "No problem." But he did have a problem, a big one.

Buzz Sperrick phoned him at five and left a message. Jack didn't get back to him. There was nothing he could say. The next call he got was from Stewart Raskin, the morning of the tenth, saying he wanted to see Jack immediately about a matter of extreme urgency. Stu had obviously been contacted by Buzz Sperrick, reviewed the Sperrick statement, and noticed the discrepancy: funds had inexplicably been withdrawn and had disappeared.

Jack told Mary, his assistant, he had to have a root canal that day.

She said, "You have clients coming in at three and five."

"Call them and cancel. Say it's an emergency."

"Want me to reschedule?"

"Tell them we'll get back to them."

"Jack, are you okay? Is everything all right?"

"I'll see you in the morning."

He took the elevator to the lobby, walked up the street, and grabbed a cab to Vicki's apartment.

He could hear the shower when he walked in. He took off his suit coat, folded it on the back of a chair, and went in the kitchen. He opened the refrigerator, scanned the contents. There was half a bottle of Cuvaison chardonnay. He took it out, pulled the cork, and poured a glass. He felt like a fool. Why did he think he could get away with it? He drank the wine and poured another glass. Everything he had done was to help Vicki, but he couldn't tell anyone.

"I thought I heard somebody." Vicki walked into the room, wearing a robe, drying her hair with a towel. "What're you doing here so early?"

"I thought you'd be glad to see me. I decided to take the day off." Jack wasn't going to tell her about embezzling money from Barbara Sperrick to pay off the debt or that he was going to be fired in the morning and would probably be arrested and taken to jail.

He saw himself flanked by detectives, escorted out of the office in handcuffs, passing a waiting news crew in the plaza. But first, Cobb or Ruben would stop by his office and he'd hand over the cashier's check.

Jack said, "Can you call in sick?"

"Really?"

"Why not?"

"You said you had meetings all day. What's gotten into you?"

"How about a glass of wine?"

"It's ten to eleven. I usually wait till at least eleven fifteen."

"Let's go to bed," Jack said, thinking it might be the last time.

"What's going on, Jack? You're acting strange."

Vicki untied the sash, opened the robe, and let it slide off her shoulders onto the wood plank floor. She walked naked toward the bedroom, stopped, looked over her shoulders and said, "Jack, you coming?"

TWENTY-FOUR

Cobb watched Sculley get out of a taxi and move quickly to the apartment building entrance.

"Let's go," Ruben said.

"What about the doorman?"

Ruben frowned. "You worried about that guy in the clown outfit?"

That was the one thing about Ruben he liked; the dude had confidence. Cobb got out and waited for traffic to clear. Ruben came around the car and moved up next to him, the two of them walking side by side to the building. Cobb went in first. The doorman, wearing a green double-breasted coat with gold trim, gave him a concerned look, checking out Cobb, then Ruben.

"Can I help you gentlemen?"

"We're visiting our friend, Joe Sculley," Cobb said in a friendly, down-home voice.

"I'll give Mr. Sculley a call. Can I have your names, please?"

Ruben said, "Hey, where you get that outfit at? You going to a costume party, or you like looking like a clown?"

The doorman gave him a nervous smile. His name tag said Pat. What kind of pussy name was that?

"I'll tell Mr. Sculley you're here."

"We want to surprise him," Ruben said.

"I have to announce you. It's a rule."

Ruben took a step toward him. "Go take a leak, you never saw us. That's the rule I'd follow I was you. What apartment's he in?"

"Four D." Pat the doorman looked like he was going to be sick.

"Why don't you come up and show us where it's at," Cobb said. Put him to work, put Sculley at ease.

In the elevator, Cobb said, "Like being a doorman?" He imagined himself standing in the lobby in that outfit all day, opening the door and having to be nice, walking tenants out to a taxi under an umbrella on rainy days and helping them with their groceries, but mostly taking a lot of shit.

"It's not too bad."

"Yeah, what do you like about it?"

"It pays pretty good, but sometimes people will ask you to do things that aren't part of your job description."

"Like what?"

"Like washing their windows and walking their dog. One time, a woman asked me to do her dishes."

"Any of the ladies ever ask you to come upstairs and take care of their personal needs?" Cobb winked and punched his open palm with a fist a couple times, one guy to another.

Pat the doorman shrugged and said, "No sir, nothing like that."

The bell sounded and the elevator doors opened.

"It's this way," Pat the doorman said, directing them to the left. "Last one at the end of the hall."

Now, standing in front of Sculley's door, Cobb said, "Knock, say you have a package for him, but don't mention us. It's a surprise, remember?"

Pat did as he was told, and the door opened. Sculley saw them and backed away into the living room. Ruben went after him.

"If that's all, I have to get back to work."

"We'd like the pleasure of your company a while longer. People can open their own fucking door." Cobb grabbed the doorman's collar, pulled him into the apartment.

Ruben had Sculley on the couch in the living room, standing over him, the skyline of Lower Manhattan minus the Trade Center in the background. Cobb took the doorman into a bedroom, opened the closet. "Take off your clothes and get in there."

"Why? I did what you asked. I have a job to do."

Cobb drew the Ruger. "'Cause I have this. I'm your new boss, and I'm telling you to."

Pat undressed. His body was pale and thin, looked like he'd never been in the sun in his life. Pat walked in the closet. Cobb closed the door and locked it. He went into the living room. Sculley glanced at him. There was a deep purple bruise along his jawline. Cobb slapped the side of Sculley's swollen face with an open hand.

"Ahh, Jesus." Sculley ducked and put his arms up to protect himself.

Cobb said, "You gonna call security?"

"I don't know where Jack is. Do you hear me?"

"I hear you, but I don't believe you," Cobb said.

"What do you want me to do, make something up?"

Cobb said, "I believe that's what you're doing." He aimed the Ruger, held it six inches from Sculley's face and cocked the hammer. "What do you think's gonna happen here? You think we're just gonna go away, forget about you?"

"Eventually," Sculley said.

"You trying to be funny? Let me tell you, this is no fucking joke."

"Well, it is a little absurd, don't you agree? You're threatening to shoot me but you can't 'cause you believe I know where Jack is. Does that about sum it up?"

Ruben bent down and pulled Sculley up off the couch and hit him in the gut. Sculley grunted and fell back on the cushions, holding his stomach.

"Last time I talked to him, he was in Florida, a town called Pompano Beach," Sculley said, breathing hard.

Cobb said, "What's the address?"

"It was a post office box."

"Where's he staying?"

Sculley answered the question just as Dominic "Dapper Dom" Benigno walked into the room pointing a silenced semiautomatic at them.

TWENTY-FIVE

Diane sat in the car, watching people walk by. She was across the street from Cobb's apartment building. She wouldn't have guessed Duane Cobb lived in Chelsea, but then he was something of an enigma.

Midafternoon, Cobb came out of the building and walked down 21st Street past his car. Diane crossed the street and followed him. She wondered what she'd say if he saw her. He was seventy to a hundred feet ahead of her on the crowded sidewalk, Diane trying to keep an eye on Cobb, and then she lost him.

She walked half a block, stopped, moved close to a building, and waited a few minutes. The street was lined with cars, the sidewalk packed with people. She looked again and saw him coming toward her, carrying dry cleaning wrapped in plastic draped over his arm. Diane ducked into a cluttered indie bookstore, saw Cobb walk past the window, gave him thirty seconds, and went after him.

Cobb disappeared in his building and Diane went back to her car. The hard part was waiting, not knowing what he was going to do.

It was getting dark when someone tapped on the side window. A homeless man was saying something she couldn't understand. There was a shopping cart filled with plastic bags, his meager possessions on the sidewalk next to him. Lights were on in the shop behind him.

She lowered the window a couple inches and now caught a whiff of the man and had to breathe through her mouth. He mumbled something unintelligible. She had to get rid of him. As she reached for her purse on the passenger seat, Cobb appeared again in front of the building.

Diane took out her wallet, grabbed a ten-dollar bill, and fed it through the opening at the top of the window. She climbed over the center console onto the passenger seat, opened the door, and saw Cobb walk past his car still parked where he'd left it hours earlier. She waited for traffic to clear, and ran across the street and down the sidewalk dodging pedestrians.

She didn't see Cobb again till he was ten yards ahead of her. She followed him into a restaurant and saw him sit at the bar. Diane ran back to his apartment building, stepped into the vestibule, and pressed the button for the super, Z. Korab.

"Yes? Hello." He had an Eastern European accent.

"I'm sorry to bother you. I'm Diane, Duane Cobb's girlfriend. Duane was supposed to leave a key to his apartment in my mailbox, and I guess he forgot."

"He say nothing about this."

"I just need you to let me in his apartment."

The super didn't respond, and in the silence, she thought he had cut her off, disconnected, but then the door buzzed. She slipped inside and saw a man coming out of a ground-floor apartment to meet her. "You have identification?" He was bald down the middle of his head and suspicious and smelled of BO, garlic, and sharp spices like paprika and cumin.

Diane opened her wallet and showed him her Connecticut driver's license, now glad she hadn't given him a fake name. He stared at the license and then at her. "Live in Connecticut," he nodded, "very nice." She put her wallet away and the super pressed the button for the elevator. The doors opened and he swung his right arm toward the open car like an impresario.

Riding up to the third floor, he said, "I never see you here before."

"That's because I've never been here."

"You don't mind my saying, I don't see you and Mr. Cobb together."

"Sometimes opposites attract."

He gave her a look that said he didn't believe it. They walked down the hall to 312. The super unlocked the door. "You need anything else, pretty lady, come see Zoltan Korab."

She went in and closed the door. She was able to hide her nervousness with the super and now felt relieved to be alone. She had no idea when Duane Cobb would come back or what he would do if he found her in his apartment.

There was a cheap blue leather couch facing a Sony Trinitron on an end table, and a coffee table cluttered with newspapers and copies of *Playboy* and *Penthouse* and a paperback titled *The Seven Stages of Grief.*

Across the room there was a PC and a printer on a desk. Diane walked over and booted up the computer. She checked Cobb's e-mails but didn't see any familiar names. She checked the drawers and found a manila envelope full of photographs. There were shots of Jack taken at various locations in the city, close-ups and long shots. Jack getting out of a cab; Jack crossing the Trade Center Plaza; Jack getting off the train in Darien and pulling into the driveway at home.

There were shots of Jack and Vicki laughing, hugging, holding hands, kissing—the man she married and thought she knew, captured on film in the arms of another woman. The images seemed surreal. This wasn't really Jack; it was someone who looked like him.

There were also shots of the funeral procession and shots taken at the rainy gravesite, everyone huddled under umbrellas. The last one was a close-up of Ruben Diaz scowling at the camera or, more likely, Cobb. She put the photographs back in the envelope and left it on top of the desk. She would take it with her, show Detective Brown. He wanted proof, well, here it was. Maybe now he would believe her.

In another drawer, she found a notebook that had Jack's contact information, e-mail address, home address, and phone numbers, including Diane's cell, and there was a piece of note paper with an address in Florida: 300 Briny Avenue, Pompano Beach.

Diane and Jack had gone to Pompano before they were married and stayed in a motel on Briny Avenue. Was it a coincidence? She didn't think so. She put the notebook back and closed the drawer. In the printer next to the computer was a piece of paper that Cobb had probably forgotten about. It was from the Delta Airlines website, a morning flight from LaGuardia to Fort Lauderdale scheduled to leave the next day at nine thirty. For weeks she'd been grief-stricken, thinking Jack was dead, and now she believed he might be alive.

Cobb ordered a 7 and 7 and sipped it sitting at the bar, eating pretzels, studying the profile of a blonde in a gray business suit, sitting next to him. "How was your day?" Cobb said, trying to be friendly.

She turned and glanced at him. "What're you taking a poll?"

Her body looked okay; it was her face that needed help. She'd look better after a couple more drinks. "What're you having, let me buy you one."

She sat there frozen, pretending he didn't exist. Cobb finished the 7 and 7 and signaled the bartender. "A refill for me, and get my stressed-out friend one." She was drinking white wine in a stemmed glass.

"I'm not stressed out and I'm not your friend," she said with the same angry tone.

"I was gonna invite you back to my place, offer to give you a back rub, but not now."

The girl gave him a nervous grin. "You've got to be kidding. Does that lame come-on really work? Women fall for that, I can't imagine. How gullible do you think I am?"

Cobb had her full attention now. "You want to be cranky and unpleasant, go right ahead, be my guest." He turned and looked away.

The bartender came with the drinks, put a 7 and 7 on the bar top in front of Cobb and a glass of white in front of the girl.

"You're right," Cobb said. "This is out of character for me. I was being a little forward, a little bold. Usually when I see a girl as good-looking as you, I freeze up." She picked up her wine glass, and he noticed the engagement ring on her finger. "Oh, I'm sorry, I didn't realize you were betrothed."

"What're you talking about?" she said in a softer voice.

"Engaged. Someone's fiancée."

The girl frowned. "I'm not. This is my mother's ring."

"Well, it wouldn't have surprised me."

The girl smiled.

"I think we got off on the wrong foot. Let's start over, what do you say? I'm Duane." He offered his hand.

"Mara."

"No kidding? That's a great name. Mara, what do you do?"

Diane walked through the apartment looking at things: a framed photo of a little boy dressed as a cowboy, and another of a teenager driving a tractor. There were four yearbooks from Carbondale Community High School. She took out the one from 1984 and found Cobb's senior picture. He was named Class Flirt and had been a member of the band and choir club. She closed the book, put it back on the shelf, and went into the bedroom.

Duane Cobb was neat, she had to give him that. The apartment, although weak in decor, was immaculate. He even made his bed, a queen with a green comforter. There was a small suitcase on one side of the bed that he had started to pack with shorts and golf shirts for the trip to Florida.

She checked the closet, looking at Western shirts on hangers lined up next to oxford-cloth button-downs, cowboy boots sharing the floor with penny loafers, cowboy hats next to sport caps. In the top drawer of the dresser, she found a matte black semiautomatic. It was a Ruger Lc9. Diane ejected the magazine, removed the cartridges, flushed them down the toilet, and put the gun back.

Cobb unlocked the building door and held it open for Mara, the editorial assistant who seemed like she had a stick up her ass when he first met her, but after two glasses of wine had mellowed, turned into a different person. "I've never done this before," she said as they waited for the elevator. Yeah, Cobb was thinking. Next she'd tell him she was saving herself for Mr. Right. Jesus. His plan was to take Mara upstairs, skip the foreplay, bang her, and say good night.

Mr. K., the super, came up behind them, glanced at Cobb, and said, "I let girl in apartment."

Cobb had no idea what this crazy Hungarian was talking about. "What're you saying?"

"Girl come to see you, I open door for her."

"What girl?"

"Diane from Connecticut."

"How do you know her name's Diane?"

"I see driving license."

He knew only one Diane from Connecticut. How in the hell'd she find him? She must've followed them and he hadn't noticed, wasn't paying attention. That seemed hard to believe. Now Mara made a face, gave him a dirty look. "You have a girlfriend? I knew this was a bad idea." She moved past him and walked out the door.

He fixed his attention on Mr. K. "You're saying you let her in my apartment?" Cobb couldn't believe it. "What's she look like?"

Mr. K. made a curvy female shape with his hands and grinned, something Cobb had never seen him do, not that Cobb saw him that often.

"What color hair?"

"Blonde."

"You think she's still up there?"

Diane was conscious of the time and felt she had been in the apartment too long already. She picked the envelope full of photos off the desk and moved to the door, opening it a couple inches, glancing right down the empty hall to the elevator.

She was about to walk out, go left to the stairs, when she heard something and hesitated. The elevator bell sounded and the doors opened and Duane Cobb charged down the hall. Diane ran into the bedroom, went in the closet, and closed the door but left it open a crack.

She heard him come in and move through the main room, shoes clicking on the hardwood, and then he stood in the doorway to the bedroom, three feet away, looking in the room. She moved deeper into the closet and got on her knees behind a row of jeans on hangers.

Cobb thought he smelled perfume when he came in, a hint of it still in the air. Who'd this bitch think she was, coming to his place, fucking with him? He went through the apartment, looked in the bed-room, checked under the bed, looked in the closet. He went in the bathroom, pulled the shower curtain back. She wasn't there, and there was no other place to hide.

After the drinks, he had to piss so bad his eyes were yellow, his teeth were floating—things his father used to say when Duane was a kid and had to go. He stood in front of the toilet and let fly, and Jesus if he wasn't there a good three minutes.

Cobb went back in the bedroom, opened the top drawer of the dresser, and grabbed the Ruger. He knew guns and could tell some-thing wasn't right and ejected the magazine. It was empty. He had a strange feeling he was being watched, moved to the closet, swung the door open, and smelled perfume. Cobb grabbed the softball bat leaning against the wall and brought it to his shoulder, took a beat, and swung through his Western shirts on hangers, sending them sideways. Now he parted a row of Levis on hangers with the barrel of the bat, looking behind them. She wasn't there.

He went back through the apartment to the front door. It wasn't closed all the way. Did he do that, or was Diane McCann in the apart-ment when he came home? He took the stairs to the lobby and went outside, looking down the sidewalk in both directions and at the cars on both sides of the street and saw a silver BMW pull out of a parking space. Didn't Jack have a car like that?

Back in the apartment, Cobb closed the door and locked it. He sat at the desk, opened the top drawer, and noticed the photographs were missing. He'd have sworn he left the envelope right there. He went through the other drawers but didn't see it. He was tense till he reasoned that the photos, without the negatives and the camera, didn't prove anything, didn't implicate him or Ruben.

There was a piece of paper in the printer he'd forgotten about. Cobb pulled it out, looking at the flight information, wondering if Diane had seen it. What if she had, it wasn't gonna help her. She didn't know where they were going.

TWENTY-SIX

Diane slid what was left of her turkey sandwich into the sink and saw Detective Brown coming around the back of the house. He nodded at her in the window, walked to the patio, and knocked on the French doors. Shit. What did he want? She unlocked the door and opened it. "Don't tell me: you were in the neighborhood, decided to stop by, say hello?"

"Your gun wasn't the murder weapon."

"Isn't that what I said to you when you took it?"

She felt a blast of cold air hit her in the face. "You want to come in, or is that it?"

He stepped into the breakfast room, the stale smell of cigarettes on him as he walked past her, and she closed the door. "Winter's on its way, huh?" He reached into an overcoat pocket and brought out her Beretta in a Ziploc bag. "Here you go."

Walking into the kitchen, she took the gun out of the bag, ejected the magazine.

Coming behind her Detective Brown said, "Think we took your cartridges? They're all there."

"Have you arrested anyone?"

"Not yet. We're working on it."

"Did you talk to Ruben Diaz or Duane Cobb?" He slipped off the overcoat and folded it on the back of one of the chairs. He was wearing a wrinkled brown suit.

Diane was already tired of his low-key delivery, waiting for him to get to it.

"They still contacting you, still hanging around?"

"Cobb came by yesterday and for the first time admitted he worked for Frank DiCicco." She was about to offer him their addresses, but caught herself. She didn't want Cobb and Diaz picked up and detained.

"Frankie Cheech, huh?" Detective Brown held her in his gaze for a couple of beats. "Tell me what's going on. I think you know more than you're saying."

"Cobb asked for Jack's life insurance money to cover the debt. Then Cobb said Jack's alive, got out of Tower One before it collapsed."

"Is that what you think, or do you know?"

"I thought so on nine-eleven, watching it on TV. I prayed Jack was okay and he was going to walk through the door any minute. After a couple days, I knew I was kidding myself. He wasn't coming back."

"But now you think it's possible, huh?"

"I don't know what I think."

"Let's say Jack's alive. Where would he go?"

Diane shrugged.

"You have a cottage somewhere?"

"No."

"Where's your husband from?"

"A suburb of Detroit."

"He have any sibs?"

"Jack was an only child. His mother had him when she was forty-seven."

"How 'bout his parents? They still around?"

"Both passed away. Jack's dad had a heart attack when he was ninety, and his mom died of a brain aneurysm, a massive stroke."

"Anywhere you talked about moving when you all retired?"

"Jack liked Charleston."

"South Carolina, huh?"

"And he liked Captiva, talked about maybe living there part-time."

"Where's Captiva at?"

TWENTY-SEVEN

Ruben was hungry, thinking about what he was going to have for dinner, seeing a plate of grilled octopus and then roast chicken stuffed with chorizo, and flan for dessert. He looked out the window at the blur of taillights ahead of them, traffic still heavy at almost seven o'clock.

Cobb's cell phone rang. He took it out of his shirt pocket, flipped it open, and listened, keeping one hand on the steering wheel. Ruben could hear a man's voice talking but not what he was saying.

"Uh-huh. Okay. We'll be right there." Cobb closed the phone and slid it in his shirt pocket and glanced at Ruben. "Frank wants to see us."

"When?"

"Now," Cobb said, keeping his eyes on the road.

"I don't want to see that asshole. I want my dinner. Drop me off. You do it."

"He wants us both."

"What you gonna tell him?"

"We don't know anything, remember?"

"We know Jack McCann's alive. You gonna say that?"

"Are you kidding? I'm not gonna tell him a thing. We're gonna find Jack, get the money, split it, and live happily ever after."

"Well, here they are," Frank said as they walked in the living room of his townhouse, "the hillbilly and the spic."

Frank's bodyguard Val, a big dude with a ponytail, was a Hollywood heavy. But the other one, Santo, looked like he just walked out of an olive grove. Ruben pictured him in a beret with a shotgun slung over his shoulder. The bodyguards stood at attention on opposite sides of the couch, Frank sitting between them.

"Hey, Ruben, look at you. Trying to dress like a white man, huh?"

In his high-waisted Italian pants, hiked up near his armpits, Val grinned. He grinned at everything Frank said. He was a professional grinner. Ruben had spent nineteen years fighting tough guys and now had to listen to this, the man talking down to him, treating him like a fool. "What can I do for you?"

"Ruben, with that skin, you must have some native blood, uh? Who was the eggplant, your mother or father? Next time, I'm gonna have you come to the back door."

Ruben looked at him, wondering why he was saying these things, thinking he could get to Frank, bust him up before the bodyguards could stop him. "You bring me here, disrespect my family."

The bigger of the two bodyguards, Val, came toward Ruben. "You don't talk to Mr. DiCicco like that. Where's your manners at?"

Frank said, "It's okay. He's a PR, what's he know about manners?"

Val reached out to grab his coat. Ruben blocked his hand and stepped in, hit him with a straight shot to the solar plexus. The middleweights he'd fought would've taken the punch and several more just like it, and kept coming, but the bodyguard dropped to his knees, trying to draw a breath.

Vincent was late getting to Frank's for the delivery, Vincent bringing a week's worth of profits from the poker room in a canvas duffle bag on a strap over his shoulder, three hundred grand and change: counted, banded, and ready to hand over.

He stood on the porch and rang the bell, glanced behind him at Renzo, his driver, standing next to the Caddy, smoking a cigarette. He rang the bell again, and when no one came, he knocked on the door. It was strange, usually one of Frank's bodyguards, Val or Santo, was right there. He never waited more than a minute. Vincent took out his cell phone and dialed Frank's number and heard the phone ringing inside the townhouse, but no one answered it. There was a chill in the air, and he could see his breath. The bag was getting heavy, and he slid it off his shoulder, resting it on the porch but still holding the strap.

He glanced at Renzo again, saw him flick the cigarette. It hit the street and sparked. He waved him to the porch, and when Renzo came up the steps, Vincent said, "Something isn't right. I need you to go around back, see if you see anything and call me."

Vincent left the bag of money where it was, walked down the steps, and pushed through the waist-high shrubs, trying to look in the window. On his tiptoes he could just see over the top of the window ledge. He grabbed the brick ledge and tried to hoist himself up, but he was too heavy. He jumped and thought he saw something on the Oriental rug. He jumped again and was able to hang from the window ledge for a second. Jesus. Unless he was seeing things, Santo was unconscious or dead on the floor.

His phone rang. Renzo said, "I don't see nothing."

"I want you to break in. Bust a window, whatever you have to do."

"Break in Frank DiCicco's, you serious?"

"Something's happened. We have to get in there."

Vincent went back to the porch and waited. A few minutes later the front door opened. Renzo looked like he had seen a ghost. "Mio Dio."

"What is it?"

Vincent walked in and saw Frank on the couch and the bodyguards on the floor, blood everywhere, the smell of death in the air. Frank had enemies for sure, but who would have the balls to do this? Not only shoot them but robbed them too, took their money and tossed their wallets on the floor. Could that have been the motive? He doubted it. They'd have to know Frank to get in. Vincent glanced at Renzo, picking his teeth with a toothpick, looking at the bodies with a bored expression.

"Go wait in the car," Vincent said. "And don't say a word about this, you understand?"

Renzo gave him a nod, toothpick in the corner of his mouth now, black hair slicked back, sparse stubble on his upper lip. "What're you gonna do? Need something done?"

"I'll let you know. Now go wait in the fucking car like I told you."

Vincent went into Frank's study, opened the cabinets, and saw the safe, a big old Mosler, looked like it weighed as much as a car, and filled with money. Frank didn't believe in banks. Vincent's guess, the robbers didn't know about the safe, or they would've tried to open it, would've banged on it with sledgehammers till they were too tired to lift their arms.

He sat at Frank's desk and turned on the computer. Frank had installed surveillance cameras at the front and back doors, so he could see who came to his house when he wasn't there. It was also to keep tabs on the maid, the cook, and his assistant, a nice-looking Sicilian girl named Concetta, Frank was knifing on the side.

The computer booted up and he clicked on the security icon, clicked on the front-door camera, scrolled back to midday. There was a time code on each frame. A UPS man delivered a package at 2:31 PM; Concetta opened the door and signed for it. There was no other activity till Concetta left for the day at 5:37. Frank and the bodyguards arrived at 6:23. And then nothing till Cobb and Diaz showed up at 6:56, which surprised him. Why did they come to see Frank? Frank didn't usually deal with the collectors. That was Vincent's job. He watched the video. Cobb rang the bell, and Val opened the door and let them in. Twelve minutes later, Cobb and Diaz left the townhouse in a hurry, moving quickly down the steps and then out of view.

Next, Vincent saw himself ringing the bell, knocking on the door, and turning to look at Renzo. Now he checked the camera at the rear entrance, saw the maid leave at 4:31, and no one else until Renzo appeared lighting a cigarette, looking in windows.

TWENTY-EIGHT

Vincent, sitting in the back of the Cadillac, was thinking about the girl as they drove through Manhattan. God, did he have a thing for her. Vicki was all he thought about. He'd been trying to get in her pants since the day he hired her, waited to make a move and she brushed him off. Every time he tried, she shut him down. Vicki would say something like "Vincent, I'm seeing someone, okay?" Or, "Vincent, I'm sorry, you're not my type."

Vicki had come highly recommended by Panetta, one of the older dealers, knew Vicki's old man, who'd run a game. Panetta said she knew cards, knew how to deal, and she did. Vicki said she knew how to play too and for a while did okay. But then she started losing and quickly got in over her head. Vincent told her before he lent her the first fifteen, "You sure you want to do this? It can get out of control fast."

"Yeah, but I won't," Vicki had said, flashing that sexy smile.

He secretly hoped she'd get in trouble and come to him for help, but it didn't happen that way. In trouble or not, she didn't want anything to do with him.

Within a couple weeks, what Vicki owed had turned over a couple times and it didn't look like there was any way she could pay it off. That's when Duane Cobb approached him with a plan. Get a rich guy to fall for her and take over the debt. Vincent liked the idea, and it would get Frank off his back.

Vicki'd hooked a Wall Street dude right away, and after they'd gone out for a while, she told him the situation she was in, and the man said he'd help her. She didn't even ask; he offered. They'd tacked four hundred grand onto what Vicki owed, Vincent's idea. She went along with it 'cause she was afraid, and now she was dead. If Vincent couldn't have her, no one was gonna.

Ruben was packing his suitcase, thinking about what happened at Frank DiCicco's earlier, the situation going sideways right away. Ruben picturing the scene in his head. After he hit Val, Santo pulled a gun from behind his back, holding it down his leg, seeing that Cobb had already drawn his, a black semiautomatic he held at arm's length, aimed at Santo's chest.

"The fuck's going on? Put it down," Frank said to Cobb. "Are you crazy? Put it on the floor."

"I do that, he's gonna shoot me." Cobb was talking to Frank but had his eyes glued to the bodyguard. "Tell him to put his down first."

"Listen to me," Frank said. "You gotta be outta your fucking head, you bring a gun in my house. I ain't gonna tell you again. Drop it."

"You want to walk out of here," Ruben said, "shoot him."

"Put the fucking gun down," Frank said. "You hear me?"

"Shoot him," Ruben said to Cobb.

Santo brought the gun up now and Cobb shot him, turned and shot the one with the ponytail, reaching behind his back, the hard ring of the gunshots filling the room. Frank got off the couch, put his hands up. "That's enough."

Cobb turned his gun on Frank.

"Listen to me," Frank said, "It's over, what happened here. It ends now."

Ruben said, "How dumb you think we are, uh?"

"The fuck you doing? I'm made, you know what that means? They gonna come at you with everything they got." Getting tough, 'cause that's all he had left.

Ruben glanced at Cobb. "You hear what he's saying? Do it, man. Leave him like this, we're dead."

"You're dead anyway," Frank said. "You just don't know it."

Cobb shot Frank twice in the chest and he fell back on the couch, his white shirt turning red, the sounds of the gunshots bouncing off the walls of the big room.

Ruben thought he heard someone at his apartment door. He put his glass of tequila on the table, and stood looking through the peephole at Vincent. There was someone next to him in a gray jacket. Ruben could see only part of the man, but not his face. How'd they figure it out so fast? Vincent knocked again.

"Ruben, hey, you in there? I need to talk."

"Tell me what it is. What do you want?"

"Open the door, come on. Something's happened. I have to talk to you."

"I can hear you." Ruben had his eye in the peephole. He should not have come back here. He should have left town. There were others next to Vincent. He could see parts of them. He could see one of them holding a sledgehammer, and another a gun.

Ruben waited till he saw someone raise the sledgehammer, and went left into the tiny kitchen as the door crashed open and three men came through the entryway. The first one was Renzo, holding a gun, looking straight ahead into the main room. Ruben stepped in and hit him with everything he had, felt the man's jaw break and his legs give out, and saw him drop to the floor.

Ruben backed into the kitchen, grabbed the handle of the cast-iron skillet from the stovetop, two of Vincent's men—he had never seen—moving toward him, single file in the narrow room, the first one swinging the sledgehammer, sounding like a gunshot as it missed Ruben and struck a cabinet door, punching a hole in the wood. Ruben, his back against the refrigerator, threw the skillet. It crashed into the man's forehead, blood mixing with grilled meat and chipotle peppers. The man yelling something in Italian as he went down.

Now Ruben felt the sting of a bat as it slammed into his ribs. Jesus, the pain taking his breath away. Ruben covered his face and head with his arms as if he were in the ring, against the ropes. He moved left, threw a combination: straight right that broke the second man's nose, followed by a right hook to the body that dropped him and almost dropped Ruben, the pain like a hot poker in his ribs.

Vincent looked surprised to see him come out of the apartment, Vincent raising his hands in surrender, backing away. "I just want to talk."

"You bring all these men with weapons to talk? What you want to know?" Before this Ruben had liked Vincent, thought of him as a friend.

"Why'd you kill Frank?"

"It just happened."

"How am I gonna explain this?"

Ruben had no idea.

"You gotta get out of here. You gotta go somewhere, disappear, don't come back."

Ruben walked to the elevator, holding his side, looking over his shoulder. Was Vincent being straight, saying they weren't going to come after him? He didn't say it exactly, but that's what Ruben understood, or wanted to.

He rode down and went outside, waited for traffic to clear, and crossed the street. Hiding in the shadows of a darkened storefront, keeping an eye on his building. He phoned Cobb, told him what happened, told him to get out of his apartment and do it fast.

Cobb said, "Where you gonna go?"

"I don't know. I'll meet you in the morning." He could feel the cool night air go right through him, his damaged ribs tightening, spasming. He could feel the sweat on his forehead getting cold.

Maybe fifteen minutes later, he saw them come out of the building, Vincent steering the three tough guys as they wobbled, unsteady like drunks, to a black Cadillac parked on the street. Ruben watched them climb into the car and drive away.

He waited until they were out of sight, crossed the street, and went back to his apartment. The door was open, the molding cracked and splintered where the door had been busted open. He went in, saw the baseball bat on the kitchen floor, grabbed the bottle of tequila from the cupboard, unscrewed the cap and took a long drink, feeling the liquid burn his throat and the alcohol relax him.

In the bathroom, Ruben unbuttoned his shirt and took it off, the pain shooting through him like someone stabbing his insides. He had a bruise on his left side where the bat had landed. He touched his damaged ribs, checking to see if any were broken, but couldn't tell.

There was a roll of surgical tape in the medicine cabinet. He pulled off long strips, wrapping them around his ribs and torso, stopping to take drinks of tequila when the pain was too much. When he was finished, the layers of tape looked like a cast. Ruben opened a bottle of aspirin, poured four in his hand, and washed the pills down with a swallow of tequila.

When the pain lessened, Ruben went in the bedroom closet, loosened the floorboards, and took out plastic-wrapped bundles of cash, fifty-seven grand. He finished packing, taking just the clothes for warm weather, guayabera shirts, cotton pants and sandals, his watches and jewelry, and a straw porkpie.

Ruben felt free for the first time in years. He didn't like what he was doing and wondered why he had not quit on his own, walked away instead of running from the Italians. He was better than this, dealing with Frank and Vincent, collecting from losers. When they found McCann and got the money, he'd be set, could take it easy for a while, maybe even retire. Get a little place in Ponce, fish during the day, chase women and drink rum at night.

It hurt to put on the blue overcoat, but that was okay. Pain had always been part of his life. It kept you honest, made you tougher.

Ruben studied his beat-up face in the mirror, thinking he looked distinguished. People still recognized him in the old neighborhood. He squared the hat on his head and carried the suitcase out of his apartment for the last time.

Ruben saw him in a car parked on the street when he came out of the building. It was cold and the window was down, the man smoking a cigarette. Ruben started down the sidewalk with the suitcase, looked over his shoulder, saw the car following him and then moving up next to him. He could not see the driver but had an idea who he was. The man's arm came through the window, glove on his hand, aiming a gun. Ruben lifted the suitcase, a reflex to protect himself, felt the impact of silenced rounds tear through it and thought he was hit, but he wasn't. He ran back the way he came, the suitcase slowing him, his bruised ribs on fire. He saw the car backing up, trying to stay with him, until it was struck by oncoming traffic. Ruben, still moving, saw the collision, thinking it was over until Dominic Benigno got out of the car.

Ruben moved toward the subway entrance at the end of the block, walking as fast as he could, took the stairs down to the row of turnstiles, slid the suitcase under one and lifted himself over it, the pain taking his breath away. There were people on both sides of him but no one gave him a second look.

Now he was on the platform, moving through the people waiting for the train. He glanced over his shoulder and saw Dominic Benigno coming down the stairs. Ruben thinking about what Dapper Dom had said that day in the restaurant with Frank. Something about Mickey Ward kicking his ass and something else about tiptoeing for chili that he did not understand, but it was not said in admiration, he was sure of that.

Ruben ducked into a janitor room that said Authorized Personnel Only above the entrance. There was a closet door on the right side, a big sink straight ahead with buckets under it, mops and cleaning supplies hanging in fixtures on the walls. He put the suitcase on the floor, picked up a broom, and unscrewed the pole. He took out a pocket knife and shaved the grooved tip into a sharp point. Ruben opened the closet door, pushed in the suitcase, and stood just inside. He looked out the doorway and saw Dominic Benigno walk past him, moving along the subway platform. A couple minutes later, Dapper Dom, aiming the pistol, walked into the janitor's room. From his hidden position in the closet, Ruben waited till he was right there before lunging with the pole, driving it into the meat of his side. Ruben hearing him grunt, hearing the pistol hit the floor. Watching him try to pull out the spear as Ruben pushed it deeper into him. Seeing his suit and hands wet with blood.

And then Dapper Dom was on the floor, Ruben standing over him, hearing his raspy breathing, seeing the pain in his eyes. Ruben's damaged ribs had slowed him, but the rush of adrenalin kept him focused. "Listen, you hear me? Mickey Ward didn't kick my ass. Was a draw, but I kick yours, uh? *Cono* motherfucker."

PART
THREE

TWENTY-NINE

Jack drove up the coast past Delray, Boca, and Boynton Beach to West Palm and took the Flagler Memorial Bridge across the Intracoastal to Palm Beach. He went south on County Road past the Breakers, where he had stayed with Diane a couple times over the years, and past Royal Palm Way, looking at the tall groomed palm trees lining the boulevard.

He parked on Worth Avenue and walked down the street to Ta-boo. Inside it was cool and dark. Jack sat at the bar. There was an empty seat to his left, and to his right was a fiftyish woman with big hair and a lot of diamonds. She was having an afternoon martini in a stemmed cocktail glass, and he could see an olive submerged in the translucent depths.

Jack ordered a Stoli and tonic and looked at a menu until the woman said, "Are you going to nosh?"

"What do you recommend?"

"The crab cake is to die for."

Even in the subdued light, he could see she'd had a lot of work done on her face. It looked like you could bounce a quarter off the skin on her cheeks, and her lips were curled up like a duck's.

"So what are you, a tourist?" she said, reminding Jack of a ventriloquist, talking without her lips moving.

"How can you tell?"

"How can I tell? You've got a sign on you. Your clothes are brand-new like you just unwrapped them. I can see the creases where your shirt was folded."

"I live down here."

"Since when, this morning? I'll tell you one thing, you don't look like Palm Beach. Delray maybe, although you need a shirt with an alligator on it, but not Palm Beach."

Jack sipped his drink, thinking this snippy Palm Beach bitch had sized him up, pegged him perfectly. He saw someone sit in the chair to his left and turned, staring at a sultry girl in a sundress, midthirties, tan legs crossed, sunglasses on her head, angled into dark, curly hair. For a split second he thought it was Vicki.

The girl looked at him and smiled. "Sorry I'm late, I got here as soon as I could."

"Yeah, I was starting to wonder." He was wondering all right, who was she? "What're you drinking?"

"The usual."

"Oh, the usual." Jack raised his hand and signaled the bartender. "Cosmo up for the lady and another one for me." He turned his back to the rude woman on his right. "Don't keep me in suspense any longer."

The bartender put the drinks in front of them on Ta-boo napkins.

"You look like you needed to be saved. Joan Rivers was all over you, in case you didn't notice."

"She was giving me a hard time for not measuring up to Palm Beach standards. Based on the way I'm dressed, she thought I was from Delray. What a slap in the face, huh?"

"I can see that."

"Is everyone in Palm Beach a snob?"

"I don't know. I don't live in Palm Beach."

"Since we're going out, tell me your name."

"Rita Najjir."

"Where you from, Rita?"

"Jounieh, originally. It's in Lebanon."

"I've been there."

"Come on?"

"I flew to Tel Aviv after college and drove up the coast and went around Beirut. The city had been destroyed by civil war." He paused. "I'm . . ."—he almost said Jack McCann, but caught himself—"Richard Keefer." She looked him in the eye as he shook her soft hand with pink nails.

"We're not very popular after nine-eleven. I guess that's an understatement."

"You can't blame all Arabs for what a small group of lunatics did."

"It hasn't been easy." She paused. "You want to get out of here?"

"What about your drink?"

"I prefer arak with ice and water."

"Who doesn't."

Rita smiled. "Ready?"

"You go ahead. I'm going to finish my drink." After everything that had happened, going with this girl didn't feel right.

Rita said, "You sure?"

"Yeah, another time maybe." He sipped the fresh drink and watched her walk out.

Twenty minutes later, Jack was about to get in his car and saw Rita on the sidewalk, carrying a shopping bag, coming toward him. She stopped at a red Mercedes SL convertible, two cars behind his, popped the trunk and put the bag in. Now she noticed him. "Sorry if I did something to offend you. I was going to invite you to lunch. I'm usually not that forward."

"Why did you sit next to me?"

"I watched you for a while in the bar, talking to Joan Rivers. I wondered if you were a gigolo."

"Maybe it was our first date, we met online."

"She looked ten years older than you, at least."

He went back to a previous statement. "A gigolo, huh?"

"You're a hunk. You have a hunkiness about you. You're big and you look like you're in good shape." Rita smiled. "But, if you don't want to come with me, that's fine. I'm not going to beg you."

Jack said, "Where do you want to go?"

"My place."

He followed her driving south, passing mansions with water views on both sides: the Intracoastal on the right and the Atlantic Ocean on the left. Then for a stretch the mansions were replaced by immense gated estates. He followed her over a bridge and saw high-rises with ocean views and more ostentatious mansions that rivaled those he had seen in Palm Beach.

How they met seemed believable, but he couldn't shake the feeling of paranoia. Was it happening again? Did Frank's men get to Sculley? Jack should never have involved him. Now he saw it: Sculley, under duress, told them where he was and gave them his alias. Jack could see it happening that way. They saw him lying by the pool at the Sands in Pompano, followed him up the coast to Palm Beach, and sent in Rita, another good-looking young girl. *Pick him up and bring him to us.* After what had happened to Vicki, that scenario seemed plausible.

Rita turned off the highway into a gated community called Palm Cove. He could see a high-rise sticking up over a pink stucco wall surrounded by palm trees. A guard wearing khakis and a golf shirt came out of the gatehouse. Rita said something to him. The gate went up and then he waved Jack through.

They curved around a palm-lined boulevard to the high-rise. Jack parked next to her and stepped out of the car. "Are they upstairs waiting for us?"

Rita gave him a puzzled look. "What're you talking about?"

"Frank DiCicco." He watched her as he said it, but her expression didn't change.

"Who's that?" She glanced his way, still confused. "And why would he be at my place?" Rita hesitated. "Oh, I get it, you're messing with me, aren't you? You were kidding when you mentioned this guy, Frank, right? It sounded like you were serious. And if you are, you think I'm involved in something." She moved toward him, held his hand in both of hers. "Which is pretty crazy since I've never seen you before today, and I've never heard your name. You've got nothing to worry about. I'm Rita Najjir. Grew up in Dearborn, Michigan. I'm thirty-one, divorced, no children, no boyfriends, no pets. I worked for Microsoft ten years, retired six months ago, bought the condo. Want to come up and see it, or go back to Palm Beach? Richard, it's up to you."

THIRTY

Six fifteen in the morning, Duane Cobb checked out of the airport hotel and took a shuttle to Newark. After what happened to Ruben and almost happened to him, LaGuardia was too risky. He still had the Ruger but couldn't risk bringing it in his suitcase even though he was checking the bag. He dropped the reloaded gun in a trash bin outside the terminal, checked his bag at the Delta counter, and went through security that took forever after 9/11.

At the gate Cobb hid behind a newspaper, thinking about last night, picturing the anger on Frankie Cheech's face when the gun was pointed at him.

Nobody'd ever done that and lived to tell about it. And then the adrenalin rush as he shot them. Christ, he was still high. Feeling no remorse then or now. Ruben had been right—there was only one way out of that situation.

After Ruben called, he'd wheeled his suitcase to his neighbor Cindy's apartment. He knew they'd be coming for him anytime and didn't want to risk going outside. She'd opened the door and said, "Duane, what's up? Where're you going?"

"Out of town."

"Well, I can see that."

"Just wanted to say good-bye."

She invited him in and they stood next to the door. "Wanna have a drink and sit?"

"I only have a few minutes."

"Where're you going?"

"Florida."

"Can I go?" She grinned. "Just kidding. I couldn't get time off work anyway."

Cobb gave her a fake smile. The little blonde-haired flirt had been hitting on him since he'd moved in six months earlier. He didn't believe in tapping co-workers or neighbors, thinking that when the relationship soured, he'd regret it. Cindy worked in customer service for an airline and used to tell him the odd names of people who'd call up and complain. One time a black woman named Clammy Weary, another time a guy named Justin Case. Were they putting Cindy on or what?

Cobb could hear footsteps coming down the hall and saw the blur of movement as they passed by the peephole. He could hear them bust open his apartment door and tear up the interior.

Cindy made a face and said, "Duane, what's going on? Who is that?"

"Some men coming to kill me."

She looked afraid now. "I'm calling the police."

Then someone was pounding on her door. He put his index finger up to his mouth, stepped back, and drew the Ruger Lc9. When the pounding stopped, he heard them walking away.

Cobb scanned the gate area looking for Ruben, checking out people waiting to board, a couple of good-looking broads laughing, sitting next to two guys with short hair, wearing golf shirts, looked like insurance salesmen letting loose.

He barely recognized Ruben entering the gate area a few minutes later in sunglasses and an overcoat. Ruben looked like he was limping, glanced at Cobb, made eye contact, but didn't say anything, and sat away from him on the other side of the gate. No reason to talk or call attention to themselves.

When Cobb was in line ready to board, he noticed a dark-haired girl wearing sunglasses standing in line several people behind him. He wondered if she was a movie star. She had that look about her, nice body in tight jeans and a lightweight jacket, something familiar about her like he'd seen her on TV or in a movie. The girl was talking to Ruben when Cobb walked into the Jetway, and he saw Ruben sitting next to her on the flight.

Cobb saw them again when they walked off the plane, and it bothered him. Ruben, this fucking Neanderthal, dealing a hot-looking babe who seemed interested. He went to baggage claim, got his suitcase, and waited for Ruben, who appeared five minutes later and now looked like a plantation owner in sunglasses, a straw porkpie, and one of those white shirts with vents on the sides barbers wore. The girl wasn't with him. Cobb said, "Do I know you?"

Ruben gave him a sour look.

"The hell's wrong?" Cobb said. "Still tense after what happened last night, huh? I don't blame you. I'd say you're real lucky."

"They were punks."

"Well, it's a good thing. They were tough, you might not be here." Cobb paused. "Where's your girlfriend at?"

In the motel office, Cobb showed a photograph of Jack McCann to the manager, a fat guy looked like he was trying to eat himself to death. "Our buddy Jack show up yet?"

The manager looked at him like Cobb was speaking Urdu.

"Big guy, six feet, two hundred."

"You're not talking about Mr. Keefer, are you? I think his first name is Richard." He turned to a fat woman with a Crisco ass standing at a file cabinet in the office behind the counter. "Candy, what's that fella Keefer's first name?"

"Pretty sure it's Richard." She had a tiny voice for a girl her size.

"That's what I told him."

Cobb said, "Let's not make a federal fucking case out of it, okay? Jack's his nickname."

"You don't have to use language like that. You can call him late for dinner for all I care. And yes, he arrived. Been here about a week." He turned looking at the fat girl again. "Candy, how long's Mr. Keefer been here?"

"Be a week tomorrow."

"That's what I told him." The manager turned back to Cobb. "Although I ain't seen him around much lately."

"When you do, don't say anything about us. He's not gonna believe his buds from back home are here. What room's he in?"

Sitting by the pool a half hour later, Cobb saw the maid knock on Jack's door a couple times, wait, knock again, and use her key to go into the room. Cobb walked up the stairs and hung around the balcony outside Jack's room, heard the vacuum cleaner, and when it turned off, he glanced in the room and saw the maid take her bucket of cleaning products in the bathroom. He went in and tried not to make any noise. He checked the dresser. There were clothes in the drawers and shirts hanging in the closet.

The maid came out of the bathroom carrying a pile of dirty towels, gave Cobb a suspicious look, or maybe she didn't expect anyone to be standing there. "Looking for my buddy. Seen Mr. Keefer around?"

"I no see today," she said with an island accent.

THIRTY-ONE

Diane, in her new disguise, looked for them in the terminal. There was a guy in jeans, cowboy boots, and a Western shirt, but it wasn't Duane Cobb. He and Ruben weren't on the flight. She flew first class, was third in line getting off the plane in Fort Lauderdale. She sat at the gate, waited till everyone walked out of the Jetway.

She went to baggage claim, pulled her bag off the conveyor, and rolled it outside to the National car rental stop, boarded a green bus, took it to the lot, and rented a Chrysler sedan.

Diane stared at her face in the rearview mirror, barely recognized herself, and doubted that Cobb or Ruben would, either. She had cut her hair last night and dyed it, a color called medium ash brown.

She followed the map north on Federal Highway, and then east to the ocean and found 300 Briny Avenue. It was a classic two-story 1960s motel called the Sands. This was the address Duane Cobb had in a desk drawer in his apartment. What did it mean? Did Jack rent a room? Were Cobb and Ruben staying here? Diane had no idea. But she'd find out soon enough.

She drove past the Sands, went around the block, and parked on the side of the street just south of the motel, lowered the front windows and felt a warm ocean breeze blow through the interior. Now she was hot and took off her sweater and folded it on the seat next to her.

Diane looked north toward downtown Pompano. There were one- and two-story motels lining both sides of the street and, in the distance, high-rise condos painted in pastel colors. Old folks coming down to take up residence and live out what was left of their time.

To her right was an empty lot with beach access. Across the street and one motel over was the Ebb Tide, a small place with a swimming pool in front and a view of the Sands.

She checked in. There was a pickup truck with a silver tool box across the bed parked in front, and a minivan with a luggage rack. A couple with two young kids were playing in the water, making a lot of noise. Diane went to her room, which was cheap and small, faded robin's egg blue walls and white trim. She put her suitcase on the second twin bed and changed into shorts and a tank top, fit a New York Mets cap on her head, grabbed her sunglasses, and went out the door.

She walked down the street, crossed just south of the Sands, and headed to the beach. It was a perfect blue-sky day, sun high, a slight breeze. Diane stood by the lifeguard shack, looking at the ocean. There were sunbathers and joggers and two kids throwing a Frisbee and a group of teenagers playing volleyball.

Diane stepped out of her sandals, picked them up, and walked toward the Sands, seeing the renters on lounge chairs around the pool, too far away to recognize anyone. She spread her towel on the sand and lay down on her stomach, felt the sun on her neck and the back of her legs. This wasn't going to work. Even if Cobb was out by the pool, she wouldn't be able to see him.

After a few minutes, Diane stood up, grabbed her towel, and went back to the Ebb Tide. She grabbed a magazine from her room and sat in an aluminum lawn chair by the pool, paging through *Vanity Fair*, looking at pictures and articles, too distracted to read, the reality of what she was doing finally weighing on her.

The family came out of the pool a little after three. The mom dried off the kids, and they all went to their room. Diane was relieved; they were loud and annoying and she was tense. The manager came out of the office, crossed the pool enclosure, and waved. "How you doing? Soaking up some of our Florida sun, huh?" Like it was his. He got in an SUV parked in the driveway and drove away.

Now a guy in frayed blue jean shorts came out of one of the rooms with a can of beer in one hand and a small plastic cooler with a handle in his other. He was stripped to the waist, his white body showing half a dozen bluish tattoos and a farmer's tan. She fixed her attention on the magazine and saw him glance over a couple times. He walked around the pool and came toward her, put the cooler down, and sat back in a lounge chair about fifteen feet away, no towel, bare, tattooed skin on sunbaked vinyl.

He looked up and squinted, made a visor with his hand and said, "Hey, you ready for a cold one?"

Diane laid the open magazine on her lap, the pages curving over her thighs. "Not yet."

"Let me know when you are."

She nodded and went back to *Vanity Fair*. He was quiet for a while, sat there drinking a beer, but she could see he was restless. He got up gripping the can and walked in the shallow end of the pool.

"I don't know it gets any better than this." He drank some beer. "Where you from?"

Diane didn't answer, hoped he wasn't a talker.

"You here on vacation, or what?"

"My husband had to work. He's either coming down tonight or tomorrow morning. We're from Connecticut."

"I hear it's real nice up there." He paused. "I'm working a construction job up in Belle Glade, got a couple days off, drove south, and ended up here. Looked okay, and the price is right."

"Enjoy yourself." She hoped that was the end of it.

"I'm Larry Fish, by the way. But everyone just calls me Fish. Need anything, don't hesitate."

Was he looking for some action, or just being friendly? Diane went back to the magazine, occasionally looking across the street. She saw Cobb come through the archway at the Sands and felt a jolt of adrenalin. He was standing next to a red Mustang convertible that had been parked in one of the spaces since she'd arrived. He opened the door and got in the car.

If she hoped to follow Cobb, Diane knew she didn't have time to go back to her room and get the key to the rental car. She got up and approached Larry Fish. "Is that your pickup truck?"

"Maybe," he said, grinning. "Who wants to know?"

"You mind if I borrow it for a little while?"

He got up, reached into one of the jean pockets, took out a key ring and threw it to her. "Knock yourself out. Just be back by midnight." He grinned.

The Mustang was almost to Atlantic Boulevard when she put the Ford F 150 in gear and pulled out. She floored the accelerator, and the tires squealed. She caught up to the Mustang at A1A, still thinking about Fish lending his truck to a stranger. She wouldn't have been so trusting.

She followed the Mustang west to Dixie Highway and then south to Dixie Guns and Ammo. Cobb parked and went in. She waited in the truck, listening to outlaw country. The DJ said, "We're bringing you the best of Waylon, Willy, Merle, Billy Joe, and more," cold air blasting her. Diane hated country music but didn't want to change Fish's station.

Half an hour later, Cobb reappeared, carrying something wrapped in brown paper a couple feet long. Next she followed Cobb to a hardware store, waited till he came out with something in a paper bag, then to a uniform supply store and back to the motel, giving him time to get out and go to his room before she parked the truck.

Fish was where she'd left him, four beer cans next to his chair. "That was quick."

"I told you."

"Listen, you're not doing anything this evening, I'd like to buy you dinner."

"Thanks for the offer, but I am going to relax, take it easy."

"Change your mind, you know where to find me."

Half an hour later, Diane put on running shoes. She looked at herself in the mirror, still not used to the short, dark hair, and fit the Mets cap on her head.

Fish was picking up empties, dropping them in the cooler, when she walked back out by the pool. He had finished the six-pack and was holding another beer, looked like number seven.

"Where you going?"

"For a run."

"What do you want to do that for?" He sounded buzzed now. "Don't tell me you're a Mets fan. They ever won anything?"

Her dad had been a diehard Mets fan, keeping the faith even through the lean years. "How about the World Series in sixty-nine? They beat Baltimore in five. Won again in eighty-six, beat the Astros. You obviously don't follow baseball."

"Not the National League, if that's what you mean." Fish fit the top on the cooler and slid the handle up from the side and lifted it. "So you gonna have dinner with me or what?"

Diane jogged down to the pier and came back along the ocean, ran up past the Sands—no one out by the pool—and went back to her room to take a shower. She was drying herself in front of the fogged-up mirror, wiped it with a towel, but still couldn't see her face well enough to put on makeup. There was a knock on the door, and then another one, harder this time, and louder.

"Hey, I know you're in there. I seen you come back."

Diane had a feeling Fish was going to be a problem. She slipped on shorts and a tank top, pulled a comb through damp hair, and stepped into her Jimmy Choo sandals. He knocked again. She went to the door and opened it. "I was taking a shower." That would've been enough explanation for most civilized humans, but not Fish.

"Gonna invite me in?"

He was holding a can of beer and still hadn't put on a shirt, his bleached skin now pink with sunburn. She got a gamey whiff of him as he pushed past her into the room, and sat on the twin bed with the floral comforter, staring at her suitcase.

"Ain't even unpacked, huh?"

Fish patted the mattress next to his leg. "Why don't you come over here, join me." He had a drunk grin plastered on his red face and couldn't have been more of a fool as he slurred his words.

"Listen, Fish. I like you, you're a nice guy, but you've got to go. I have to get dressed."

"That's okay with me. I won't look." He grinned again, eyes swollen. "The hell I won't."

He drank some beer and fit the can between his legs, slid a half pint of whiskey out of his back pocket, unscrewed the cap, and took a drink. He exhaled and shook his head. "Lord almighty. That shit'll set you free."

"What is it you don't understand?" Diane said, hands on her hips.

"Huh?" Fish held her in his bleary gaze. "Know what I think? I think you're down here by yourself and no one's coming to meet you, is what I think."

Was it dumb luck, or was Diane giving off some kind of loser vibe? "You can think anything you want as long as you do it somewhere else."

He drank the beer. "Oh, you got spunk, don't you? I like my whiskey strong and my women feisty."

"Fish," she said raising her voice, "I've had it. I'm out of patience." She opened the door. "Get the hell out of here. I see you again I'm going to call the police."

"All you had to do was ask."

He got up, staggered past her, and she closed the door.

THIRTY-TWO

"It's a double," Ted Lafrance said.

Coming into the room, looking at two naked white guys, bodies bent and angled in death on the blood-soaked king-size bed, Marquis Brown said, "How'd you figure that out?"

Ted Lafrance frowned. "What do you mean?"

"I'm fucking with you, rookie. Who are they?"

"Guy on the right's Joseph Sculley, the condo owner. Other one's Patrick Linehan, the building doorman.

Marquis studied the scene. The murders had the look of a pro, shot precisely, one round in the forehead, one in the heart. There was a window above the headboard, Marquis looking out at Lower Manhattan, still not used to the big opening in the skyline the Trade Center had occupied.

"I think it was a love triangle," Ted Lafrance said. "Sculley's wife came home unexpectedly, found them in the marital bed, lost it, pulled a semiautomatic."

Marquis shook his head. "Why do you say that?"

"Knowing what I do, that's what it looks like."

Huh? Marquis was thinking. "You an expert on love triangles?" Ted—smart as he thought he was—was a dumb motherfucker when it came to solving murders.

"It's an assumption, a supposition."

"I know what it means," Marquis said. "What else you got?"

"One of the tenants, Charlene Lemmer, remembers seeing two guys talking to the doorman in the lobby about six o'clock, and the three of them got in the elevator together."

"Think one of them could be the shooter?"

"I don't know." Ted was five-five, the shoulders of his blazer covered with dandruff.

"Call Ms. Lemmer," Marquis said. "I want to talk to her."

"I suggest we divide and conquer. I'll question Charlene Lemmer. You talk to the other witnesses."

"Hold on. You said only one person saw them talking to the doorman? Now you saying they're others?"

"There's bound to be, don't you think? I mean, it's a busy time of day, people are coming home from work, people are going out for drinks and dinner."

"How many tenants in the building?"

"No idea."

"Why don't you go find that out, leave the Q and A to me." Marquis took out a notebook. "What's Mr. Sculley's profession?"

"He's a lawyer." Ted handed Marquis a business card. "Works for Baskin Williams, one of the top firms in the city."

"Isn't that what you were gonna be, a lawyer?"

"I am a lawyer."

"What the hell you doing with homicide?"

"This is more interesting, and I want to make a difference."

Ted walked out of the room, saying he was going to call the witness, set up a time to talk. Marquis wrote the crime scene report, noting the positions of the bodies, the gunshot wounds, the degree of rigor, the four shell casings on the floor that Ted had tagged with orange Post-it notes. A white shirt and dark slacks had been tossed on an antique trunk at the foot of the bed. There was no mystery. He could see the manner of death and ruled it a homicide.

"Charlene Lemmer's gonna meet you in the lobby at four thirty," Ted said, coming back in the bedroom.

Marquis glanced at him. "What's she look like?"

"Bottle blonde, a little on the chunky side."

Marquis pictured Patricia Arquette in *True Romance*. "I'll look for her."

The evidence tech showed up a few minutes later, a pale thin cadaver of a man with jet black hair. Marquis had never met him. The guy said his name was Staley. He walked into the master bedroom and went to work. Marquis went into the study and continued writing his report. He finished at four twenty-five and took the elevator down to the lobby.

When she showed up fifteen minutes late, he didn't think Charlene Lemmer was chunky. Marquis liked women with curves and a booty. After introductions, Marquis said, "Tell me what you saw."

"Pat, the doorman, talking to two men. I've never seen them before. I'm positive they don't live here."

"What'd they look like?"

"One was Puerto Rican or Mexican and rough-looking."

The PR again, Marquis thought. The dude got around.

"His face was a mess. The other one wore jeans and cowboy boots. They didn't go together, that's the first thing I thought."

"Where'd you see them?"

"Over by the entrance. Pat looked afraid, like they were threatening him, giving him a hard time about something."

"Did you tell the manager?"

"I didn't have a chance. I went over and got my mail and saw the three of them get in the elevator together."

"Anyone else there?"

"I saw Al Melfi and Cindy Petty while the two men were talking to Pat."

Marquis wrote their names in his notebook. "You know them?"

"I see them around. I talk to them at the Christmas party. Al's an ad executive, works for one of the big agencies in town. Cindy's a model. She's from Bottineau, North Dakota, goes by her model name, Eden. She's always posing but trying to look natural. She's a little full of herself, thinks she's entitled, the world owes her 'cause she's skinny and good-looking."

Across the lobby, the elevator doors opened; the bodies of Sculley and the doorman, in black body bags, were wheeled on gurneys through the entrance outside to a van parked on the street.

Marquis had Ted Lafrance set up meetings with Mr. Melfi and Ms. Petty for later that evening.

First he met again with Charlene, this time in the kitchen in her apartment. He stood on the other side of an island counter while she drank wine and made dinner. He could smell onions and garlic. She was sautéing vegetables and chicken in a wok.

"How about a glass of wine or a drink, Detective?"

"I'm still on the clock, got two more Q & As to do. Don't want to interrupt your meal. Just a couple more things." He took the mug shot of Ruben Diaz out of his shirt pocket. It was taken in 1979, when Ruben was seventeen. Now he was thirty-nine. Marquis handed the picture to Charlene. "This guy look familiar?"

She studied the black-and-white photo. "Yeah, I think he was one of them. But he looks a lot different now. Who is he?"

"Ruben Diaz, ex-fighter works for a loan shark with ties to the Mafia."

"Do you think he killed Pat and Mr. Sculley?"

That's what Marquis was asking himself as he rode the elevator up a couple floors to Cindy Petty's apartment. If the medical examiner determined the time of death was around six in the evening the day before, Ruben and the cowboy were the most likely suspects.

Cindy, in her socks, was as tall as he was, a little under six feet. They sat in her living room, Cindy at one end of the couch with her long, skinny legs bent under her, Marquis in a chair on the other side of a glass coffee table. He wanted a cigarette bad, wondered what the model would do if he lit up. "I hear your stage name's Eden? That have something to do with the garden?"

"I think of Eden as the epitome of innocence. There was no sin."

"Until Adam and Eve went against God's law and ate the fruit from the forbidden tree, and God booted 'em out."

Cindy smiled. "You know your Bible, Detective."

"I do okay. You know why I'm here?"

"I heard about the murders. I can't believe it happened in our building."

"Did you know Mr. Sculley and Mr. Linehan?"

"Not really."

"What time'd you get home yesterday?"

"Five after six. I'd been at a shoot all afternoon. I was exhausted."

"What was being shot?"

"It was a magazine cover."

Marquis studied her perfect features and perfect skin, her perfect nose and perfect teeth. "So I'll see you, huh?"

"If you look at *Vogue*."

"My subscription ran out." Marquis grinned. "What'd you see when you walked in the lobby?"

Cindy stared out the window for a while and looked back at him. "There were a couple people getting their mail, and two guys talking to the doorman."

"Look to you like they was having an argument?"

"I didn't pay that much attention."

"Nobody talking loud?"

Cindy shook her perfect head.

Marquis got up and handed her the mug shot of Ruben. "This one of them talking to the doorman?"

She looked at it. "I think so." And handed it back.

Marquis leaned forward in the chair. "Mr. Sculley lives right down the hall from you. Hear anything sounded like gunshots?"

"No. I came up here and went in my apartment."

"Any kind of commotion?"

"What do you mean?"

"Somebody falling, banging into a wall. People yelling, shouting, angry."

"Nothing like that. But I saw a man wearing gloves, I'd swear he came out of Mr. Sculley's apartment. He was right there. It was the gloves that caught my eye. You don't see men wearing gloves inside."

"What'd he look like?"

"He was well-dressed. I saw his face, but he was far away."

"Say anything to him?"

"No."

"Ever see him before?"

Cindy shook her head.

"What time was that?"

"Five forty-seven. I had just returned after meeting a friend for a drink. My boyfriend called." Cindy took out her cell phone, pressed a couple buttons, and showed him. On the screen, it said TOM. Under the name he saw: INCOMING CALLS and the date: SEPTEMBER 26, 5:47 PM, 01:12. "I told him I'd call back."

"So you were in the hall at the time?"

She nodded.

"Show me, will you?" Marquis got up and Cindy led him across the living room to the front door and out of the apartment. He looked down the hall at Sculley's door one hundred feet away, yellow crime-scene tape crisscrossed in front of it. "Where were you at?"

Cindy Petty walked down the hall to where the elevators were, stopped, turned and faced him. "I was right here. I heard a door close. Looked over my shoulder and saw him."

"Maybe he came out of another apartment."

"The closest door was Mr. Sculley's."

"I'd like to have a police artist come by, have you describe the man."

"Like in the movies, huh?" Cindy looked like a little girl now, smiling. "But as I said, he was too far away. I didn't really get a good look at him."

Next Marquis visited Al Melfi on the third floor. He sat in Mr. Melfi's wood-paneled study with framed ads on the walls. "These all yours? I've seen some of them." There were ads for Absolut Vodka, one for "Coke the real thing," "This Bud's for you," and Viagra. Headline said: "You need wood?" A gray-haired dude with a grin on his face was carrying a pile of logs he'd just cut, looking at a gray-haired woman like he was going to pounce on her. "Viagra for erectile dysfunction," it said at the bottom.

Al Melfi made a face. "What can I do for you, Detective?"

"You know Mr. Sculley and Patrick Linehan, the doorman?"

"In passing. I heard what happened."

"In your profession, you must be an observer, always checking things out, looking for ideas. Tell me what you remember when you walked in the lobby after work yesterday."

"The doorman was talking to two guys."

"What were they talking about?"

"How do I know? It looked to me like he knew them. I stopped to pick up my mail. A few minutes later, they got in the elevator. I tried to get in with them but the doors closed. Are they suspects?"

"At the moment, prime."

"When I was coming down the sidewalk from the subway, I saw them get out of a Toyota sedan, cross the street, and go in the building."

"Sure it was a Toyota?"

"Positive. A Corolla, black and tan."

"You see the tag?"

"No."

Marquis handed him a card. "Call me, you remember anything else."

THIRTY-THREE

It was Chet Karvatski's crime scene. Chet, who everyone called Chetter, knew Marquis had questioned Frankie Cheech in connection with the murder of Vicki Ross, and called him. The room was big and ornate, with a high ceiling and a couple furniture groupings, a fireplace, and tall windows that faced the street. Marquis studied the positions of the three bodies: Frankie Cheech, white shirt soaked with blood, sitting on a couch with his head back, and the two bodyguards, one facedown, the other faceup on the Oriental rug. He tried to picture the scene, imagine what had happened.

"Who found them?"

"Housekeeper, broad's in Frank's office, crying."

Across the room, Ted Lafrance, in a custom-made suit, said, "You ask me, the shooters stood here, came in firing."

Marquis said, "Ted, go out back, look for any evidence of force-ful entry."

When Ted was gone, Chetter said to Marquis, "Who's that?"

"New guy, Ted Lafrance. Graduated law school, decided to become a cop."

"He's full of shit. There was one shooter, stood in front of the couch. Four casings—all from the same gun. Let me show you something."

Marquis followed Chetter into Frank DiCicco's office. A dark-haired woman about forty, sitting behind the desk, got up and walked out of the room.

"The housekeeper," Chetter said. "I wouldn't kick her out of bed for eating crackers." He sat at the desk, looking at a computer.

"Showing your age with that line." Marquis walked over and stood behind him. "Last time I heard it, I was in grade school."

Chetter turned, glanced at him. "Footage from the security cameras. Check it out."

Marquis watched, and Chetter froze the frame when two men appeared at the front door, 6:56 PM on the time code in the left-hand corner of the screen.

"Know them?" Chetter said.

"The PR's Ruben Diaz. I believe the other one is Duane Cobb. Collectors work for Vincent Gallo, who worked for Frankie Cheech. Let's see what else you got."

Marquis watched Diaz and Cobb come out in a hurry at 7:12. Fifteen minutes later, Vincent Gallo and his driver showed up, Gallo carrying a duffle bag. "You know the time of death?"

"M.E. said between six thirty and eight thirty, but it was a guess."

"Say it was Diaz and Cobb, why they do it?"

"Money would be my first guess. Or something happened. Killing a made man is a death sentence." Chetter studied the screen. "This is the camera in back."

Gallo's driver was behind the townhouse, smoking a cigarette, looking in windows. He busted a glass pane in the door with his elbow, reached in, unlocked it, and went inside.

Now they were watching Vincent Gallo on the front porch. The driver opened the door.

"Look, he says something to Vincent. See his face? The dude's worried."

"Maybe he's the shooter," Marquis said. "With Frankie Cheech out of the way, Gallo moves up the ranks."

"I don't think so," Chetter said. "First of all, he didn't have time. Second, you kill a made man, you don't bring a witness."

At 8:09, Vincent Gallo and the driver exited the townhouse as fast as Ruben and Cobb had about an hour earlier.

"Let's say Gallo's innocent," Marquis said. "Why didn't he call the police?"

"They take care of their own problems," Chetter said. "They must know who did it. I should follow them, see who they got in mind."

Next stop was the subway. Transit Police had secured this crime scene. Staley, the evidence tech, was dusting a broom handle for prints when Marquis arrived. "Apparent murder weapon. Killer used it like a spear."

"What, you think we're looking for a Zulu warrior?"

"Or maybe a Hutu," Staley said, his cadaverous face showing signs of life, breaking into a grin. He reminded Marquis of Steve Buscemi without the bug eyes.

The room smelled like a butcher shop. The body of a dark-haired man was on his back on the concrete floor, a hole in his side, body resting in a pool of coagulated blood. "Who is he?"

"Dominic Benigno," Staley said. "Forty-two, lives in Brooklyn. AKA Dapper Dom, know him?

Marquis was acquainted with him, crazy motherfucker, Sicilian, Frankie Cheech's trigger. Benigno had done time for assault with intent. His gun, a silenced Beretta semiautomatic, was on the floor ten feet from the body, and he was wearing gloves. Marquis remembered the model at Sculley's apartment building saying she saw a dude wearing gloves. "Any witnesses? Anyone see anything?"

"Busy subway platform," a transit cop named Kohl said, "someone had to hear it, had to see it, something this crazy and violent. But no one's come forward. Janitor found the body this morning. And look at this: wood shavings from the killer sharpening the broom pole."

Marquis was looking at the bloody footprints all over the floor, and more heading toward the exit.

Staley said, "We're looking for a dude wears a nine Benny."

"Huh?"

"It's a shoe size, nine B. I measured the print; I used to sell shoes."

"That shouldn't be a problem." Marquis grinned. "Can't be many men in New York City wear a size nine, huh."

Staley said, "Less than a million, I'd guess."

The For Sale sign on the front lawn surprised him. Mrs. hadn't said nothing about selling the house. Marquis Brown rang the bell and waited. He walked up the driveway behind the house to the garage, opened the door, saw that Jack's BMW was missing. He walked back to the house, stood at the side door. Mrs. hadn't had the broken windowpane repaired yet; a piece of cardboard was taped in place where the glass had been knocked out. He pushed through it, unlocked the door, and went in, thinking this was one of the strangest cases he'd ever worked.

Here's what he knew: the husband allegedly had an affair with a young girl in debt to a loan shark. McCann agreed to pay the debt but died when Tower One collapsed on 9/11. Now two of Frank DiCicco's collectors were trying to strong-arm Mrs. for the money. Three people connected with the case had been murdered: Vicki Ross, Joe Sculley, and Patrick Linehan, and this morning, Frankie Cheech and his bodyguards were found shot to death in Cheech's townhouse. Add Dominic Benigno to the list, and there were seven dead. With all that had transpired, Diane was off his list of suspects in Vicki Ross's murder. But he still thought she knew something.

Marquis walked through the kitchen and breakfast room down a hallway to the den, looked in, saw bookshelves on one of the walls and a desk with a computer on it across the room. He didn't know what he was looking for till he sat behind the desk, staring at the green and white Apple iMac. Marquis wasn't especially good with computers, had a PC at the station house. His fourteen-year-old daughter Shareeta had shown him a few things, so he knew he could at least turn the motherfucker on. He pushed the button and the screen lit up.

First thing, he started checking e-mail, saw a confirmation on an American Airlines flight: LaGuardia to Fort Lauderdale, yesterday morning. Went deeper, checked e-mails going back a week, nothing about a hotel or car rental, and then went back a month, wondering if Mrs. had been in touch with her disappeared husband. He didn't see anything that suggested it.

Marquis got up and stood in front of the bookshelves, scanning books, photographs, knickknacks, and so forth. There were three photo albums on one of the shelves. He took them down, went back to the desk, and opened the wedding album, Mrs. looking young and fine in the wedding dress, holding a bouquet of flowers, posing with Jack, starting their life together. Marquis wondered, when did it start to go bad? One day for whatever reason the dude decided to step out on her.

Or was the affair bullshit, Mrs. made it up, covering for her man? Jack went down in the tower, but walked out before it collapsed. Faked his own death, Mrs. collects the life insurance, puts the house up for sale, meets him in Florida. But why? Dude was makin' a lot of money.

He closed the wedding album, opened the next one, turning pages, looked at vacations in different places. Rome and Paris, two of them posing at the Eiffel Tower, looking all happy and such. Then on a beach in some tropical place. Heading said Captiva Island, picture taken in front of a sign that said 'Tween Waters Inn. There were other pics taken at a house on the beach, Mrs. looking sexy in a bikini, posing and lying on the sand. Why would Jack be out tomcatting he had this fine woman at home? In one of the photo sleeves was a business card with a website offering vacation rentals.

He took the card, sat in front of the computer, typed in the website, clicked on it. Marquis scrolled down till he found the house in the photograph.

Something familiar about Captiva, Marquis remembering now, Mrs. telling him it was one of the locations they talked about living at. She wouldn't have told him that if the husband was there. But if he was there, why'd she fly to Fort Lauderdale?

Marquis drove back to Manhattan, visited Vincent Gallo again at the poker club in Little Italy.

MARQUIS: Know who killed Frank DiCicco and the bodyguards?

GALLO: I might have an idea.

MARQUIS: What can we do to jog your memory?

GALLO: Was Cobb and Diaz.

MARQUIS: Came back in a hurry, huh? Why would they go after Frank?

GALLO: I think it was a misunderstanding.

MARQUIS (grinned): You think so, huh? You see the crime scene? That was some misunderstanding.

GALLO: Find Cobb and Diaz, you clear up four murders.

MARQUIS: Who else you talking about?

GALLO: Vicki Ross.

MARQUIS: (They didn't kill Vicki.) Know where they at?

GALLO: That's what I was gonna ask you.

MARQUIS: How would I know?

GALLO: Isn't that what you do, find people that don't want to be found?

MARQUIS: Tell me about Jack McCann.

GALLO: Owes us a lot of money.

MARQUIS: He's alive?

GALLO: Course he's alive.

THIRTY-FOUR

Jack cruised through Pompano past the pier and the public beach. It was four o'clock; the sun was starting its descent over the rooftops of the city. He turned onto Briny Avenue and pulled into a space behind the motel. Jack decided to pack first and then check out. He opened the gate and walked by the pool, saw a couple playing cards at one of the tables, glanced at the empty beach and the ocean, and walked up the stairway to his room.

His suitcase was in the closet. He took it out, put it on the bed, and unzipped the top. He grabbed piles of clothes from the dresser drawers and fit them in. He pulled his shirts off hangers and folded them on top, got his toiletries from the bathroom, and zipped the suitcase closed. He carried the suitcase down the stairs and put it in his car trunk.

The manager was behind the counter, his big body leaning forward, hands splayed on Formica, looking down at a newspaper that was folded in half, when Jack stepped in the office and closed the door.

The fat man looked up and said, "Your friends find you?"

"What friends?"

"Two fellas came in asking for you."

Jack turned and walked out, looking around as he got in the car, and saw Cobb through the windshield coming toward him, bringing a shotgun up from his leg, racking it as Jack turned the key. Cobb came around on his side of the car, and then Ruben appeared on the passenger side, reaching for the door handle. Jack pushing the lock button, but too late, shifting into reverse now, the door was opening, the scene in Jack's mind happening in slow motion, Ruben hanging on as Jack backed out of the parking space, the door opening all the way.

Cobb was moving with the car, slamming the sawed-off end of the shotgun into the side window, the glass cobwebbing. Across the way, Ruben regained his balance for an instant. Jack shifted into drive, saw Ruben let go of the window frame as the car bolted forward. He glanced in the rearview mirror, saw Cobb getting into a red Mustang, backing out, seeing Ruben get in next to him. They'd obviously gotten to Sculley.

He went left on Atlantic and got caught in traffic, waiting for the bridge to go down. There were cars in front of him, cars on both sides and behind him. He saw the mast of a sailboat going through the opening, moving past him on the Intracoastal.

The bridge was going down when he saw Ruben in the rearview, moving between cars, looking for him. Then seeing Ruben in the side mirror, getting closer, two cars away as the bridge came down with a clang and the crossing gates lifted, and now Ruben stopped, ran back to the Mustang.

Jack floored it, weaving in and out of traffic all the way to I-95.

When Fish left, Diane dried her hair, changed into jeans and a tank top, and went outside. No sign of him, thank God. It was almost dark. She looked down the street at the Sands. The Mustang was gone. The time spent trying to get rid of Fish, she had missed them.

She walked across the street to the Sands, opened the gate, and went out to the pool. There was no one around. The wind had picked up, the sea rough, beach deserted.

Diane walked around to the office and went in. There was a heavy blonde sitting at a desk in a room behind the counter, putting on makeup, holding a pink Betty Boop compact in one of her hands, tracing a line of lipstick on her mouth with the other. The blonde glanced at Diane, closed the compact, and with considerable effort, stood up and moved to the counter, breathing hard.

"I am sorry, we have no vacancies whatsoever," she said in a Southern accent. "This time a year, you know." The woman was chewing gum, and it looked like it was going to fall out of her mouth when she talked.

"My boyfriend's staying here. Can you tell me what room Duane's in?" She smiled. "Duane Cobb. He loves surprises." And thought, *get ready.*

The blinds were closed but she could see there wasn't a light on in the room. She knocked on the door, heard muffled voices, turned, and saw a young couple crossing the pool area. She decided to go for it, slid the key in the lock, opened the door, and turned on the light.

Cobb's airline ticket from Newark to Fort Lauderdale was on the desk. That's why she didn't see him at the airport; she had flown from LaGuardia. His clothes were in a suitcase on the floor. She ran her hands under the layers, found an envelope with a couple thousand dollars in it. She folded the money and put it in the back pocket of her jeans.

There was an assault rifle wrapped in a blanket in the corner of the closet next to Cobb's cowboy boots. She picked up the AR-15, ejected the magazine, rewrapped the gun, and put it back. She fit the magazine in the waist of her jeans under the tank top, turned off the light, and walked out the door.

Jack got off the freeway, went east to Dixie Highway, and took a left. He thought for sure he'd lost them till he saw the Mustang coming up on his right approaching PGA Boulevard, blew through a red light, swerving around a car going left.

The police cruiser came out of nowhere, Jack seeing its grille fill the rearview mirror and hearing the loud yelp of the siren. He pulled over on the gravel side road, lowered the damaged side window, and watched the trooper get out of the car, square his Sam Browne, and come up next to Jack, bending his tall frame to look inside. The Mustang passed by at that instant, Ruben making eye contact with him for a split second, and Jack thought, wait a minute, maybe this was a blessing in disguise.

The trooper said, "License and registration."

Jack handed him his Richard Keefer New York driver's license, wondering where this would lead, thinking he could be in deep shit.

"What the hell you doing, Richard Keefer from New York City, running a red, jeopardizing the citizens of North Palm Beach? You want to tell me what that bonehead move was about?"

Jack, with his hands still gripping the steering wheel, said, "I lost my concentration for a second. Looked up I was halfway through the intersection."

"Lost your concentration, huh?" The trooper, a young guy in a tan uniform with brown trim, maybe thirty, said, "Mr. Keefer, you been drinking?"

It was hard to hear with the traffic so close. "No sir."

"Stay right where you're at. I'll be back."

Jack watched him in the side mirror, moving back to the cruiser, traffic zipping by. Jack wondered what was going to happen when the trooper ran Richard Alan Keefer in the computer, wondered if he should put it in gear and take off, then abandon the car, and take his chances. Or get out and run for the mall parking lot that was fifty yards to his right, hop the chain-link fence.

It seemed like it took forever but it had been only seven minutes. Now the trooper was getting out of the cruiser, adjusting his hat, a piece of paper in his hand. At the window, the trooper bent his tall frame till he was eye level with Jack.

"What's strange, there's a Richard Alan Keefer in New York City, but he doesn't look anything like you and has a different license number and different address. What do you make of that?"

Be cool, Jack told himself. This thing could blow up right here. "If you're asking me to explain how bureaucracy works, why I don't show up in the system, I can't. New York's a big city."

"This your current address?"

"Yes, it is."

"What're you doing down here?"

"Working."

"What sort of work you do?"

"I give seminars to brokerage firms like Merrill Lynch, Morgan Stanley, and others. I show them my forecast for the market, what I think is going to happen."

"You talking about stock brokers?"

Jack nodded.

"What should I buy?"

"Gold. I don't think you can lose."

"Gold, huh? Thanks for the tip. Now let me give you one." He handed Jack a ticket. "Observe the traffic laws of North Palm Beach, you won't get another one of these."

Why'd the trooper let him go? Probably 'cause the situation was too complicated to pursue. Why waste time getting involved? Palm Beach County would make their money off the ticket, and the trooper would get the credit. That's probably all that mattered.

Jack took the first right, got off the highway, looking for a red Mustang, and drove toward the ocean, considering his options.

THIRTY-FIVE

Cobb had gone back around and parked on the side of the road, a hundred yards or so behind Jack McCann and the cop.

Ruben said, "What're you doing?"

As if it wasn't obvious. "Waiting to see what happens."

When Jack went through the red light, they were too far back, Cobb thinking at the time, Jesus Christ, this boy's gone. And then, like divine intervention, a police officer mercifully appeared and pulled the traffic offender over.

It took fucking forever to play out, Cobb thinking the cop was making a career out of stopping Jack. For the love of God. Finally, the trooper gave him a ticket, went back to his cruiser, and drove away. Jack took off right after the cop, and they followed him up the coast to a gated development with a pink wall around it on the ocean, the southern end of Palm Beach called Palm Cove. Duane got a kick out of the name: Palm Cove.

It sounded like a place you'd want to live, you were a senior citizen, a mellow retirement community on the ocean. He pictured smiling residents with capped teeth and tight, surgically enhanced faces, wearing slick sportswear, saying, "Seventy is the new fifty. Let's party."

He was surprised when Jack's car pulled in at the gatehouse and was met by a guard wearing khakis and a pink golf shirt with a little palm tree on the upper right side. Guy talked to Jack, and the security gate went up. Cobb drove down the road, turned around in a condo lot, and glanced at Ruben.

In the sunglasses and guayabera shirt, he looked like a barber on vacation. "Got any ideas?"

Ruben took off the sunglasses, bewilderment on his face, like Cobb had asked him how to split an atom. "Wait till he comes out."

It sounded like a question. "Okay. But when's that gonna be?" Cobb didn't see it as a problem, though. He enjoyed the competitive nature of the situation. Who was gonna get to the red zone first, take it to the house?

Was Jack visiting someone, shacking up, or was he now living here? And where was he hiding the money? They agreed to see it through a while longer, got a carryout from a Mex restaurant several miles down the road, Ruben's suggestion, what a surprise.

They parked in a marina lot on the Intracoastal across from the Palm Cove entrance. Cobb sat there, Ruben's aftershave mixing with the smell of enchiladas and refried beans, Cobb's stomach making noises. He cracked the window and let the ocean breeze clear out the car.

When Ruben finished eating, he wedged his body between the seat and the door and put his head back. A few minutes later, he was snoring, taking a siesta.

Cobb got out of the car, laid the shotgun in the trunk next to the spare. He walked south down the beach road, crossed over to the Palm Cove property, and moved through a flower bed to the pink stucco wall that was about as tall as he was. He reached up, got a reasonable grip on the cement cap, and hoisted himself up, running shoes kicking, trying to grip the smooth stucco, got enough purchase, and went up and over.

The complex was much bigger than it appeared. There was a ten-story high-rise and three smaller buildings—all built close to the water. On the north side of the property was a private marina. He could see dozens of yachts and pleasure craft.

Cobb pictured himself cruising around in a yacht, pounding down 7 and 7s, surrounded by knockout babes. When they got out to sea, girls had to take their suits off. Captain's rule.

It was a good thing Ruben wasn't with him. Guy that looked like him, wasn't wearing a uniform, his name on the shirt, someone'd see him, call security: *There's a spic, looks like a serial killer, just hopped the wall, Jesus, get over here quick.* Cobb walked through the parking lot behind the high-rise, and there was Jack's rental car with the cracked side window. He walked to the building, went in the lobby, and looked around. No one there except an old-timer, had to be seventy-five, in a blue suit coat, eyeing him from behind the reception counter.

Cobb walked toward the guy and said, "You seen Mr. McCann this evening?"

"Sir, I don't believe I know a Mr. McCann. Does he live here in the tower?"

"I thought so." Cobb frowned. "You have a directory I could take a look at?"

The man reached under the counter and handed him a booklet with a photograph of the Palm Cove complex shot from the ocean side. Duane opened to *M* and went down the list, didn't see McCann. So Jack was visiting someone.

"Sir, will you describe him?"

Cobb looked up. "He's good size, tall as me with about thirty-five more pounds, has light brown hair, dresses like he's screwing the pooch." The old man glanced at him as though he was having memory failure, and then surprised Cobb.

"I believe the gentleman you are looking for was accompanied by Ms. Najjir, one of our tenants."

"Sounds A-rab. You let them in here after what happened on nine-eleven?"

"Sir, I don't have anything to do with that."

"Oh. I thought you owned the place."

"No, sir."

"Where's Ms. Najj-ir live at, exactly?"

"Sir, I'm not at liberty to give out that information."

Duane grinned. This old buzzard was a piece of work. "She live in this building?"

"I'm not allowed to say."

"She live in this complex? You can tell me that, can't you?"

Shook his old gray head.

"But you gave me her name."

"I know. It doesn't make any sense."

"Well, we agree on something."

The old boy wrote on a Post-it note. "You can phone Ms. Najjir, and she can give you her address."

This was some crazy shit, but okay.

Ruben was still snoring when he got back to the car. Cobb slammed the door hard. Ruben's eyes opened and his body jerked forward. "Jesus, the fuck's going on?"

"I wake you? Sorry. Go back to sleep."

"Where you been, uh?"

"Looking around."

Ruben was snoring when Cobb drove through Pompano, deserted at ten forty-five. He parked behind the motel, Ruben, head back, mouth open, making sounds Cobb had never heard before. He left Ruben in the car and went up to his room, turned on the TV, and took his clothes off, folded the shirt and shorts on the spare bed. He brushed his teeth, looking at himself in the mirror, flexed his biceps a couple times. Good muscle tone but he needed color. Take care of Jack, put in some serious pool time.

The closet door slid open; Cobb reached in and grabbed the AR-15, sat on the bed, unwrapped the gun, and saw the magazine was missing. What the hell? Did he put it somewhere? Searched his mind, saw himself bringing the gun in the room, popping the mag in, and wrapping the AR in a blanket that was on a shelf in the closet. Who did it? Couldn't have been Jack. It wasn't the Eye-talians. They'd have been waiting in the room for him.

So who was it?

Cobb didn't much like the idea of someone watching him and thought about Diane McCann. Not a chance it was her, right? The way things had been going, he couldn't be sure of anything.

He checked his suitcase, found the empty envelope. The hell's going on? Cobb picked up the shotgun, a High-Standard Flite King he'd bought at the store on Dixie Highway—no three-day waiting period on shotguns and long guns in Florida. Was that civilized or what?

He racked a shell in the chamber. Put the gun on the bed, slipped on blue jeans, a black T-shirt, and a Chicago Bears cap. He tied two pieces of rope around the trigger guard and fit the looped end over his left shoulder. He had cut the barrel down and the stock off.

Now he swung the gun up with his left hand, caught the fore-end with his right, and was ready to fire in like a second. He slipped on the windbreaker, glanced in the full-length mirror, and saw a small-town high school football coach.

From the balcony outside his room, he scanned the pool area and the beach. It was warm and quiet. He walked down the stairs and out to the Mustang. Ruben was gone, must've woke up, went to his room. Cobb wandered south fifty yards or so, checking parked cars on both sides of the street. No one in any of them sitting there spying on him.

Back in the room, Cobb slept in his clothes on a mattress between the beds, the shotgun next to him. Ruben, the tough guy who didn't need a gun, was on his own.

THIRTY-SIX

Ruben opened the door a crack, rubbing his eyes, silver rings on mangled fingers. Cobb could see a bluish bruise sticking out of white surgical tape wrapped around his rib cage. Cobb made a face. "How's it feel?"

"I've been hurt worse than this."

A foot away, and Cobb could smell his sour morning breath. Ruben swung the door open and backed into the room. He was naked. The ex-fighter had put on some weight in the five years since he'd stopped training, but still looked like he could handle himself.

There was a girl in bed behind him. She pulled the sheet off and sat on the side of the bed, nude, and lit a cigarette. The girl had a decent rack, dark hair streaked blonde, and a line of Chinese characters tattooed low just above her naughty meat. "Hey, what's your tat say?"

"To know the road ahead, ask those coming back. It's a Chinese proverb."

Ruben glanced at her and said, "Hey, you better go."

The girl balanced her cigarette on the end table, picked her underwear up off the floor, and slipped it on. She dressed quickly, got the cigarette, and kissed Ruben on the cheek. He slapped her butt, and she walked to the door, stopped and looked back. "So, you gonna call me?"

"You'll find out."

The girl smiled and closed the door.

"Who's that?"

"I met her in the airport, hairdresser lives down here. I called, she come over."

Again, Cobb couldn't believe it. Sure he remembered her, the girl Ruben was talking to in Newark. She was a quality piece of ass. What'd she see in this barbarian? "Hey, Ruben, would you put some fucking clothes on, or wrap a towel around you?" He was uncomfortable standing next to this naked Neanderthal.

Ruben got dressed and came back, staring at the dark green khaki uniform Cobb had taken out of the bag and unfolded on the bed, sleeves and pant legs spread out like whoever was wearing it had evaporated. The name over the pocket said Manny.

"What's that for?"

Now Cobb realized he was doing it all wrong. He should've told Ruben the plan before he showed it to him. "You want the money? This's how we're gonna get it."

"What you talking about?"

Cobb told him what he was thinking, but Ruben was stuck on the uniform. "Where you get it at? You steal it? I ain't wearing somebody's dirty fucking clothes."

"I got it at a uniform supply place," Cobb said. "It's brand-new, okay? Never been violated by a spic laborer." He'd bought it earlier at a store on Dixie Highway. "In this, nobody gives you a second look."

"Why don't you wear it, then?"

"It wouldn't look right on me." Nobody'd believe it, Cobb wanted to tell him. Why was that hard to understand? It was so obvious.

Thirty minutes later they walked down to the car, Cobb in a yellow golf shirt and white pants, Ruben in the uniform, wearing sunglasses and a straw porkpie. Cobb couldn't talk him out of the hat, and thought, fuck it.

They headed north to Palm Beach, Duane having a hell of a time looking at Ruben in the uniform without laughing, biting his lip or he'd have lost it for sure. The florist was on Worth Avenue. Cobb went in and bought a dozen long-stemmed red roses. He bought a Show Your Love bouquet with blue orchids and a vase that weighed as much as a cinderblock. And he bought a Love You Fur-ever stuffed bear.

The woman behind the counter said, "Sir, if you don't mind my saying, you have exquisite taste. Most men who come here don't have a clue." The woman paused. "How many notes will you need?"

"One."

"Oh my. One truly special person." She handed him a little card and an envelope.

He slid it back to her. "Would you mind? My handwriting isn't too good."

"Not at all. What would you like to say?" The woman picked up a pen and looked at him.

Cobb had thought about it and come up with something earlier. "When you look at them, think of me."

The woman smiled. "Very romantic."

With the flowers in the backseat, Cobb drove down the coast past these big goddamn mansions, and when they were close to the condo, he said, "You got to get in the back, lay down on the floor. I'll cover you with the blanket. Guard sees you, he's gonna think you're Freddy Kruger."

"What if it don't work?"

"We drive away, think of something else."

It was amazing, Ruben always took the negative point of view. Probably 'cause his parents never gave him confidence. In Cobb's experience, that's where it started—when you were a little kid. His own folks, Herb and Donna, treated him like a little prince. His mother told her friends she thought Duane was truly gifted. "He was a genius or something."

Cobb drove in the Palm Cove entrance and stopped behind the security gate next to the gatehouse. The guard, a doughy fifty-year-old with a gut, came out and said, "Can I help you?"

"Delivering flowers." Cobb pointed over his shoulder with his right thumb.

The guard looked in the backseat. "Where you from?"

Duane handed him a business card from the flower shop called Fleur-de-Lis. The guard studied it and handed it back. "Who you delivering to?"

It sounded like the guy was accusing him. "A Ms. Najj-ir. You know her?"

"How come you don't have a van?"

"Man, we're busy, got three drivers out. I've got to run back, pick up another load."

"Ms. Najjir's in the tower." The guard pointed. "Park in front by the door, go in the lobby."

The security gate went up. "Thank you, officer." Cobb grinned and took off. "Ruben, how you doing back there? Don't go to sleep on me."

There was a lot of activity in the lobby, groups of seniors sitting around talking and playing cards. Cobb led the way, carrying the roses and the pump gun wrapped in decorative paper, Ruben behind him with the vase of orchids and the stuffed bear. They stopped at the reception counter, and Cobb said, "Delivery for Ms. Najj-ir." He handed the receptionist the flower shop business card, but she fixed her attention on Ruben, the humble laborer, holding him in her gaze. "Hope you don't mind," Cobb said, "I borrowed Manny from your landscaping crew to help." The girl, who had dark hair pulled back in a ponytail, seemed worried, as if Ruben being in the building was breaking some Palm Cove rule.

"I guess it's okay if you make it quick. Ms. Najjir is on the fourth floor. Four oh three." She pointed. "The elevators are over there."

That's what Cobb wanted to hear.

"Hey, buddy, you did good," Cobb said to Ruben when the doors closed and they started up. "Ever decide to hang it up as a collector, I think you could make it as an actor in Hollywood." Ruben stared at him, the flowers and stuffed animal not going with the uniform, Cobb letting a little grin slip out, trying to pull it back.

He set the roses on the elevator floor, undid the tape at the end of the paper around the shotgun, gripped the handle, and picked up the flowers as the elevator stopped and the doors opened.

Duane Cobb found 403, positioned himself in front of the peephole, holding the roses, and knocked on the door. The girl downstairs said she was going to call Ms. Najj-ir, tell her they were on their way.

The door opened, Cobb was staring at a nice-looking dark-haired girl. He handed her the roses. She cradled the bouquet and smiled. "Who're they from?"

"I'm only the driver. They don't tell us that." He paused. "And look, there's more." Cobb pushed the door open farther, and she saw Ruben. "Manny here was kind enough to help me. Where do you want us to put everything?"

"Come this way."

They followed her across the marble foyer into the kitchen. He saw Jack through the window stretched out on a lounge chair on a huge balcony, reading the paper, a view of the ocean that could've been on a postcard.

"Anywhere is fine." She placed the roses on the counter next to an industrial stove, pulled off the envelope that was taped to the paper, and read the note. "Oh my god," she said, excited, sounding like a young girl. Ruben was still holding the vase and teddy bear. She said, "Bring those over here." Ruben did and put them next to the roses. She picked up the bear and hugged it. "Isn't he cute? So cute, so cute."

That's all it took. Give a girl a stuffed animal, she went fucking goofy, started saying shit that didn't make sense. He looked out at Jack, relaxed, no clue what was about to happen. Now Ms. Najj-ir glanced at the package Cobb held wrapped in decorative paper, and said, "What's that?"

"It's a surprise."

"Another one?"

"I'll hold it, you pull off the paper." She grabbed a fistful, and it came off in one piece. She frowned looking at the shotgun, trying to make sense of what was happening, and was about to say something when Ruben put his hand over her mouth and held her in place.

"Do what you're told, nothing's gonna happen. We're not here for you." Cobb paused. "You got any duct tape?" Something they forgot. He felt like an amateur having to ask.

She nodded and pointed at a closet door on the other side of the kitchen.

Cobb found the roll, ripped off a piece, and wrapped it around her wrists.

He ripped off another piece and put it over her mouth. Then he looked outside at the balcony. Jack was gone.

Jack heard the phone ringing in the kitchen, and then heard Rita's voice. She came out to the balcony where he was sitting, reading the *Palm Beach Post*, drinking strong Lebanese coffee Rita called *kawha*.

"I just got a call from the receptionist. Someone sent flowers." She smiled. "That's so nice. You're full of surprises, aren't you, Richard Keefer?"

Jack had no idea what she was talking about. He was going to tell her he was leaving. It didn't feel right, and Rita was clearly into it, talking about places they should go. "All right, my short list is Lyon, St. Tropez, Barcelona, and Istanbul." She was coming on too strong, and they had just met.

Jack finished the last of the coffee and felt a jolt of energy, like taking a hit of speed in college to study for finals. The view was spectacular, ocean on one side, Intracoastal on the other. He could feel the morning sun on his face. It was beautiful here, but it was time to go.

He heard Rita's voice, thought she was talking to him. He sat up, looked into the kitchen, morning sun reflecting off the glass making it difficult to see inside. He made a visor with his hand, saw Rita directing two guys carrying flowers. Two guys delivering flowers. That struck him as odd.

Jack moved along the balcony around the side of the building to the master bedroom, opened the sliding door, and slipped in. He walked through the bedroom into the hallway, heard a man's voice that sounded familiar, and then saw Ruben holding Rita from behind and Cobb wrapping duct tape around her wrists.

Jack went back in the bedroom, grabbed his wallet and car keys, looked out the sliding door and saw Cobb coming toward him. He ran into the hallway, saw Ruben coming out of the kitchen, and took off for the front door forty feet away.

"Is him," Ruben yelled behind Jack.

The stairs were close. Jack swung the door open and went down, two steps at a time. He was halfway to the third floor when he heard them, looked up and saw Ruben and behind him Cobb holding a sawed-off shotgun. Cobb fired before he got to the third floor, the heavy sound echoing through the stairwell, buckshot pinging off the railing and stairs in front of him.

He went down another flight. The door to the second floor opened as Jack approached, and he squeezed past a silver-haired couple startled by his presence, standing there frozen. He heard Cobb say, "Get the fuck out of the way."

Jack ran down two more flights to the parking garage filled with light-colored, late-model luxury cars, passed a white Cadillac pulling in and glanced over his shoulder at Cobb and Ruben. He ran to the entrance and came out looking at the ocean to his right and went left into the parking lot, looking for his car.

Cobb, moving toward the oncoming Cadillac, leveled the shotgun. The car stopped. Cobb opened the driver's door, reached in, grabbed a tan, gray-haired senior by the shirt collar, and pulled the man out of the vehicle. The senior went down on the concrete floor. Cobb slid in behind the wheel. Ruben got in on the other side and said, "Why'd you hurt the old man?"

"All we got going on, you're worried about some senior citizen might have a couple months to live? Why don't you worry about finding Jack? That make any sense to you? 'Cause we're about to fucking lose him."

Cobb did a U-turn, tires squealing, racing out of the garage.

THIRTY-SEVEN

Diane had just seen Cobb and Ruben get in the Mustang, Ruben wearing a uniform. She had to move fast if she was going to catch them. She ran across the street, got in her car, and took off speeding up the coast, no idea where Cobb and Ruben had gone, surprised when she saw a red Mustang waiting for the bridge to go down at Hillsboro.

She heard her cell phone ring, reached in her purse, and grabbed it.

"Mrs. McCann, it's Detective Brown. How you doing today? I stopped by earlier, no one was home, 'less you saw me, didn't answer the door. I see you're sellin' the house."

"What can I do for you? I'm out of town."

"Yeah, where you at?" She could hear him drawing on a cigarette, blowing out smoke.

"Florida," she said without thinking. Why did she tell him that? "I needed to get away for a few days."

"Everything okay?"

"Yeah, everything's fine." She tried to say it calm, but it didn't come out that way.

"Took your advice, went to visit Duane Cobb and Ruben Diaz. Both looked like they cleared out in a hurry. You wouldn't know nothing about that, would you?"

"Their line of work, I'm sure they've made enemies."

"I'm talking to one, isn't that right?"

"You think they're running from me?"

"Well, they're running from someone." She heard Detective Brown exhale and pictured him with a cigarette in his hand, smoke drifting up.

"You know a Joseph Sculley?"

"You know I do. He was Jack's best friend."

"Mr. Sculley was murdered a couple nights ago."

"Not Sculley. Jesus." Her eyes welled up and Diane felt tears roll down her cheeks. "Sculley was a good guy. Why would anyone want to kill him?"

"I don't know." Marquis paused. "Let me ask you something. Was Mr. Sculley gay?"

"Why would you say that?"

"Found him naked in bed with Mr. Linehan, the doorman. Like the shooter came in, caught them in the act, and shot them."

"I'm not an expert on Sculley's sex life, but I can't imagine. He's married, and his wife Ilene is a good friend. If something wasn't right, I've got to believe I would have heard about it."

"Two men that fit your description of Duane Cobb and Ruben Diaz were seen entering the building where Mr. Sculley lived, talking to the doorman, and seen leaving sometime later. You know something about this? Are you holding back on me?"

"Why would I be holding back on you." She paused looking ahead, lost sight of the Mustang. "Listen, I'm in the middle of something. I have to go."

"Hang on, where in Florida you at?" Detective Brown said as she disconnected. He called back and she let it ring.

Diane followed the Mustang into Palm Beach, parked and waited while Cobb went into a flower shop and came out with roses, orchids, and a stuffed animal. What was this? What was going on? She followed the Mustang south along the coast and watched it drive into a condominium complex.

She waited till the Mustang was out of sight and drove up to the gatehouse. The guard came out and said, "Good morning, how may I help you?"

"I'm interested in buying or renting, who should I talk to?"

He made a copy of Diane's driver's license and directed her to the sales office in the lobby of the high-rise and said, "Have a nice day."

"I just saw a fella with a gun in the stairwell," a tall silver-haired man in golf attire said, walking into the lobby. There was a collective murmur from the dozen or so seniors sitting nearby. The ponytailed girl behind the reception counter picked up the phone and said, "Jerry, we've got a situation. Someone's running around with a loaded gun." The girl listened. "I have no idea." To the people in the lobby she said, "Security's on their way."

Diane had been waiting for something to happen, but not this. She got up and went outside, felt the tropical heat after being in the chilly air-conditioning. She walked to her car and sat with the engine running, not sure what to do next. She saw a man running, coming toward her. He stopped in the next row of cars twenty feet away, his size and the way he moved holding her attention, and her heart started to race.

She was looking at a guy with Jack's muscular legs and broad shoulders, a guy with Jack's light brown hair and chiseled features, Jack, who she thought was dead, his unknown remains buried in the rubble of the Trade Center. It seemed surreal, and yet there he was, the man she had loved and had been married to for twelve years. Diane thought he was alive, but seeing him now, she couldn't believe it.

She sat there frozen for a couple beats, reached for the door handle, and stopped. What was she going to say to him? *Why did you have an affair, you son of a bitch?* No, she had to do better than that. *Why didn't you come home, admit what you did, and handle it like a man?* That's what the Jack McCann she thought she knew would've done.

And as if he had heard her, Jack turned, squinting in the morning sun, looking at her in the car. Did he recognize her? And if he did, what was he thinking? Now something caught his attention and he turned, glancing toward the high-rise. She saw it too, a white car speeding across the parking lot. Coming from the opposite direction was a security vehicle. The two cars screeched to a stop, almost collided in front of her.

THIRTY-EIGHT

Cobb got out of the white Cadillac with a sawed-off shotgun, held it across his body, and blew out the windshield of the security vehicle. Jack jumped in his car and drove out of the parking space as Cobb turned, pumped, and fired two times, blowing out one of the taillights. Cobb got back in the Cadillac, floored it in reverse, tires squealing, turned the car ninety degrees, and took off.

A dazed, over-the-hill security man, windshield glass covering his pink uniform shirt, got out of the damaged vehicle, talking fast into a two-way radio.

"Goddamn it, get the PD over here posthaste. White Caddy coming your way, two Caucasian males, one of them has a shotgun."

Cobb raced through the complex, knees under the steering wheel, trying to keep the car in a straight line, trying to feed shells into the shotgun. He glanced at Ruben. "Hate to bother you, think maybe you could give me some assistance here?"

"Looks like you doing all right to me. What you want?"

"Would it be too much to ask you to hold the fucking steering wheel?"

Ruben slid over in the seat and gripped the side of the wheel.

Cobb let go, fed shells into the loading flap till he heard each one click. He held the action release button, pumped the slide, loading a shell in the chamber.

Now he took the steering wheel back. Up ahead, Jack's car was almost to the gatehouse. Cobb heard a siren in the distance.

"You make all the plans, what next?"

"We'll find out, won't we?" Cobb was jacked, revved up. "Got a problem, you can leave anytime." Ruben didn't like it, too bad. The shotgun barrel was wedged at an angle on the floor mat, the rounded grip sticking up over the bottom of his seat. If Ruben tried anything, Cobb wondered, could he bring it up and pull the trigger?

The guard was standing in the exit lane next to the gatehouse as Jack approached. The guard stepped back in, and the security gate went up. Jack turned right on the beach road. The siren was getting louder, closer. The guard saw Cobb and Ruben coming and drew a revolver, holding it down his leg. Cobb lowered the side window and rested the shotgun barrel on the sill. The guard saw it and dropped the revolver, taking a step back, ran into the gatehouse and out the other side, moving along the boulevard entrance to the complex. Cobb busted through the security gate and turned right on the beach road just before a speeding Palm Beach County Sheriff's cruiser, lights flashing, entered the complex.

"Believe that? Old Duane came through again, didn't he? There was never a doubt in my mind." But there was. Jesus, that was close.

"Is not over yet," Ruben said, going negative on him again.

"I had hoped my earnest vibes would rub off on you, turn your contrary outlook around, but it doesn't seem to be working."

"I don't know what you saying. Man, you like to talk, uh? Try not to open your mouth, try not to say nothing for five minutes. I bet you can't do it."

"What's the point?"

"What I tell you, uh?"

No matter what happened, this was the last time he'd be dealing with Ruben Diaz.

They caught up to Jack a couple minutes later on a narrow stretch of beach road, the southern part of Palm Beach, Cobb hanging back in the Caddy. "Want to take him now, or see what he does?"

"Think he got the money with him?"

"Where else is he gonna keep it?"

"I don't know, man. Maybe he buried it. I saw that one time in a movie."

Duane wanted to give Ruben an IQ test, wondering what his score would be, remembering from high school that most Americans were between 85 and 115. Considering how many times Ruben had been hit in the head, Cobb wouldn't be surprised if Ruben's IQ had dipped below 80, borderline deficiency in intelligence, not feebleminded, but he might get there yet. Cobb's, on the other hand, had been 130, but he thought it was higher now. He just plain felt smarter. "I think we let him get comfortable, see what he does."

"Why ask, you already make up your mind?"

"I thought you might surprise me."

"Lose the tone, or I'm gonna surprise you." Ruben reminded him of Charles Bronson now, Charles delivering a line in a movie, saying it straight, but there was menace in his voice. You believed Bronson just as Cobb believed Ruben.

They followed Jack to the airport in West Palm and into short-term parking, Jack driving like a maniac through the structure, tires squealing around turns, dodging people rolling their suitcases, jumping out of the way. Cobb and Ruben were on the third level passing the elevators. Ruben said, "Stop, there he is." Jack was wheeling a suitcase into the elevator.

Ruben ran for the stairs, went down to the second level, where the gates were, ran to security. It was packed. He was out of breath, out of shape, sweating under the guayabera. He scanned people in the roped-off area six rows deep that reminded him of a livestock pen, everyone angry, taking off their shoes, coats, belts, rings, Jesus, practically undressing to get on a fucking airplane. McCann could not have gone through that fast. Ruben didn't see him.

He went down to the lower level and ran outside. Glanced toward the taxis lined up, no sign of him. He looked left at the car rental pickup lane, saw Jack in a crowd, getting on a Hertz bus. "I find him," Ruben said, calling Cobb on his cell phone. The Hertz bus took off.

THIRTY-NINE

Driving out of the complex, Diane passed a Palm Beach Police car, lights flashing, speeding by. She slowed down and watched it pull up to the high-rise entrance. The security gate had been broken off, no sign of the guard. Diane stopped at the road, no idea where Jack was, but maybe she knew where he was going. It was a long shot, but it was the only one she had.

Three hours later, she crossed the bridge to Captiva Island, driving on a narrow strip of land, houses on both sides of the road set back behind tropical foliage. Diane was thinking about the two times she had been here with Jack. They had been deeply in love then, couldn't get enough of each other. They had stayed at Jensen's On the Gulf the first time.

Captiva was sleepy, old Florida, the pace so slow Jack thought someone had slipped a Quaalude in his orange juice. The first time, it took him a few days to adjust and realize he didn't have to be anywhere. He wasn't on a schedule. "This is the most relaxed I've been in ten years," he said after a couple days.

They stayed in a cottage on the beach, smoked weed, lay in the sun, and read paperback thrillers. They went to the Mucky Duck, drank shells of beer, and ate grouper sandwiches. They made love in the afternoon and took naps. When did things between them begin to change? Diane never noticed. Though when he took the job at Sterns & Morrison, they saw each other less often. Jack was gone three or four nights a week, and that went on for years.

The bottom line was that in spite of the affair, Diane thought she still loved him. At first it bothered her. She had run the gamut of emotions from anger to forgiveness. Jack had cheated on her. Diane thought she could handle that and maybe let it go and move on. But now the situation was a lot more complicated. Vicki and Sculley were dead. And Jack had stolen money from one of his clients. But worst of all, he let her think he had been killed on 9/11.

She stopped at Jensen's, went to the reception desk, and asked if Jack McCann had checked in. He hadn't, and now she was thinking, coming here was crazy. She got in the car and decided to drive to Fort Myers, drop the rental off, and fly home. Passing the 'Tween Waters Inn, she thought about the last time she had been there with Jack, pictured him having a Stoli and tonic, talking to locals and tourists, Jack the all-purpose conversationalist.

Diane hit the brakes, made a U-turn, and pulled into the 'TWI parking lot. She grabbed her purse, went into the crowded restaurant, and sat at the bar, a three-sided rectangle. She looked across at two fifty-year-old guys in golf shirts, drinking white wine, self-conscious sitting by herself. One of the guys raised his glass to her, and she looked away.

The bartender, wearing a Drive-by Truckers T-shirt, said, "What can I get you?"

She ordered a Coke and opened a menu that was on the bar top next to her. Diane had not eaten anything all day and was thinking about a hamburger when she heard him say, "Anyone sitting there?" She turned and saw Jack behind her in shorts and a T-shirt, looking tan and healthy like he was the Captiva poster boy.

"You remind me of someone, but the girl I know has blonde hair."

Diane thought there might be a slim chance he'd be here but now was surprised to see him. "You finally got the nerve to face me, huh? I had to come all the way down here."

"How'd you figure it out?" He sat next to her.

"It seemed like the logical choice knowing the trouble you're in. This is the end of the line. Who would think to look for you here?"

Jack raised his hand, got the bartender's attention, and ordered a Stoli and tonic. He turned in Diane's direction, eyes meeting hers, then glancing down at the bar top, head bent forward, avoiding her.

"Look at me." She said it angry, wondering what had happened to Jack, the stand-up guy she married.

He fixed his attention on her. "I owe you an apology."

Diane shook her head. "You owe me a helluva lot more than that."

The bartender set Jack's drink down in front of him. He looked relieved to escape the hot glare of her gaze for a few seconds. Jack picked up the cocktail, took two big gulps, and put it back on the napkin. He faced her again. "I got involved in something that blew up on me." He paused, glancing at his vodka and tonic, picked it up, and took another long drink.

"I think I know a lot of it. The affair with Vicki, the money you took from one of your clients. When I first heard it, I thought, no way. But it's true, isn't it? I met with Mel Hoberman and Barry Zitter. They wanted me to pay them back what you stole out of your life insurance. I know Cobb and Diaz, the two guys looking for you, and I don't think they're going to give up. What I don't know is why."

"I made a mistake."

"A mistake? I'd say it's a little more serious than that." Diane paused. "Why didn't you call me when you got out of the Trade Center? Why did you let me think you were dead?"

Jack finished his cocktail, the booze loosening him up, and signaled the bartender for another.

"Forget about your drink and talk to me."

"I was in trouble."

"Are you talking about San Marino Equity?"

"I don't know what that is. Never heard of it."

"Ruben Diaz said you owed them seven hundred and fifty thousand dollars."

"He was scamming you."

"He showed me a contract that had my signature that wasn't even close, telling me I was responsible for the debt. Any of this sound familiar?"

Marquis Brown landed in Fort Myers, went to the rental place, and they gave him a Chevrolet.

It took an hour to get there, going over the bridge from the mainland, Marquis driving on a thin strip of land now, water on both sides, windows down, a warm breeze blowing through the interior. The idea of coming here was triggered by a conversation with Diane after seeing a For Sale sign in the front yard. Marquis had wondered, was she in on the scam?—and he was still wondering. Called her, she said she was in Florida, and it all started to make sense.

His conclusion: her husband, caught in a terrorist attack, saw opportunity, faked his death, wife collected the life insurance. Marquis was thinking about the photos of Diane posing in the bikini at the rental house on Captiva Island and hearing Diane say "Captiva" when he'd asked where they had talked about retiring.

"Why did you have an affair?"

"I don't know."

Diane frowned. "Come on. What happened, were you tired of me?"

"It had nothing to do with you."

She wanted to reach over and punch him. "If you loved me, if you were happy, you wouldn't have done it." She picked up her Coke and held it. "Who made the first move?"

"It wasn't like that." He had that guilty look on his face again.

"What was it like?"

"It just happened. I was at Ulysses. She walked by me, and we started talking, had a couple drinks, that was it. She told me where she worked, and a week or so later, I stopped in for lunch and saw her, and saw her again that night."

"Is that code for you slept with her?"

"Why think about it?

"You didn't think it was wrong, did you?"

The bartender put a fresh cocktail in front of Jack and grabbed his empty glass. Jack picked it up and took a drink.

"You don't want to answer that one, huh?"

"I can't explain why it happened. I don't know. A good-looking girl came on to me. It made me feel good. It made me feel young."

"Do you know why you cashed in most of our savings and stole money from one of your clients? Who are you?" He looked like Jack but didn't sound like him. He glanced at the cocktail. Diane could see he wanted it and didn't want to answer the question.

"Vicki was in serious debt, owed a loan shark a lot of money."

"Why was that your problem?"

"I felt sorry for her."

"She's dead, so you can put her out of your mind. And now you can add Sculley to the list. They shot him in his apartment." Diane paused. "What do you have to say for yourself?"

Jack didn't want to answer that one either, picked up the drink, and brought it to his mouth, stopped, and looked at her. "I feel terrible."

"I hope so. What do you feel for me?"

"The same as I always have."

"What does that mean?"

"I love you," he said, with no emotion behind it, and drank his drink.

She wanted to punch him, knock that stupid look off his face.

"Vicki didn't mean anything to me."

"That's worse. You risked everything for something that didn't mean anything?"

Jack wasn't expecting that. "I don't know."

"Now you sound like a dumb-ass."

"That's what I am."

"Why didn't you call me? Why did you let me think you were dead?"

"I already told you."

"Tell me again."

"The whole thing got out of control. I was trying to protect you. I didn't want you involved."

"You don't think I was involved? You have no idea."

"I know you were, and I'm sorry." He put his hand over hers and she pulled away.

"Want me to go, I'll go. Walk out of your life for good."

"Didn't you already do that?"

Jack finished his second drink. The bartender approached, Jack shook his head. "I told you, I didn't have a choice."

"Sure you did."

"Okay, if that's how you feel."

"Don't put this on me. I didn't have anything to do with it."

Jack slid off the bar stool, stood next to her, took a wad of bills out of his pocket, peeled off a ten and a twenty, and left them on the bar top. "I know you're not going to believe this. I've missed you. You're all I've thought about. But I don't think that's enough, is it? I don't think there's anything I can say or do that is."

Hearing him confess, hearing him tell her that he had screwed up helped, but it wasn't enough. Not even close. Diane watched Jack walk out the door.

FORTY

Ruben's stomach was making noises. He was so hungry, sitting in the dusty lot with the windows down, sweating, the afternoon sun turning the car into an oven. They were in Captiva, outside the hotel restaurant, waiting for Jack to appear, Cobb, fingertips drumming on the top of the steering wheel, singing some country tune.

Ruben's head hurt from the music and the sound of Cobb's voice, the Southern twang getting to him. He reached over, turned off the radio, and saw McCann come out of the restaurant, hand up shielding his eyes from the afternoon sun. "You see him?"

Cobb turned, looked through the windshield. "It's McCann."

"Before you do anything, wait till I get close. I'm gonna surprise him." Ruben got out of the car and followed McCann, moving in a row, between cars, going through the parking lot, ducking behind a minivan.

McCann was forty feet away when Cobb, the idiot, backed out of the parking space, gunning it, speeding toward them, kicking up sand from the hard-packed lot. McCann saw the Caddy coming toward him and started running. Ruben chased him around the restaurant building, past the tennis courts and the pool, lounge chairs lined up, people lying in the sun, and people in the swimming pool. It was loud and hot, Ruben, sweating and short of breath, felt tightness in his legs, hoping McCann would get tired and slow down, but he didn't and Ruben lost sight of him for a time, then picked him up running between two hotel buildings.

Ruben stopped, upper body bent forward, hands on his knees, sucking in air, taking long, deep breaths, been years since he done road work. When he could, he took out his cell phone, dialed Cobb, and told him the direction McCann was going.

Diane, standing just inside the door, had seen everything. She ran to her car and got in. Cobb, in the white Cadillac, was parked on the other side of the small dusty lot. She didn't think he'd seen her. If he did, he wasn't doing anything about it.

She went left on Captiva Drive, heading north, sure Jack would go this way, and just beyond the 'Tween Waters Inn property line, he appeared, running toward the road on the hard-packed sand. She hit the brake and lowered her window as he approached. "You better get in."

"I'm okay," Jack said, standing next to the car, leaning with his hands on the door sill, breathing hard.

"You're not going to be for long." Diane glanced in the rearview mirror and saw the white Cadillac in the distance coming after them.

Now Jack looked and saw them. He opened the door and got in. The tires spun on the hard sand and squealed, making contact with the blacktop.

"Why're you doing this?"

"I don't know." Even after all he had done, she didn't want anything bad to happen to him. The Caddy was down the road a couple hundred yards and closing fast. She was going fifty, twenty over the speed limit.

Up ahead the road jogged right ninety degrees, going from the ocean to the gulf side of the island, and then a sharp left turn as the road curved again.

She went right on South Seas Plantation Road. Now they were on a narrow strip of land with water on both sides, the aquamarine ocean to the left with beach houses tucked behind walls of foliage and stands of palm trees, and to the right the deep blue gulf, pelicans gliding through the thermals high above.

Jack said, "You see them?"

Diane, glancing in the rearview mirror, said no.

"Maybe we lost them."

She gave him a questioning look.

"Take the next left and we'll find out."

Diane slowed down and turned onto a hard-packed sand path barely wide enough for a car, drove thirty yards, kicking up a trail of dust, and took another left, now seeing glimpses of beach houses set back from the ocean behind sea grape, dogwoods, and coco plum. She stopped behind a sand berm that ran parallel to the road. A white Cadillac zoomed by and Diane thought they were safe, till she saw brake lights.

The Caddy turned around. She floored it and they took off. "There's a turnaround up here that'll take us back to the main road."

She went left around the circle and then up a short rise to the road. Diane glanced in the rearview mirror; all she saw was a wake of dust behind them, no sign of Cobb and Ruben, and she felt relieved. "I think we should go to the police."

"And say what?" Jack paused. "I'd rather have you drop me off, and take my chances."

"Drop you off where?"

"The beach house."

"I called and asked if you had rented a place. They said no."

"I did under a different name."

"That's right; you're a fugitive. Who're you pretending to be?"

"Richard Alan Keefer."

"Come on? All the names, that's the one you pick?"

"I didn't have a chance to consult with you."

"That's the first thing you've said that sounds like you. I was starting to wonder."

Diane glanced in the rearview mirror. There was a silver SUV maybe a hundred yards behind them. "You've had a lot of time to think. What's your plan? What're you going to do with the rest of your life—aside from running away from your problems?"

She glanced at Jack. He was clearly annoyed, or angry. That's how he reacted when he didn't get his way, like there was a boy still inside of him. He didn't say anything else till Diane pulled up in front of the beach house. She had a lot of good memories staying here.

"Want to come in?"

Diane pictured them sitting on the deck, drinking wine, watching the sun set. They were in love then. Their life together was perfect and she couldn't imagine it ever changing.

"I don't want you to leave like this," Jack said.

"What did you think was going to happen?"

"I don't know. I didn't think I would ever see you again, and here you are." Jack was laying it on heavy. "You can even stay with me if you want."

"And forget everything else?"

"Why not?"

"I can think of a few reasons."

"Why don't you see how it goes. You never know, you might be surprised." Jack, used to getting what he wanted in life, was selling hard now.

"I don't think so." She didn't know what else to say.

He opened the door, got out, and hesitated. "You sure?"

"Yeah. I'm sure."

"Well, if you change your mind, you know where to find me."

Diane watched him walk to the front door and go inside.

FORTY-ONE

Jack was positive she was going to follow him to the house they'd rented on their last Captiva vacation. He left the door unlocked, grabbed a beer, and sat on the deck, looking out at the ocean fifty yards away.

Thirty minutes later, Jack knew he was kidding himself. Diane wasn't coming. She'd had enough. He didn't blame her for taking off. He was the one who'd screwed everything up. He'd been through it enough times and decided not to beat himself up anymore. He tried. There was nothing more he could do.

The sun was resting on the horizon when Jack started down the beach, walking on the hard, wet sand along the water's edge, carrying his sandals and a can of beer. There was a warm breeze coming off the ocean. The beach was deserted except for joggers and dog walkers. He was thinking about Ruben and Cobb. No way they'd find him on this secluded part of the island. No way anyone could see the house from the road. You had to know where you were going to find it.

Jack had the beach house for a week. After that, he was going to pack up and head north across the Florida Panhandle, through stretches of Alabama and Mississippi into Louisiana, stop in New Orleans for a couple days, eat oysters, redfish, and étouffée. From there, he didn't know where he was going or what he was going to do. Ahead he could see the outlines of buildings in the 'Tween complex, picturing two football fields end to end, thinking that's how far away it looked.

Diane sat in the car for a few minutes not sure what to do. Was she really going to let him go? It sounded like a song. She drove to the south end of the island, took the bridge to Sanibel, pulled into the public beach parking lot, and looked at herself in the rearview mirror. What was she doing? This was it, the moment of truth. She either went back and worked things out with Jack, or she'd never see him again.

Of course there were other issues. Could she ever trust him after what he had done? But how would she ever know for sure unless she tried? If things didn't work out, would she be any worse off than she was now? Probably not. The most important question: Did she still love him?

Jack moved through the alley behind the 'Tween complex used by the maintenance staff. He stood at the edge of a building, scanning the parking lot. It was dark now, incoming headlights making it difficult to focus on anything or anyone. He moved closer, stood in shadow along the side of the building, the sound of rock music coming from unseen speakers, people everywhere. He had a good angle now, saw his rental car where he'd left it earlier. Didn't see a white Caddy, but that didn't mean anything. His gut told him Cobb and Diaz were still around. They'd expended considerable effort to find him, and he didn't think they would give up that easy. Not with this much money at stake.

He needed his car and thought this would be a good time to get it. Jack walked behind the building, crossed the complex, and came out on the opposite side of the parking lot, standing behind the tall smooth trunk of a palm tree. He watched for a while and moved through a row of cars to his, got in, turned the key, and put it in gear, creeping through the lot with the lights off.

Jack waited till he was on the road before he turned his lights on, checking the rearview mirror. He drove past where he was staying, went down another mile or so. He could see headlights in the rearview mirror. He pulled over on the side of the road, let the car pass. It was an SUV. He made a U-turn and drove to the beach house.

He unlocked the door and turned on a couple lights, feeling relieved. Cobb and Ruben hadn't caught him, and now they weren't gonna. He cracked a beer, opened the sliding door, felt the breeze, heard waves breaking on shore. He walked down to the beach, drinking a beer, staring out at the water for a while, then went back to the cottage and sat at a table on the deck.

Earlier Cobb had boosted a Mazda MDX in a strip mall parking lot. Jack had made the Caddy, so they didn't have a choice. Scanning the cool interior, thinking the Japs had really got their shit together. Cobb was checking out the instrument cluster when Ruben surprised him, saying, "You want him? He has to go back to the restaurant to get his car."

First time ever Ruben had suggested something Cobb hadn't already thought of. Well, Jesus H. Christ, mark this day on the calendar with a fucking star.

Fifteen minutes later, they were sitting in the dusty lot, watching the sun go over the motel buildings, watching cars pull in, watching people go in the restaurant. Ruben telling him he should come down to Puerto Rico. "Man, beautiful women, beautiful beaches, great food, gambling, fishing. The place is alive."

"What do you think, we're gonna hang out?" Cobb pictured them walking around Old San Juan, Ruben introducing him to his greaser buddies. "This is my American friend, Duane."

Cobb saw someone moving on the other side of the parking lot, car lights illuminating him. Looked like he was sneaking around, didn't want to be seen. Then he was hiding behind a palm tree. "See him over there?" Cobb pointed.

"I don't see nothing."

There were cars pulling into the lot one after another. "Keep watching."

A few minutes later, McCann appeared moving through the parking lot, ducking behind cars.

"Yeah, there he is," Ruben said.

FORTY-TWO

Diane walked around to the back of the beach house, felt the wind coming off the water. Jack, with a can of beer in his hand, was sitting at the small round table. "I don't know if this is a good idea," Diane said, walking up the steps to the deck.

"We'll find out." Jack paused. "How about a drink?"

"Bourbon would be good, on the rocks."

"I'll be right back." He got up, slid the screen door open, looked back at her. "I'm glad you're here." And went inside.

Diane wasn't so sure. She leaned against the railing, looking out at the ocean. Five minutes later, when he wasn't back, she wondered what he was up to.

Diane stepped into the room and saw Duane Cobb pointing a shotgun at Jack. Ruben came behind her, grabbed her biceps, pushed her deeper into the room, closed the door, and locked it.

Cobb said, "Where's our money at?"

Jack said, "You didn't see what happened on nine-eleven?"

Cobb said, "The hell's that mean?"

"The cashier's check was in my sport coat."

"Uh-huh."

"The coat's gone, blown to dust."

"Oh, okay," Cobb said. "Well, thanks anyway. I guess we'll be going." Cobb jabbed Jack's chest with the shotgun. "Let's try it again, Slick. Where's our money at?"

Jack said, "You set me up, didn't you? Why'd you pick me?"

"You picked yourself. Vicki was the bait, and you went after her like a hungry dog," Cobb said, glancing at Diane. "You can't blame Jack—everyone wanted her."

Diane shrugged. "You're defending him now?"

"I'm just saying," Cobb said.

"You remind me of frat boys talking about a cheerleader. You all wanted her, but Jack got her. What a lucky guy, huh?" Diane said, glancing at her husband. "All we've been through, I hope she was worth it."

"Myself, I always thought you were the keeper. And I like your new look," Cobb said, moving next to her, pressing the barrel of the shotgun against the small of her back, moving down her butt, caressing her with the hard steel. "I was hoping for a shot at you." Cobb glanced at Jack when he said it. "She thought you'd kicked and still wouldn't fool around. That's devotion, my friend." Cobb paused. "Now here's the deal. Jack, you don't fetch the money, and I mean quick, I guarantee I will pull the trigger and never think about it."

"It's outside," Jack said. "I buried it."

Cobb shifted his weight from one leg to the other. "Think I just fell out the hayloft?" He racked the slide. "I don't know if I'll be doing you a favor, or you still want her, but she's gonna be all over this wall you don't start talking."

"Come out, I'll show you."

Cobb nodded. "Well, all right. Ruben, why don't you keep Lady Di here company till we get back."

Diane said to Ruben, "I'm going to make myself a drink. You want something?"

"I don't know it's a good idea."

"That's right. You better keep an eye on me. I'm going to try to get you drunk and take off."

Ruben smiled and followed her into the kitchen, which had a half wall separating it from the dining room. There were fifths of booze on the counter: Stoli and Maker's and small bottles of mixers.

Diane said, "What do you want?"

"Vodka."

She opened the cupboard, took out two lowball glasses, opened the refrigerator, and filled them with ice and his with Stoli, and handed it to him. Diane filled hers halfway with Maker's and took a sip.

Ruben was somehow different. Maybe it was the island clothes. He didn't seem as tough, didn't seem as hard-edged in the guayabera shirt, blousy pants, sandals, and black socks, the outfit reminding her of German tourists she'd seen on holiday in Rome.

Diane said, "How'd you get involved in this mess?"

"After I stop fighting I needed a job. I was a bodyguard for a few years, working for a rich Cuban in Miami."

"What does a bodyguard do beyond the obvious?"

"Take the man's wife to the beauty parlor, wait while she get her hair done. Take her to the club, wait while she eat lunch. Take her shopping, wait while she try on outfits."

"I can see how that would get to you, particularly if you're not patient."

"You know me a little, uh? What do you think?" He sipped the vodka and put the glass on the counter.

"After chasing me through the supermarket and breaking into my house, I have to say no."

Ruben smiled, and for the first time, she noticed a diamond pattern on his front teeth. "Yeah, I have to scare you."

"You did a good job." Diane sipped her bourbon, thinking this lunatic who'd terrified her seemed kind of normal now.

Ruben drank some vodka. "You gonna stay with your husband?" he said, changing the subject.

The question surprised her. "I don't know. Things are pretty screwed up right now. Jack's in a lot of trouble. He can't go back."

"So you start over. How many people would go for that, uh?" Ruben picked up his glass, drank his drink. "Is the same for me. I can't go back."

She wasn't expecting that. It sounded as though he was confessing. "What happened?"

"It doesn't matter."

"What's San Marino Equity?"

Ruben grinned. "Is nothing."

"Was Vicki Ross really in debt to a loan shark?"

"Yes, of course."

"So Jack does owe the money?" Diane paused. "Something tells me you're working for yourself. You're not going to give the money to the Italians, are you?"

"You figure that out, uh?"

"As far as I'm concerned, it's yours. You know Jack won't say anything, and I won't either." She sipped her drink. "Where you going? No, I don't want to know."

"Why, you gonna come visit?" Ruben grinned, showing his glitzy front teeth again.

Jack led Cobb across the sand path behind the cottage to a wide stand of high shrubs, sea grape, dogwoods, and palm trees that separated the beach from the house.

"Don't even think about trying to get away. I'll go back in there—"

"You're not gonna do anything," Jack said, cutting him off. "I'm gonna give you the money, and you're gonna leave here and we're never gonna see you again."

"Where do you get your confidence at? A shotgun in your face, you're telling me the way it is?"

Jack ignored him, found the spot and knelt in the sand, Cobb standing a few feet away as he started digging, knew it was right in this general area, about five feet from the palm trees. He knifed the sand with his fingertips in different places, but didn't feel anything. He was thinking about Vicki. He was gonna give her the cashier's check the night she was shot.

After she was murdered, he ended up depositing the money in the Pompano Beach bank. A week and a half later, he tried to withdraw it. The manager said no customer had ever taken out that much. The bank didn't have enough cash on hand, had to order it from the Federal Reserve, and it would take a couple days. The manager also said it was dangerous to carry that much cash and suggested Jack hire armed security.

Marquis Brown had stopped at the vacation rental agency on Sanibel Island and was told the house he was inquiring about had been rented for the week. "Who rented it?" Marquis asked the office manager, a foxy Hispanic babe about his age, said her name was Carmen.

"Due to a citizen's right to privacy, I'm not at liberty to give you that information."

"Not at liberty, huh?" Marquis took out his detective shield, flashed it at her. "Somebody's life's at stake. You want that on your conscience?"

"Oh, it's a police matter; that's different," the woman said. "The house is on Captiva Island, the main road, ocean side. We rented it to a Mr. Richard Keefer."

"What's the address?"

It was dark when Marquis arrived at the rental house. He parked on the side of the main road. There were two cars sitting on the hard-packed sand and trampled sea grass in front of a thick wall of vegetation. Could be Mrs. and her man reunited, or someone entirely different. If it was the McCanns, Marquis believed Cobb and Ruben would be close by.

He walked along the north side of the house, catching glimpses of the beach and ocean, another wall of green separating this property from the neighbor's.

Looking around the back corner of the house, Marquis felt the wind and heard waves breaking on shore. He thought he heard voices, but couldn't hear what they were saying. Thought he saw something move, and yeah, there was a dude on his knees digging in the high shrubs behind the house about twenty yards away.

Marquis walked straight toward the ocean, went left around the vegetation, ducked behind palm trees, and saw another dude holding a sawed-off shotgun. Then a third dude appeared, slid the screen open, and stepped out on the deck. "Man, what you doing out there?" This one had a Spanish accent. Had to be the PR, who else?

"Says he can't find it."

The PR said, "Want me to come out there, help you?"

"You just watch her. I'll handle this."

A couple minutes later, Marquis saw the digger pull a gym bag out of the sand like a magic trick. The digger stood up, gripping the strap. It was Jack McCann. The dude holding the sawed-off walked McCann to the deck, and they went in the house.

Marquis crouched on the outside of the deck railing. The sliding door was closed and the blinds had been pulled down. He went around to the south side of the house, looked through the window into the kitchen, and beyond it into the main room and saw them all: Mrs., Jack, Ruben, and Cobb. He walked around the house to the front door and drew the Glock.

Diane was surprised when Jack said he hid the money, and thought it was a ploy to get away from Cobb and call the police. She was more surprised when he came in with the black nylon bag still covered in sand. Jack placed the bag on the wooden dining table, which had three chairs on each side. Ruben was next to him, Cobb across the table, and Diane stood at one of the ends, everyone staring at the bag as Jack unzipped it.

"I'll take it from here," Cobb said, pointing the shotgun at Jack, motioning him away from the table. Jack took a couple steps back, and Ruben moved closer, unzipped the bag, reached in, and took out a banded stack of bills, fanning the end. Cobb was grinning, took his left hand off the shotgun, and grabbed a couple bundles of cash like he had just won the lottery.

"The surprises keep on coming, don't they?" Diane said, directing the question at Jack. "This is what he embezzled from one of his clients, an old woman who can't think straight."

Cobb glanced at Ruben. "Put it back in the bag, will you?" Aiming the shotgun at him now.

"What is this?"

"Change in the plan," Cobb said. "Should've done it a while ago. I don't need a partner, and this seems like a good time to sever ties and move on."

Ruben, no expression, dropped the money in the bag and stared at the shotgun. In Diane's mind, it was all over for everyone except Cobb until she saw Detective Marquis Brown come into the kitchen with a pistol in his hand. So unexpected, it seemed as though she was hallucinating.

"Drop the sawed-off," Marquis said.

Cobb turned, fired, and blew a hole in the cabinet where Marquis had been standing.

Diane went down on the floor, ears ringing. She heard Cobb rack the shotgun again, but couldn't see him.

"Throw out your weapon," Cobb said.

Now she saw Marquis rise up over the counter, aiming the Glock, squeezing the trigger: *Bam, bam,* followed by the *boom* of the shotgun, and Marquis was blown off his feet. She could see him on his back on the kitchen floor. Cobb was feeding shells into the shotgun.

Diane scrambled on hands and knees into the kitchen, picked up Marquis's Glock from the floor next to him. He opened his eyes and looked at her. His sport coat was spread open across his chest, and the top two buttons of his bloodstained, buckshot-puckered dress shirt were undone. She could see the outline of the vest beneath it.

Cobb racked the shotgun and came around the counter. Diane was on her knees, two hands on the Glock the way her father had taught her. "Put it down, Duane."

"You've got to be kidding me." Cobb grinned. "Think you can play with the big boys?" He held the shotgun barrel pointed at the floor.

Diane felt her hands shaking, finger on the trigger, fifteen feet from Cobb, who was grinning. "Ever shot somebody? Ain't like shootin' at a target. Now drop the gun, you might live to tell about it."

She centered the site on Cobb's chest, trying to steady her hands.

"You don't have the nerve." Cobb brought the shotgun up, aimed it at her, and Diane fired twice. Cobb went down on the living room floor and didn't move.

She stood over him, a look of surprise on Cobb's face, eyes open, two holes in his chest, blood soaking his yellow golf shirt and white pants. She crouched and picked up the shotgun, walked into the kitchen, and rested it on the counter. Diane was surprised to see Marquis sitting on the floor with his back against the cabinet doors. He tried to get up.

"Easy now, sure you should be doing that?"

"I'm fine."

"Yeah, you could've fooled me. You might be fine after we get you to a hospital. You've been shot. You're probably in shock."

He was unsteady trying to stand, back sliding up the doors below the counter, and then resting elbows on the granite. There was blood on his collarbone above the vest.

"I'm all right."

"You don't look all right. You look like you're going to fall over. I'm going to call an ambulance."

"Relax." Marquis smiled. "You can shoot. Man, can you shoot. I'm not surprised, girl as tough as you. You can give that back now 'less you're gonna shoot someone else."

"I think I'm all done for tonight." Diane handed the Glock to him, and he slid it in the holster on his hip. "Still think I had something to do with Vicki Ross's death?"

Marquis Brown shook his head. "You been cleared."

"Who did it?"

"Shooter worked for Frankie Cheech."

"You come all the way down here to tell me that?"

"Cobb and Diaz are wanted for murder. I figured, I find you, I'm gonna find them. Remember, you told me you liked Captiva, told me where you stayed, said you could even live here part of the year. Remember that?"

Yeah, she remembered. It was when he asked where Jack might go. "Well, here he is." Jack came over and stood where the carpet and linoleum met. "Jack, this is Detective Brown, New York Police Homicide."

"Found him, huh? Knew where he'd be. That was the plan, I gotta believe."

"There was no plan. It happened the way I told you."

Marquis seemed distracted, looked through the kitchen into the living room. "Where's Diaz?"

Now Diane looked too. Ruben was gone and so was the black nylon bag.

Marquis moved slowly past Jack into the living room, glanced down at Cobb, drew the Glock, crossed the floor and went in the bedroom, Diane behind him, seeing the open window. Marquis walked over and looked out at the darkness. He smiled and slid the Glock in his holster. "Listen, you've got to get out of here."

"You're not going to arrest Jack?"

"For what?"

"I should stay and tell the police what happened."

"You don't think I can do that? Now take your man and go."

They drove in silence to the end of the island, Diane picturing Cobb, eyes open, dead on the floor. Why did it have to end this way? She could feel Jack staring at her. He finally broke the silence. "You all right?"

"No, I'm not all right. I'm not close to being all right. I just killed someone."

"Who was going to kill you, who was probably gonna kill all of us. You didn't have a choice."

Hearing that made her feel a little better. The tires whined as they went over the bridge. Jack, still staring, said, "What do you want to do?"

Diane pulled over in the deserted beach parking lot, looking at the ocean.

It was hot, stuffy in the car. She put the window down and felt a warm breeze and heard waves breaking on shore. She turned in the seat and faced him.

"Let me say something." Jack paused. "Look, I screwed up, I can't change that, but I can tell you it won't happen again." His eyes held on her. "If that sounds like I'm giving you a line, I'm not. I mean it. You're gonna have to go with your instinct on this. Either I'm worth another chance, or I'm not."

Diane had made up her mind. "It isn't going to work. I don't know you anymore. I don't trust you."

"You're gonna throw away twelve years of marriage just like that?"

"You already did, remember?"

"What do you want me to do?"

"Get out of the car."

"Come on. We can work things out. I know it."

"I would always wonder about you, and I don't want to live that way."

"I do love you," Jack said, giving it one more try, but there was no sincerity or emotion in his voice. He sounded like he was recommending a mutual fund.

"You'll get over it."

Jack got out. Diane pulled away, left him standing in the parking lot and knew it was the right thing, the only thing. She got on the road to the mainland and never looked back.

FORTY-THREE

Ruben shaved and poured cologne in his hand, patted his face, and felt his skin sting a little. He picked up the Cuba Libre and, in a white hotel robe, walked out on the balcony, staring at the dark ocean in the distance, feeling the breeze and listening to the night sounds of San Juan below him.

He put on a crisp white shirt and the new linen suit. It was nine forty-five. Ruben would start at Club Brava and go from there. He would drink rum and the local men would come up to him and say, *Ruben, hey man, how you doing? I saw you fight so-and-so. Man, you knock him out in the . . .*

He would meet a woman, dance, and bring her back to his wonderful luxury room that had a bathtub and a shower. For the first time in his life, Ruben had money and nothing to worry about. *La vida era buena.*

When he finished dressing, Ruben stood in front of the full-length mirror admiring himself in the white suit. He thought he heard a door close and saw a man appear behind him holding a gun, and he knew he should've been more careful.

"Where is the money?"

"In the closet," Ruben said. With what he had saved and what he took from Jack McCann, there was more than eight hundred thousand.

"Vincent Gallo sends his regards." The man raised the pistol now and shot him in the back, the bullet going through his body, coming out his chest, and shattering the mirror. Ruben, not sure how he was still standing, looked at himself in the fractured slivers of glass. There was a hole in his suit jacket, the white fabric turning red. Ruben dropped to his knees and fell backward, the man standing over him aiming the pistol again.

ACKNOWLEDGMENTS

A week before my father passed away, he was at my house for dinner. Elmore was telling me about the book he was writing called *Blue Dreams*. He paused, smoking a Virginia Slims 100 and said, "How's your book coming?" I said, "I'm in the middle of act two." Elmore said, "What's your title?" I said, *"Unidentified Remains."* He brought the cigarette to his mouth, inhaled, glanced across the room, blew out smoke and said, "How about *Unknown Remains?*"

I want to thank my agents Andrew Wylie and Jeff Posternak for connecting me with Counterpoint, my new publisher, and for getting *Unknown Remains* in the hands of editor Dan Smetanka. Dan is extraordinarily good at keeping a story moving, hitting on all cylinders.